SOMETHING FISHY

I found a plastic memo clip and clamped it tightly over my nose. The envelope was easy enough to open with my desk scissors, but there was no need to open the newspaper package inside. By then the smell of dead fish was too strong to be stopped by a nose clip.

There was a folded sheet of white paper attached to the newspaper with a small strip of masking tape along the spine. The words, "SORRY CHARLIE," were scrawled on the outside in green crayon, and the words, "IT'S YOUR TURN NEXT," on the inside in red.

I began to shake, faster and harder than any paint mixer I'd ever seen. It took me several minutes before I had a grip on myself.

Someone had just threatened my son. And if that someone was the same person who'd taken a bellpull to my aunt's neck, they meant business.

Den of Antiquity Mysteries by
Tamar Myers
from Avon Books

LARCENY
AND
OLD LACE

TAMAR MYERS

AVON BOOKS
An Imprint of HarperCollinsPublishers

AVON BOOKS
An Imprint of HarperCollins*Publishers*
10 East 53rd Street
New York, New York 10022-5299

Copyright © 1996 by Tamar Myers
ISBN 978-0-380-78239-0
www.avonbooks.com

First Avon Books paperback printing: November 2000
First Avon Twilight paperback printing: June 1996

Avon Trademark Reg. U.S. Pat. Off. and in Other Countries, Marca Registrada, Hecho en U.S.A.
HarperCollins® is a registered trademark of HarperCollins Publishers.

Printed in the U.S.A.

20   19   18   17   16   15   14   13   12   11

For my husband, Jeff

I would like to acknowledge my editor, Carrie Feron; her assistant, Ann McKay Thoroman; and my agent, Nancy Yost. In addition to these three ladies in the publishing business, I owe a debt of gratitude to Page Hendrix at the York County Library in Rock Hill, South Carolina.

Now, as for all you antique dealers out there whose shops I have frequented all these years—I *will* be back shortly, and *this* time I will buy something.

ON LACE

Of many Arts, one surpasses all. For the maiden seated at her work flashes the smooth balls and thousand threads into the circle, . . . and from this, her amusement, makes as much profit as a man earns by the sweat of his brow, and no maiden ever complains, at even, of the length of the day. The issue is a fine web, which feeds the pride of the whole globe; which surrounds with its fine border cloaks and tuckers, and shows grandly round the throats and hands of kings.

—JACOB VAN EYCK

The real good of a piece of lace, then, you will find, is that it should show, first, that the designer of it had a pretty fancy; next, that the maker of it had fine fingers; lastly, that the weaver of it has worthiness or dignity enough to obtain, and common sense enough not to wear it on all occasions.

—JOHN RUSKIN

And here the needle plies its busy task,
The pattern grows, the well-depicted flower,
Wrought patiently into the snowy lawn,
Unfolds its bosom, buds and leaves and sprigs,
And curling tendrils, gracefully dispersed,
Follow the nimble fingers of the fair—
A wreath that cannot fade of flowers that blow
With most success when all besides decay.

—WILLIAM COWPER

At christenings lace was always abundantly used. In 1778 the infant daughter of the Duke and Duchess of Chandos was so weighed down by the immense amount of lace on her robes that she fainted. George III and Queen Charlotte stood as sponsors, and although the child's mother observed her condition she said nothing, so that the dignity of the christening, with Majesty in attendance, should not be disturbed. As the Archbishop of Canterbury gave the child back to its mother he remarked that it was the quietest child he ever held. It died soon after, having never recovered from the effects of its christening.

—From *The Lace Book*, by N. Hudson Moore,
Tudor Publishing Company, New York 1937
(copyright© 1904 by Frederick A. Stokes Company)

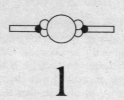

1

Eulonia Wiggins was found strangled to death by an antique bellpull. It was a fine example of nineteenth-century needlework. On the blue velvet background, a splendid red rooster paraded, his comb erect, his spurs as long as talons. An elaborate crest of one of the finest noble families in England was displayed proudly above the cock. I would have charged at least $200 for the pull, more to the right customer. I suppose if my aunt had to die by strangulation, the pull was as suitable an implement as any. But I can't help thinking that if I had reacted in a more rational and placating manner, my aunt might still be alive.

We—the members of Selwyn Avenue Antique Dealers Association—had gathered together for our monthly breakfast at the local Denny's restaurant. Normally this is just a social event, since our organization is too small to have any real business. Today, however, the business was my aunt.

I must immediately point out that my aunt was the first of our group to open a shop on prestigious Selwyn Avenue. If it hadn't been for her pioneering spirit, and persuasive tongue (the zoning board was slow to come around), none of us would have our shops today. Plainly put, we all owed her a great deal.

In the interest of fairness, I am compelled to say that her shop, Feathers 'N Treasures, had seen better days. Okay, to put it frankly, it was an eyesore, but she didn't deserve to die for it. Lightly flogged, maybe. I mean, since when is peeling paint a capital crime? As for those tacky cardboard signs in the windows, she did change them every time she ran a sale. I'll even admit that most of her merchandise was garage sale leftovers, but hey, this is a free country. Eulonia Wiggins, age eighty-six, had paid her dues to society. If the Selwyn Avenue Antique Dealers Association had a problem with my aunt— well, they could lump it, or else answer to me.

My name is Abigail Louise Timberlake, and I am going to tell it like it is. Call me mean-spirited if you want, but never call me dishonest. Life is too short for pretense.

I am forty-six years old, and not ashamed to admit it. I have earned every one of those years. I weigh ninety-three pounds on a good day but have been known to hit the triple digits by the time New Year's Day rolls around. My hair is naturally brown, but I purposely put a gray streak in it, so as not to be mistaken for a teenager. That is the price I pay for not smoking and staying clear of the sun. My eyes are cat green, and I have never needed glasses. That is the reward I get for having picked Hugh Wiggins and Missy Monroe Wiggins as my parents. That, and my height. I mean the lack of it.

I have one sibling, a younger brother named Toy. That's his real name. At any rate, Toy is six foot four, and not adopted. Either Mama wasn't the saint I think she is, the laws of Mendel are a bunch of bunk, or Toy is some sort of genetic throwback. I prefer to believe in choice C.

Toy lives in California and thinks of himself as an unemployed actor. In reality Toy is a busboy for a sleazy restaurant where leather ties are required. Although Mama and I write to Toy every month, neither of us have heard from him directly in several years. He has no phone.

I got married right after graduating from Winthrop College in Rock Hill, South Carolina. I met my husband, Buford Timberlake, on the water slide at an area amusement park. It was a mixed marriage. Buford was from North Carolina and a big fan of North Carolina State. I rooted for Clemson. Buford had louder lungs and we ended up settling in Charlotte.

Buford and I were lucky enough to have two children, a daughter, Susan, and a son, Charlie. I was lucky enough to be able to stay home and raise these children. I won't say I was deliriously happy, but neither did I look for a gas oven into which to stick my head. Life chugged down a fairly predictable track, and we managed to hang on for the ride.

One day our engine jumped the track. It happened right around Buford's forty-fifth birthday. The obstacle in our path was a blond bimbo with huge but perky boobs who called herself Tweetie. The boobs undoubtedly had names as well, perhaps supplied by her surgeon. Our marriage was over.

Did I mention that Buford was a lawyer? He handled personal injury cases, not divorces, but he was plugged into the good-old-boy network. The only plugs I had were connected to household appliances. To make a long and gruesome story shorter, Buford managed to keep our beautiful and expensive home in the Myers Park neighborhood of Charlotte, our two teenage children, Susan and Charlie, and our dog Scruffles. I got the cat, Dmitri.

Charlie was fifteen at the time and still lives with Buford, as does Scruffles. Fortunately for her, Susan, who was seventeen at the time, is now out of the nest and safely in college.

I said I was going to be honest, and so I will admit that Buford did offer to pay me alimony. Even before the court compelled him to. Of course, the alimony Buford volunteered wouldn't support Mother Teresa in a year full of fast days, much less yours truly. The amount he pays is nowhere close to as much as I deserve. Since I would rather suck venom from a timber snake than accept money from Buford Timberlake, I rolled up my sleeves (something people my size are used to doing) and set about finding a way to support myself.

With money my mother loaned me, and advice from my Aunt Eulonia (not always taken), I bought a failing card and gift shop on South Selwyn Avenue and turned it into an antique store. The Den of Antiquity has been a modest success. I would like to say that my life is now back on track, but I can't. Not with Charlie still in Buford's clutches.

Someday Buford Timberlake, the timber snake, is going to get what's coming to him. Frankly, I have been too busy with the shop to invest much energy into revenge—perhaps Tweetie will do it for me when she gets dumped. I was certainly far too busy to have to deal with what was about to happen.

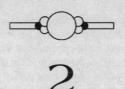

2

Again, I should have paid more attention at our monthly breakfast. Surely the signs of doom were there, like the biblical handwriting on the wall. If I had paid as much attention to what was *not* said as to what was said, my poor sweet aunt might still be alive. But oh no, I had to go on the defensive.

"I don't see any sense in complaining," I told the group, after I'd heard enough. "My aunt is who she is, and she's not about to change. Besides, we all owe her. If it wasn't for her—"

"Bullshit," somebody whispered.

I panned them with a glare. "Now that's downright ungrateful after all she's done."

"What she's done is drive away top-dollar customers." Rob Goldburg pounded the table with a fist, sending the cutlery flying. "And there's no use talking to her about it, because she won't even listen. Damn it! I could strangle that old crone!"

"Hear, hear," Major Calloway said. "Whoever bumps off that old biddy deserves a commendation. But given the fact that she's spit in all of our faces, may I suggest a firing squad?"

"I'll drink to that." Peggy Redfern held up a half-empty water glass. "To Eulonia Wiggins's hasty demise, by whatever means."

"Harm one hair on her hoary head and you all die!" I said

graciously. I hate having to curb my tongue, but my training as a southern lady is hard to counteract.

Anita Morgan, our president, tapped on her water glass. Finding it empty she tapped on Peggy's. "Quiet please, so we can start eating before our food gets cold."

By that Anita meant she wanted to say grace. In the South folks aren't shy about things like that, and Anita was less shy than most. She had taken it upon herself to see that some sort of prayer was said at each and every meeting of the Selwyn Avenue Antique Dealers Association. Of course, not everyone in our little organization is a Christian, but that's irrelevant. Southern piety, as presumptuous as it is, is well intended.

After grace, which was unusually and mercifully brief, I dug into my food. The bacon was suitably supple, the yolks in my poached eggs firm, and the biscuits slightly doughy on the inside. The grits, under their mantle of melting butter, were perfect as well. For one blissful minute I thought the subject of my aunt was behind us. I kicked off my shoes and settled in to enjoy an installment of heaven.

Gretchen Miller broke the spell. "Personally, I think Eulonia Wiggins is a jewel. Last week she sent four of her customers over to my place. Told them that I had what they really wanted. Now that's a friend, if you ask me. Although I will admit that her shop is—well, sort of run down."

"The pyramids are run down," Rob said. "Eulonia's shop is several stages beyond that."

Gretchen adjusted a pair of tortoiseshell glasses on a mere stub of a nose. "Just the same, she's a very sweet woman."

"But she's so *tacky,*" Peggy said, her mouth full of pancake.

I was surprised to see Peggy eating pancakes for breakfast. Her usual fare is men.

"So is blue eye shadow, dear," I said helpfully.

"Come, come," the Major said. "Just because she's your aunt, doesn't mean you have to be so defensive. The antique shops on Selwyn Avenue have an image to maintain. Old clothes and chipped glass don't cut the mustard."

I stared at the pale, pudgy man with the abbreviated mustache. "Hitler's pajamas don't exactly cut the mustard either, Colonel."

"That's Major, not Colonel. And I sell military artifacts. Antique military artifacts. The Führer's nightwear is for display purposes only."

Rob Goldburg's fist sent the cutlery flying a second time. "Then display them in Germany, damn it! All that fascination with Nazi crap makes me sick."

Rob is Jewish, born in Charlotte, a fact which surprises most Yankee visitors to his shop, The Finer Things. Furthermore, Rob is tall and robust, with a thick head of sandy hair, only touched by gray. The good news is that Rob is worthy of a little drool. The bad news, at least for women, is that Rob is gay.

The Major has never liked Rob. Or maybe he likes him too much. "That Nazi crap, as you call it, puts the bread on my table. A sale is a sale, after all. An S.S. insignia is every bit as legitimate as some gold-covered chair where Louis the somebody rested his ass."

I breathed a sigh of relief. Much better to be talking about some despot's pj's than my Aunt Eulonia's shop. The debate on Nazi paraphernalia didn't last long enough.

"It looks like someone dropped a bomb on the Brussels flea market," Wynnell Crawford said, referring to my aunt's shop. "Someone should set off a bomb in there. I bet she wouldn't notice the difference."

Wynnell had a lot of room to talk. If Hitler was still alive, as the tabloids claimed, then he was undoubtedly hiding in her shop, sans pajamas. Along with Elvis and Salman Rushdie. Wynnell sells period furniture, but massive pieces, like armoires and breakfronts. Because her shop, Wooden Wonders, is relatively small, and her inventory large, items are packed tighter together than Vienna sausages. On top of this leafless hardwood forest Wynnell has stacked innumerable smaller, less expensive things. We in the trade call it "fluff." You would call it clutter. Neither Wynnell's shop, nor the pitifully sewn homemade outfits she wears, are likely to win any aesthetic awards.

"People in glass houses shouldn't throw stones," I said pleasantly.

Wynnell gave me a withering look. Peggy gave me another glimpse of her pancake.

"You should talk some sense into her. Yesterday I brought an old friend over. A dealer from New York who wants a place in the sun. Eulonia wouldn't even listen to his offer."

"I am *not* my aunt's keeper," I said. I recrossed my legs then, and if I kicked Peggy in the shins, it was purely coincidental. At any rate, her yelps were far too theatrical.

"I move we vote to oust that woman from our organization," Wynnell said.

She may have given me another withering look, but I couldn't be certain without taking a hedge clipper to those eyebrows first. And anyway, some of the furrows on Wynnell's forehead have been permanently fused together.

I was prepared to apologize to Peggy's shins, when it dawned on me that it was my Aunt Eulonia that was facing the boot, not me.

"But she hardly ever attends these monthly breakfasts," I said quickly. "She isn't here today. Besides, if you kick her out, then how do you expect to talk her into doing what you want?"

"Ho, ho," the Major said. "We don't. That's your job, little lady. Think you're big enough to handle it?"

That did it. That ended breakfast for me. The nerve of Major Calloway to bring my height into our discussion! Just because I'm on the short side doesn't mean that I will tolerate being treated like a child. I slipped my three-inch heels back on, bringing my height up to five foot even, and strode from the room.

It was an action I regret to this day.

After I closed my shop for the day, I took I-77 south, past Carowinds Amusement Park and into South Carolina. My destination was Rock Hill, home of Winthrop University. Of course I'm prejudiced, having grown up there, but I think there is something special about small college towns. When all roads lead to a campus, one can't help but be the recipient of the occasional lofty thought.

I got off on the Cherry Road exit but switched over to Eden Terrace as soon as possible. Cherry is four lanes, and easy to drive on, but it isn't easy on the eyes. There are still thriving businesses on this once proud commercial strip, but signs of neglect as well. The old mall is dead, a victim of its small size (not a comfortable thought to me), and its carapace lies empty and indestructible like a katydid shell. In some places the kudzu comes too close for comfort.

For y'all who aren't from the South, kudzu is a tropical vine that was imported to control erosion and as a possible source of cattle fodder. It was very successful. Although it dies back to the ground each winter, this plant grows so fast that by the first hard frost, it will have covered an entire large tree. I know of a woman who fell asleep on her front porch after lunch, and by the time she woke up to start supper, the vine had wrapped her tight like a green mummy and all but smothered her. If killer tomatoes ever mated with kudzu, we in the South would all be goners.

Comfort, however, was what I was after. Although I live in a perfectly adequate house of my own in Charlotte, there are times when I need the comfort and security of my mother's house. My old home. That need includes my father too, but Daddy died sixteen years ago in a skiing accident on nearby Lake Wylie.

Mama lives on the south end of Eden Terrace, just a few blocks from the campus. It is a street of older brick homes and towering trees. Its gardens are bouquets of roses, petunias, gardenias, and camellias. Even in the dead of winter, pansies add a splash of color. Mama lives in the house I was born in—literally. Mama says I was so eager to join the world that I made my appearance only twenty minutes after her first labor pain. As a reward Mama stuck me with the name Abigail. Go figure. She smelled me coming.

The Monroes (Mama's maiden name) smell all impending events, especially the arrival of kinfolks. Consequently Mama met me at the door with a glass of sweet tea and minutes later forced me to choke down a supper of grilled pork chops, sweet

potatoes, and fried okra. Not that I don't love those things—
I do—but the portions Mama serves could keep a small third
world country fed for a week. Apparently Mama, who is five
foot one, feels personal guilt for the fact that I am so small.
No doubt she harbors hope that I may yet grow an inch or
two before my fiftieth birthday. Then she can relax.

"I smell trouble coming," Mama said as I walked in the
door.

I explained the situation briefly then patted her arm. "Not
to worry. Their barks are all worse than their bites. Besides,
we were all witnesses. It's not as if anybody was really going
to bump the old dear off."

Mama smoothed the skirt of her gingham apron and then
lightly fingered a strand of pearls. She wears pearls when she
cooks, just like Beaver's mother. But Mama's are real.

"I wasn't talking about the threats against your Aunt Eulonia. I was talking about your Aunt Marilyn. She's coming
up from Hilton Head for a visit next week."

I choked on a bite of chop, and Mama had to pound my
back to get me going again. "Here? Aunt Marilyn? Did she
call or write?"

Mama shook her head. The naturally brown hair swung
gracefully and then settled neatly back into place. She's sixty-
nine years old and there isn't a gray hair to be seen. The next
person who asks if we're sisters is going to get a clop in the
chops. While I am proud to own my age, I draw the line at
owning Mama's.

"She didn't call or write. But I can smell it. There's trouble
brewing for sure."

"You didn't tell her about the camellias, did you?"

As a reward for my impertinence Mama plopped another
chop on my plate. "No, I did not!"

"Next week, you say?" Mama's nose has an accuracy
range of up to two weeks if the pollen count is down, but it
was September, a bad time for nasal detecting.

"Wednesday, I think. Tuesday, at the earliest."

I breathed a huge sigh of relief. There was still time to do
something about the camellias, if I could only figure out what.
It was Buford's fault, of course. If he hadn't kept the house I

could have afforded to remain in Myers Park, near my children, and not too far from my shop.

Thank God, Aunt Marilyn came to the rescue. She owns a modest but respectable house on Ridgewood Avenue, just a skip from my shop, and two hops from my old stomping grounds in Myers Park. Aunt Marilyn wanted to retire to Hilton Head but didn't want to sell her house, "just in case the coastal scene bores me." Aunt Marilyn is Mama's sister, but you'd never know it. Mama is a *lady*. Aunt Marilyn is a *woman* who firmly believes she is God's gift to men. Any man. Her last name is Monroe, and she claims to be the inspiration for *the* Marilyn Monroe. Platinum hair and all.

"I met that Norma Jean girl at a party," she once said. "She was a frowsy little thing with dishwater hair and no attitude. She took one look at me, and immediately I could see those brain cogs turning. Next thing I knew, there she was, on the cover of *TIME,* with my name and my face. And my bosom buddies." By that she meant her breasts; Aunt Marilyn has no buddies, just lovers.

Because I am her only niece, Aunt Marilyn agreed to loan me her house—rent-free. Of course there were strings attached. The house has to be available for her exclusive use whenever she is in town (fortunately, almost never). There are other strings, but the biggest string, which is as thick as the transatlantic cable, is that I am not allowed to make any changes, no matter how temporary, in either her house or her yard. Nothing. Nada. For instance, I am allowed to cook using only her pots and pans. I may place only her dishes on the table. I may not add as much as one chair to the inventory. I have to use her linens on my bed (although I am permitted to use my own toothbrush and wear my own clothes). These restrictions, although frustrating, are manageable. They have in fact saved me oodles of money. But the stickler, the source of impending trouble, is the fact that I may not plant any new flowers or shrubs in her garden, nor remove any that are already there.

Last fall (which just goes to show you how frequently she visits) I experienced a moment of insanity in which I purchased two beautiful double camellias and planted them on either side of the front door. Last winter, despite record cold temperatures in Charlotte, they produced an abundance of exquisite blooms. Everyone on my block, and many casual passersby, complimented me on these flowers. There is no way, short of a lobotomy, that I will agree to dig these camellias up.

And don't kid yourself. Aunt Marilyn will go ballistic when she sees them. It will be either me or the camellias. Probably both. Even Mama, whom Aunt Marilyn adores, will not be able to calm her.

In all honesty, perhaps I made the situation a little worse than it needed to be. I should have left the painted plaster poodles in their places and planted the camellias off to the side. Then they might have stood a fighting chance. But the poodles were peeling and chipped, and the butt of more jokes than a blond at a MENSA convention. Then, too, I probably added insult to injury when I somehow managed to lose the pair of pink plastic flamingos that flanked the bird bath.

"Spill it," Mama said. She was washing her plate before putting it in the dishwasher.

"Camellias," I grunted.

Mama pivoted on five-inch heels. A manicured hand clutched at the cultured pearls. "You didn't!"

"I did. Two of them. Mama, you've seen them many times. You even admired their flowers. You just didn't notice they were new additions. Maybe Aunt Marilyn won't notice them either, because they're not blooming now."

"*I* don't keep a diagram of my yard with a coded and dated list of everything I ever planted," Mama said. Hers was not an encouraging tone.

"You don't suppose she'll miss those awful poodles, do you?"

Mama blanched. "You're kidding!"

"But the flamingos weren't my fault, Mama. It was like they just flew away."

Mama pulled on her pearls so hard that she began to gurgle, something the Beaver's mother never did.

"Mama, they were embarrassing. Even the garbage man cringed when he picked them up. When you think about it, I was doing Aunt Marilyn a favor. She should thank me.''

Mama let go of her pearls and began fanning herself with her apron skirt. ''My passport doesn't expire for three more years. You're welcome to borrow it, dear.''

There is a lot to be said for a positive attitude. I'm not sure just how it works, but perhaps there really is something in that mind over matter stuff. Who knows, our positive energy, if it's channelled correctly, might even be able to affect other people's actions.

But that's something mothers should teach their daughters, not the other way around. Still, it's never too late to learn, so I stood up straight, squared my shoulders back, and gave her my gummiest smile.

''Maybe Buford will have a change of heart and up my alimony. Then I could afford a place of my own.'' That I would even consider accepting more money from Buford shows you how desperate I was.

Mama turned and began to wipe down the inside walls of the dishwasher before loading it.

''Maybe your Aunt Marilyn will decide to become a missionary to Botswana. Mother Marilyn, the people will call her. When she dies, the Pope might even make her a saint.''

''I see.''

I finally did. I was a goner. If I didn't yank up the camellias by Wednesday and replace them with the poodles, I was going to have to yank up my own roots and find a new abode. Unfortunately, most of America had matured beyond pink flamingos and plaster poodles, so they would be difficult to replace.

Not that moving would be difficult; my roots on Ridgewood Avenue were rather shallow. Since Aunt Marilyn wouldn't allow me to rearrange anything in her closets, I pretty much lived from a suitcase.

''Of course, my door is always open,'' Mama said.

''Thanks, Mama,'' I said, ''but—''

I should have noticed that her nose was twitching. It must have been, because the phone rang.

''Wiggins residence, Mrs. Wiggins speaking.'' Barbara Billingsby couldn't have said it better.

There was a moment of silence while Mama listened.

"Lord have mercy," I said, imitating Mama under my breath. No doubt the aging glamour queen had outfoxed Mama's nose and was practically on her doorstep. I was up the creek without a paddle.

I had to be right. Mama was speaking in hushed tones, her expression grave. The pearls slipped through her fingers like worry beads through the hands of a Turkish pasha. She steadied herself against the wall with one hand and held the phone out to me.

I got up slowly, swallowing extra hard to push down my heart. "Don't tell me," I said, "she's already been to the house, and it's all over except for the yelling."

Mama shook her head, her eyes glistening. "That isn't your Aunt Marilyn. This is about your Aunt Eulonia, up in Charlotte." She paused and scraped at something microscopic with the toe of her pump. "Eulonia Wiggins is dead."

"Oh shit," I said.

I am not the lady my mother is.

3

"She was murdered," Anita Morgan told me over the phone.

"What?" I gripped Mama's receiver tighter.

"Strangled," she said smoothly. "I saw her myself. There was a bellpull around her neck."

"What?"

"A nineteenth-century English bellpull. Had a rooster embroidered on it. Rather nice, actually. Although some of the fringe in the tassel was matted."

"What?" Sometimes it is normal to sound stupid.

"You know, how at the end of the tassel—"

"Not that. What do you mean you *saw* her?"

"Oh that. Well, I stayed late tonight to unpack a shipment, and I decided to go straight from there to prayer meeting. You know, after that big breakfast this morning at Denny's—and then I broke down and had a hero brought in for lunch—I didn't need much of a supper. A salad at home after prayer meeting would have been just fine."

I prayed for patience. "Get back to your point, Anita. When and how did you see her?"

Anita sighed. "I was getting there. Like I started to say, I was headed out toward prayer meeting when I noticed a light on in your aunt's shop. Well, call it the Spirit moving, or whatever, but I decided to drop in and ask her along. I mean, just because a lot of people don't like her none—her being so stubborn and all—doesn't mean that the Lord don't."

"That's mighty Christian of you, Anita." I was sincere.

14

"Well, I knocked on the front door but she didn't answer. I knew she was in there, though, because your aunt ain't about to give Duke Power and Light more than their fair share."

She paused, presumably for me to agree. I didn't.

"Well, when she didn't answer I walked around to the back. I found the door halfway open so I went on inside. I started calling her name, but she didn't answer. I was just about to dial nine-one-one when I saw her lying on the floor behind her register. The bellpull was around her neck."

"She was dead? I mean, then?"

Anita coughed. Despite her convictions, she smoked like a sausage factory. "I'm not a doctor, Abigail. I didn't even want to touch her, but I did. I tried to feel for a pulse on her wrists and her neck, but I couldn't find any. When the paramedics arrived, they confirmed it. Was she saved, Abigail?"

I bit my tongue. I was raised Episcopalian. Words like "saved" and "born again" make me uncomfortable.

"She went to church, regularly," I said.

"Well, if she was saved, then we can all rejoice. She went to be with the Lord. Right now she's probably singing with the angels, or maybe out walking them golden streets. Looking for her mansion. Whatever she's doing, you can be sure she's having a wonderful time. "

"I'm sure she is," I said dryly. "What did the police have to say?"

"The police?"

"You know, the men in blue."

"Yes, well, the police asked me a bunch of questions. Was I alone when I found her? What did I touch? How well did I know her? That sort of thing."

"Did they have any ideas who might have done it?"

She coughed again. "You don't think they'd tell me if they did, do you? Except of course that whoever done it left that bellpull behind."

"They said that?"

"Not exactly. But then again, that's obvious. Your aunt didn't have anything like that in her shop. Her stuff was all— you know—junk."

I thanked Anita for calling. Perhaps I was a little curt, but that woman gets under my skin easier than fat cells. It was still sinking in that Aunt Eulonia was dead, and Anita already had her traipsing about heaven inspecting real estate. And there certainly was no need for Anita to bad-mouth a dead woman's merchandise.

The phone was on its hook three seconds before it rang again. I answered.

"I don't have time for this, Aunt Marilyn. If you want, I'll move out tomorrow and take those camellias with me. Right now I've got more important things on my mind."

"Mrs. Wiggins?" a male voice asked.

I glanced at Mama. She was sitting now and looked as pale as the pork chop bones.

"This is her daughter, Abigail Timberlake. May I take a message?"

There was a pause, accompanied by what sounded like papers rustling. "Well, yes, you'll do just fine. Even better maybe. I'm Detective—"

"Is this about my aunt, Eulonia Wiggins?"

He was silent for a few seconds. "Yes, ma'am. I'm afraid I have some bad news for you."

I let the detective tell me his version of the story. Since Anita was the source for most of it, his story matched hers pretty well. He, however, said nothing about the bellpull belonging to my aunt's killer. Neither did he try and paint pictures of her cavorting in heaven.

"I'd like to come around tomorrow and ask you a few questions," he said, without giving me a chance to ask any of my own.

"You mean to my shop?"

"The Den of Antiquity, right?"

"Yes, sir. What time?"

"Pick a time. Maybe when you generally have the least customers. That way we won't disturb them, and they won't disturb us." The words sounded ominous, but the voice didn't.

"Well, I don't know. Business tends to be pretty steady. I open the shop at nine, and I close it at five. You could come before or after those hours."

"How about over the lunch hour? Don't things slow down a bit then?"

"Twelve would be fine."

"Sorry ma'am. I'll be on another case then. I was thinking more like one o'clock."

"Well, uh, you see—I mean—"

"Don't tell me I forgot! Today is Erica's tenth wedding?"

"Excuse me?"

"On *All My Children*. I thought Dmitri would hang on to her longer than that."

"Well, it wasn't his fault!" I caught myself. Staring me in the face—rather, chatting in my ear—was a man with a pleasant voice who was obviously also a fan of *AMC*. An opportunity to meet such a man, even if (sigh) he was married, should not be missed. "Yes, well one o'clock might be fine after all."

"I promise we'll talk only during commercials," he said.

"And between customers," I reminded him gently.

The next morning I found the Major waiting outside my shop. It was one of those September mornings in Charlotte when you felt summer was never going to let go. At nine in the morning it was already eighty degrees, with the humidity high enough to poach a pedestrian in three minutes flat. And there was the Major, standing in the full sun, wearing some sort of khaki uniform, complete with a pith helmet.

"Late British Raj," he said. "Came from an English officer murdered in the Punjab. Circa nineteen thirty-nine."

I took a closer glance, looking for bloodstains. I am not a rubbernecker or a ghoul. I am, however, intensely interested in learning how to get stains lifted out of old fabric. The Major's uniform looked spotless to me. Not even sweat stains in the obvious places.

He read my mind. "The officer was garroted. Sort of like your aunt, I imagine."

"Excuse me?"

The Major put his fists together and rotated them. "You know, strangled with something."

"Excuse me!"

"Well, it's all a part of life, you know. Nothing to get so upset about."

"Well!" I fumbled, trying to find the right key to unlock the door. If I had the sense of a tadpole I'd stick bits of colored tape on my keys to make identification easier. It would be a wise thing from a safety point of view, and with shop neighbors like the Major, a personal point of view as well.

"Allow me," the Major said. He fished one of his own keys from the depths of a khaki pocket and had my door open in less time than it takes to blink in a sandstorm.

"Where the hell did you get that?" I snatched the key from him. It was identical to mine.

The Major attempted a laugh. Thank God there weren't any mockingbirds in the vicinity. It wasn't a sound I'd like to hear repeated.

"Well? Where did you get it?"

"I have keys to all the shops on Selwyn Avenue. To ones that belong to our dealers association, at any rate. Y'all gave them to me at our very first meeting, remember?"

I most certainly did not remember doing such a crazy thing. I did remember that someone had made a suggestion along those lines. Something about being able to keep an eye on each other in times of need or emergency. But I distinctly recalled that the suggestion got nowhere. After all, we didn't know each other well enough then. Had we known each other, the suggestion would never have been made.

I slipped through the door and would have locked it behind me had it not been for one of the Major's boots.

"I never gave you my key," I shouted. I was angry. I felt as if I had been violated.

The Major had to remove his helmet to get his face right up to the door. His hair, which he wore parted in the middle, remained impeccably combed.

"Ah yes, now I remember. You didn't give me your key. Your aunt did."

"What?"

In my surprise I had relaxed my diligence. The Major was now foursquare inside my shop. I picked up a heavy cut glass decanter. The time to strike was now, before he put the helmet back. Anyone who knew him would agree that it was justifiable homicide.

The Major wisely refrained from taking a step closer, thereby sparing his part, not to mention a perfectly beautiful piece of glass.

"You weren't at the second meeting, were you? Well, the subject came up again. That time we voted on the key thing. I was elected to be the key keeper, since my shop is the most centrally located."

"Except for my aunt's," I said.

"You wouldn't expect a woman her age to run up and down the street performing errands of mercy, would you? She could barely stand on her own two feet."

I drew myself up to my full four feet nine. Unfortunately I had decided to wear flats that day.

"She had no business giving you that key. I'd rather keep it under a stone. Of course, not the one you crawled out from."

I had meant to be offensive, but Major Calloway had a tough hide. When he died I wanted a pair of shoes made from it. Make that two pairs and a matching handbag.

"Ha! Good one, good one. Say, about what happened at the meeting yesterday, you aren't planning to tell anyone, are you? I mean, the police, or whoever."

I was genuinely puzzled.

"What happened that the police should know about?"

He put the helmet back on, possibly a defensive gesture. "You know, what we said about your aunt. Wishing she was dead and all."

Light dawned in the crevices of my mind, sending a myriad of fuzzy creatures scrambling. The Major's visit made sense now.

"Actually, Major, I believe you said that 'whoever bumps off that old biddy deserves a commendation.' Are you here to collect your medal?"

He took a step back, the rim of his helmet knocking against a cowbell I keep tied to the door to apprise me of customers. It was a tie as to which jangled louder, the bell or my nerves.

"Listen, Timberlake, I don't have to put up with your accusations. Everyone there said the same kind of thing. We were all sore at your aunt on account of the way she kept her place, but none of us really meant it. Hell, who would be stupid enough to make a real threat in front of a dozen witnesses?''

My glare was his answer.

"Look, girlie,'' he snarled. "I don't take this shit from anybody. I came over to offer you my condolences. Well, you can take my goddamn condolences and shove them—''

Which is what I tried to do. But the Major weighs twice as much as I, and I was barely able to push him to the door, much less have him go through it. I know that sounds a trifle mean-spirited, but with the Major's tough hide, he would only have been out the price of a couple of Band-Aids. I would have been out $32.54 for a new pane of glass.

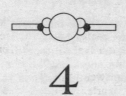

4

My phone rang off the hook. Virtually every other shop owner in the Selwyn Avenue Antique Dealers Association called with words of sympathy. Some of it heartfelt.

"Sorry to hear about your aunt," Rob Goldburg said. "I didn't mean the terrible things I said yesterday at breakfast. I really didn't. Is there something we can do to help?"

He sounded sincere. I said no, and thanked him. The "we" was undoubtedly meant to include his new partner, Bob Somebody-or-the-other. I had yet to meet the fellow, but rumor had it that he was from New York, a real expert on some of the upscale merchandise that the rest of us just dabble in. Rumor also had it that Rob and Bob were more than business partners.

The rumor-spreader must have been hard at work.

"Abigail? Wynnell here. I just heard the news and I'm sick to my stomach. How awful for you. You want me to close up shop for a few minutes and come on over?"

"Thanks, but no thanks. I'm doing fine."

"You sure, dear? I can't imagine I'd be fine if my aunt was raped and then decapitated."

"That's not what happened."

"Oh, was it the other way around? Good Lord, what's this city coming to? Charlotte used to be such a good place to live in. I'll tell you what the trouble is, Abigail. It's those damn Yankees."

"She wasn't raped or decapitated, Wynnell. She was strangled by a bellpull. And what's this about Yankees? As far as I know the police have no suspects.''

"Well, if it wasn't a Yankee, then it was someone influenced by a Yankee. If you ask me, we should build an electric fence along the Mason-Dixon line. Then you'll see. Our crime rate would plummet.''

"And so would our sales, Wynnell. What percentage of your sales is to tourists?''

"There are southern tourists as well, Abigail. We don't need murdering Yankees to survive.''

I prayed my most frequent prayer, the one for patience. "The police haven't fingered a Yankee, Wynnell. At this point the killer could turn out to be anybody. Who knows, it could even turn out to be you.''

"That isn't funny, Abigail. I was going to apologize for what I said about your aunt yesterday at breakfast, but now maybe I won't.''

I could feel Wynnell's withering look from four shops away. The woman missed her calling. Somewhere there's a classroom full of unruly kids who could benefit from the juxtaposition of Wynnell Crawford's eyebrows.

I succumbed to temptation. "Wynnell, dear, just the other day I heard that not only did you have a Yankee in your woodpile, but it was Sherman himself.''

"Why, I never!'' she said, and slammed down the phone.

Peggy got through next. She must have been horny again, because I could hear her chewing. Peggy isn't married and, unfortunately, has an exceptionally strong libido. When Peggy can't fill her sexual needs, she does the next best thing and fills her stomach. Peggy would be fat if it wasn't for the exercise she does get those times she's lucky enough to have sex.

"Abigail?''

"Is it blueberry or pumpernickel?'' Mama can smell trouble. I like to think I can smell food over a phone.

"Cinnamon raisin. Picked it up at the Bagel Works Delicatessen. There's a new guy working there who's to die for. Oops, sorry, Abigail. Sorry about your aunt, too.''

"Thanks, dear. You aren't by any chance calling because

you're nervous about something you said at breakfast yesterday?''

Who knew a bagel could be deafening? "What? I don't know what you mean, Abigail."

"I think you do, dear, but not to worry. We all shoot our mouths off from time to time, and then live to regret it."

There was a moment of silence and then the sound of throat muscles trying desperately to forward the bagel on to the stomach. Even cartoon pythons aren't that loud.

"I only said she was tacky, Abigail. I didn't threaten her."

"But you preferred her out of the way, didn't you, Peggy?"

"I'd prefer to get rid of some wrinkles, too, but I have yet to get a face-lift. And those alpha hydroxyl creams I use don't count. They're more like wishing your lines away—which is kind of like what I did to your aunt. I wished her away. I didn't kill her."

I wished Peggy a good day.

My daughter Susan called next. Susan has had one year of general studies at the University of North Carolina here in Charlotte, and already she knew more than her father and me combined. One more year and she would have been a match for Phil Donahue.

"Mama!"

"Hey, Susan. I suppose you heard the bad news about your great-aunt Eulonia. Did Grandma call you?"

"No. What's up?"

I was surprised. This semester Susan has moved out of the dorm and shares an apartment with two other girls. As part of her strategy to convince herself of her independence, she contacts her parents only when she needs money. Or someone to dump on. Since her father has oodles of money, and I don't, guess who gets dumped on. This, however, did not sound like a dumping day.

"Aunt Eulonia died last night. No, let me rephrase that. She was murdered."

"Bummer. Mama, I've got a problem you wouldn't believe."

"I said your great-aunt is dead, dear. Did you hear me?"

"Yes, I heard you. But Mama, my problem is serious. You have a minute or what?"

Actually, at the moment there was a young couple hovering around a Victorian parlor set that had been in my inventory far too long. They alternated between sitting on the pieces and carefully examining them for flaws. At one point the wife stepped back and made blocking gestures with her hands. To be sure, all five pieces were being lined up against imaginary walls. A well chosen word or two would put their cash in my coffer. I really didn't have time to be dumped on.

But I am a mother. "Spill it, dear."

The bomb dropped without further preamble. "I quit school today."

"You what?"

"I went to the registrar's this morning and withdrew. It wasn't too late. Of course I won't get all my tuition back, but who cares?"

I bit my tongue and counted to ten. Twice. Once in French and once in Spanish.

"Why did you drop out?"

"Because school's a drag. You know I've never liked school. And besides, I was at Belk's Department Store in South Park Mall last Saturday and they need someone in the cosmetics department. I've decided that's more real. School is too phony."

"If you're no longer in school you're going to need a real paycheck, dear. Didn't Dad say he was going to pay your share of the apartment only as long as you stayed in school?"

During the ensuing silence I watched the young couple slip slowly out of love with my parlor set. If I hadn't been held bondage by maternal strings, I might have been able to salvage the deal. I made a desperate attempt anyway.

"Ten percent off today," I called out cheerily.

"What?" Susan sounded aggravated with me. "Mama, my life's a mess and you're haggling with customers?"

"Oops, my mistake. It's actually twenty percent off," I yelled.

They shook their heads and walked slowly out of my shop. They had my number. Undoubtedly they'd be back the next day and try for 25 percent off. With any luck I'd be on the phone again and give them thirty.

"Mama! Don't you care?"

"Of course I care, dear. What is it you want from me?" Besides my figure, my patience, and the best years of my life. She had already taken those.

"Mama, I'm not going to be making that much at Belk's. Not to start. Aren't you going to offer to pay my rent?"

I would not. That was the *only* thing Buford and I agreed upon. We would support the children financially only as long as they remained in school. Otherwise, they were on their own. With Buford's money, Susan could have gone on to medical school or something else equally time-consuming. But since she wanted to play apartment without the benefit of an education, she was going to have to do it on her own. Maybe then she would reconsider school.

"I'm the meanest Mama in the whole world," I said, preempting my lovely daughter.

"Mama!"

"And I'm so unfair!"

Susan hung up. But what else could I do? I didn't have the money to support her while she played at having a job. If she wanted to move in with me, I'd be delighted. But Susan would rather floss three times a day than do that. After all, I'm prone to wild and wacky behavior, such as sleeping when it's dark and washing the dishes before the mold on them requires mowing. Not to mention I vacuum up my dust balls before they get too big to trip over.

During the brief respite that followed Susan's call I hurried over to the parlor set that had so intrigued the young couple. It was early Eastlake and in excellent condition. I took a minute to admire the burled walnut frames and the dusty pink velvet seats. Then I removed the old price, replacing it with a figure 30 percent higher. Even if I was caught on the phone when they returned, I could still afford to be generous.

I thought sure the next phone call was going to be from Buford. He sees it as his sacred duty to yell at me every time one of our children is unhappy or does something stupid. Even though he and I agree on Susan's education, it is undoubtedly somehow all my fault that Susan has decided to drop out of school and live in near poverty. Since I produced the egg that hatched Susan, I am responsible for her behavior. What else would one expect from a lawyer who once sued a pencil company because they didn't warn their customers that a sharpened lead can put out an eye?

"Den of Antiquity. Guilty party speaking," I said cheerfully.

Gretchen Miller gasped. "Oh, Abigail, you didn't do it, did you?"

I think as fast on my feet as a doped walrus. "You bet I did. She had to learn a lesson."

"But, Abigail, isn't decapitation a little too severe? And the rape, you didn't do that, too, did you? I mean, it isn't physically possible, is it?"

My brain had caught up with my ears. "Gretchen! Of course not! And she wasn't decapitated, she was strangled. Only I didn't do that, either. I thought you were someone else."

Gretchen's sigh of relief could have extinguished a candle a yard away. "I'm so glad, Abigail. I mean, that you're not guilty. Do the police know who is?"

"If they do, they're keeping it from me."

"Any suspects?"

"You tell me, dear. You were at that breakfast yesterday morning."

Gretchen sneezed. I imagined her pushing her round, owl glasses back up on her stub of a nose.

"Abigail, if you'll recall, I stuck up for your aunt yesterday. I said she was a 'jewel.' You remember that?"

"Yes, dear, I do. That was right before you complained about her place being run down."

She sneezed again. "Sorry Abigail. It's the pollen count. I'm almost positive it's not a cold. I usually don't get a cold until November, and then—"

"Is business slow today, dear?"

"Business is good, Abigail. I just sold that bronze statue with the you-know-what."

"The 'what' was a penis, dear. So, if business is good, why are you calling?"

I imagined Gretchen's faded gray eyes widening behind thick lenses.

"Well, I—uh—I wanted to expresses my condolences on your aunt's passing. That's really all."

I accepted her condolences gracefully, even though I would hardly refer to being strangled as "passing." Even sans the rumored rape and decapitation, my poor aunt had done more than pass from this life to the next. Catapulted was more like it. No wonder they say ghosts are usually the products of violent death. I'd have trouble finding my way through the veil, too, if my last memory was a bellpull tightening around my neck. It wouldn't surprise me a bit if Aunt Eulonia's spirit hung around her beloved Feathers 'N Treasures trying to comprehend recent events.

Perhaps it would benefit my aunt if I stopped by her shop and had a chat with her. One-sided, I hoped. You know, kind of explained what happened. And if the case ever got solved, tell her why it happened. Fortunately her shop was still off-limits to anyone but the police; the yellow tape across the doors made that perfectly clear. For the moment that was fine with me. I was in no hurry to see where dear Aunt Eulonia had lain gasping, perhaps thrashing, on the floor of her run-down shop.

To take my mind off the ghoulish spectacle I turned on the TV. *All My Children* was about to start.

5

The cowbell rang on the stroke of one. It didn't jangle this time, it rang. Bells all over heaven rang as well. God's gift to women—at least to me—had just stepped through the door.

I ran to be of service. "Yes? May I help you?"

"Ms. Abigail Timberlake?"

"Yes."

"I'm Investigator Greg Washburn, Charlotte-Mecklenberg police. We have an appointment."

I held out an eager hand. His hand may not have been so eager, but when it touched mine, electricity flowed—from my hand to my heart, to my head, to my feet. My entire body was paralyzed. It was a good thing I had worker's compensation insurance.

"Ma'am, is there someplace we could talk?"

I stared at a youthful Cary Grant. No, Greg was a little taller and broader through the shoulders, his tummy firmer. His hair was darker, curling under where it hit his collar. The chin cleft was there, but so was a dimple on his left cheek. His eyes, rimmed by long black lashes, were intensely blue.

"Contacts?" I asked. At least my mouth was working, if not my brain.

"Ma'am?"

"I mean, you must have many contacts in your line of work. Ah, yes, we can talk back there by the counter, if you like."

I willed two rubbery pedestals to move my body and my

head to the back of the shop. Somehow they made it. My brain arrived a few seconds later.

"Identification?" I asked.

It was all there. Unfortunately it didn't tell me everything I wanted to know.

"Satisfied?"

I nodded. Of course I turned off the TV. Even Tad Martin can't compete with Investigator Greg Washburn.

"Sit?" Did he think I was talking to a dog?

The blue eyes danced. There was only one chair. "Why don't you sit, ma'am? I'd prefer to stand."

I didn't need to be coaxed. I could will those rubbery pedestals to walk, but I couldn't keep them from shaking. Except that, if I sat down, those blue eyes would be too far away. I would need opera glasses to get as close as I wanted.

Investigator Washburn and I did not share the same agenda. "Ma'am, what can you tell me about your aunt?"

"She's dead," I said. So was my brain.

He smiled, flashing teeth as straight and white as piano keys. "Yes, we've determined that. Can you describe what she was like when she was alive?"

"Old."

He glanced at a pocket notepad. "She was eighty-six, right?"

"Right. She would have been eighty-seven the day after Christmas."

"A little on the senior side to still be working. Did she have plans to retire?"

I laughed and then became acutely aware that laughing can produce spittle. There are more effective ways to attract a man than drenching him.

"Let me tell you about my aunt. Her grandmother was born on a farm down near Columbia. Great-Grandma Wiggins was fourteen when the Union army swept through, burning everything in their path. She was home alone at the time but managed to save the farm. Her weapons were two muskets, a pitchfork, and a mind as sharp as a scalpel. Just how she did it is a long story, but the point is Aunt Eulonia was every bit a Wiggins. Oh yeah, Great-Grandma Wiggins died at age one hundred seven. She still lived on that farm. By herself.''

He jotted something on his pad. ''Sounds like quite a lady. You know anyone who might have had it in for your aunt. Besides the Union Army?''

I swallowed first before laughing pleasantly. ''Well, that's kind of a messy question. Can you be more specific?''

A black eyebrow arched slightly over a dancing eye. ''Is there anybody that you can think of who would have wanted your aunt dead?''

I tried not to squirm. ''Well, yes, and no.''

The blue eyes stopped dancing. ''Tell me about the yes first.''

If it was in for a penny, in for a pound, why was I always throwing my entire checkbook in the ring?

''Everybody—well, just about everyone who owns a shop on this street wanted her dead. Maybe not actually dead, but gone somehow.''

''Why?''

''It was an image thing. You've seen her shop. Aunt Eulonia had no interest in living up to anybody else's standards or expectations. She didn't give a damn about what people thought.''

''And the no part?''

The blue eyes were fixed intently on me. It might have been due to the feeble air conditioner I have out back, but I was burning up. All I could think of was jumping into those clear blue eyes and taking a swim. I had to lasso my frolicking thoughts, tie them up with words, and force them out of my mouth.

''Well, like I said, they wanted her gone, not dead. I mean, who would really want to kill an eighty-seven-year-old woman just because she kept property values down and scared off a few rich customers? At her age, how much longer could she have held out?''

''Twenty more years?''

He had a point. ''Still,'' I said, ''I can't imagine any of these people actually going ahead and doing it. Killing her, I mean. Not most of them, at any rate.''

Both eyebrows shot up. The blue intensified.

"Well, there is Major Calloway," I said. I wasn't trying to be vicious and pay back his rudeness. He really was the most likely candidate.

"Please go on."

"He collects and sells weapons and things. 'Antique military paraphernalia,' he calls it. But I don't think Hitler's pajamas count as paraphernalia, do you?"

Investigator Washburn laughed. He had a pleasant laugh, with little or no spittle.

"I think I read once that Hitler slept in the nude. Sounds like this guy's trying to pull the covers over the public's head."

"There! That's a form of strangulation, isn't it?"

He laughed again. "Did you ever hear Mr. Calloway make any threatening remarks to your aunt?"

"No. Not to her directly."

"Did he ever make threatening remarks concerning your aunt to anyone else?"

"Plenty of times. Only yesterday he told our entire group that Aunt Eulonia should be shot by a firing squad."

A smile played about the perfectly formed lips.

"What group is this?"

"The Selwyn Avenue Antique Dealers Association. We were having our monthly breakfast together at Denny's. We were all there except my Aunt Eulonia."

He jotted some more down. "Do all the antique dealers on Selwyn Avenue belong to this association?"

"All the ones concentrated in these two blocks."

"Your aunt included?"

"Aunt Eulonia was a charter member, but she stopped being active when she found out that we—well, some of us—had an agenda."

"Which was?"

I recrossed my legs. "To set and maintain standards for shops and dealers in this area."

"Did you endorse that agenda?"

"Well, I—uh, of course I'm all for standards. I mean, this is a nice part of town and we, as antique dealers, want to have a certain reputation. If this were your shop, would you want a junk shop next door?''

He shrugged. ''I've always been fond of junk shops. Found a child's pedal car in a junk shop once. It was made back in the early fifties. Always wanted one of those. Anyway, this one was in great shape. Even had all four wheels.''

My wheels were spinning. Was he a boy back in the early fifties? There wasn't a gray hair on his head that I could see, and I'd counted them twice. He had a full contingent.

''Very nice,'' I said. He could take it any way he chose.

''Ms. Timberlake, when is the last time you saw your aunt?''

''Let's see—hey, wait just one minute! You're not suggesting that I had anything to do with it?''

He displayed the piano keys casually. ''Until charges are pressed, there are no suspects. *And,* everyone is a suspect.''

Drop-dead gorgeous can go a long way, but there are limits. ''Look here, buster. She was my flesh-and-blood aunt. My father's only sister. I did not kill her.''

I leaned back in my chair huffing and puffing until it was time for round two. ''And besides, do I look like I could strangle someone?''

The piano keys disappeared. ''Your aunt was eighty-six. Almost eighty-seven. You could do it.''

I stood up. ''This interview is over. Don't let the door slam too hard behind you.''

He still towered over me. ''This isn't an interview, ma'am. It's an investigation. I can have you brought down to the station if you like.''

I didn't. I had never been to a police station, or wherever it is investigators hang out. Not even that time Buford landed in the hoosegow for goosing a housewife he thought was a stripper. I let his good-old-boy buddies bail him out. What else are his friends for?

Perhaps I'm a product of too much television, too many grade-B movies on late-night TV. Somewhere along the line I got the impression that women who visit police stations out of uniform are manhandled by monolithic matrons with flashlights in their hands. Need I say more?

"I'll sing like a canary," I said. "You just name the tune."

The blue eyes danced while the piano keys played.

"I just want the truth, ma'am. Your full cooperation."

"Ask away."

"Were you her next of kin?"

"Only blood kin she had that I know of. Me and my kids. Except for my brother, but he doesn't count."

"Why doesn't he count?"

I sighed. It seemed futile to pick open that scab again.

"Toy lives in California. But even if he were here, you could cross him off your list. Toy is about as energetic as a turtle on tranquilizers."

He nodded. "Laid-back, they call it out there. You have a key to her house?"

I scratched my head while I tried to wiggle out of that one. "Well, sort of. I mean, not exactly."

Both the eyes and the piano did a little ragtime. "I've heard high school boys in dresses come up with better explanations than you."

I felt myself blush, although it could have been a mild hot flash. Inspector Washburn had succeeded in thoroughly confusing my hormones. One minute they were happily on their way to an early retirement and the next they were doing the hundred-yard dash.

"It's like this. Aunt Eulonia gave me a key—" I paused and glanced at the front door. It was stupid of me not to have left a straight aisle between it and the register. With his long arms he could probably stop me before I got around the counter anyway. In that case, it didn't make a difference that the storeroom was cluttered as well.

"Yes? May I see the key?"

"I don't have it, sir."

"You don't?"

"No, sir. My aunt and I had this little disagreement—you know, like all families do—and I think she took the key back."

Who would have thought that blue could be a mocking color? "You *think*?"

"I have been known to, yes."

The full, perfect lips parted unevenly. I took it as a snarl.

"Well, it's hard to say," I said quickly. "I mean, I had it on my key ring, and then one day I looked, and it was gone."

"Where do you usually keep this key ring? During working hours, that is."

"Here, on this hook beneath the counter. Nobody can see it, and that way it's easy to grab when I need to unlock display cabinets for customers. I tried wearing it on my belt like some dealers do, but the jingling about drove me crazy."

"I see."

I hoped he did. I was trying my best to be cooperative, I really was. I offered to answer any other questions he had, no matter how silly or embarrassing. He took me up on my offer and asked me a billion more questions, but I seemed to disappoint him each time. I might even have confessed to something—maybe a traffic violation or two—just to get those eyes dancing again, when his beeper went off.

"May I use your phone, ma'am?"

"Please, be my guest." As soon as he left I was going to disconnect that phone. In a very dilute form Investigator Greg Washburn was going to spend the night with me.

He talked just a few seconds on my phone. His lips never touched the receiver. His hands barely held it. It was hardly going to be worth unplugging.

"Ma'am, that'll be all for today. It's been a pleasure."

"There's still five more minutes on *All My Children*," I said. Trot out the big guns when you have to.

"I'm taping it at home. Thanks, anyway."

And then he was gone. I would have kicked myself, had I not been wearing pointed shoes. I'd forgotten to look for a ring.

I am not a masochist, even though Mama thinks I am. I honestly didn't know Buford was the scum of the earth until he took up with Tweetie. The only reason I decided to drive by the homestead that evening was because I wanted to talk to our son Charlie. In person. Charlie and his great-aunt had been close. And it was more than the twenty bucks, and then fifty, Aunt Eulonia used to slip into his birthday cards. The two of them, although seventy years apart in age, were cut from the same cloth. You couldn't find fabric that wide at the Piece Goods Shop in Rock Hill.

Bob and No-Bob opened the door. Those are my names for Tweetie's breasts, although I'm sure she has her own. One of her breasts—the left, I think—bobs up and down when she walks, while the other is rigid. Her surgeon should have been more careful.

"Well, lookie what the cat drug home," Tweetie said.

I smiled pleasantly, ever the southern lady. "Is Buford here?"

At the sound of my voice, Scruffles came running. It wasn't his fault he nearly knocked Tweetie over. Good plastic surgeons should consider their patient's balance before agreeing to operate.

"Hey, boy!" I said.

"My husband is at his office," Tweetie said. She started closing the door before Scruffles could get in a single lick.

I took a cue from the Major and stuck a shoe in the door. My foot is a lot smaller than his, but then again, Tweetie is no Wiggins.

"Open that door or I'm telling Buford everything," I said.

The line works with Tweetie every time. One of these days I'm going to find out what it is she's trying to hide. At any rate, the door opened wide, leaving me face to point with Bob. Or maybe No-Bob. You get the point.

"I'm here to see my son. Is he here?"

"Maybe, maybe not. Buford said I don't have to let you in but once a week. You were already here this week."

"I was here Friday, and today is Tuesday. Anyway, I was awarded unlimited visiting privileges. Besides, Charlie is seventeen now. He can see me whenever he wants."

"I was talking about how many times I have to let you in the house. I don't care how many times you see your son. He's in the kitchen, still eating. That's all he ever does."

"That's what seventeen-year-old boys are supposed to do," I said calmly.

"And this damn dog sheds over everything. Have you ever tried getting dog hair off of white suede?"

"Not since my divorce, dear."

She lost interest in me and wandered off, the door still open. She turned around a corner, and I could see Bob bobbing and No-Bob not.

I am better behaved than most things the cat drags home, and closed the door. It was strange to be alone in my own house again—well, you know what I mean. Tweetie either had no interest in decorating or else was forbidden to do so by Buford (the man must have a little taste: he married me, didn't he?), because the only change I could see was the velvet Elvis painting above the grand piano. Even it was of better quality than most.

I gave Scruffles a big hug and let him lick my face a few times. "Next time trying chewing that white suede," I whispered.

Charlie was indeed in the kitchen, chowing down on the remains of an extra-large pizza. Tweetie undoubtedly cooked like she decorated. And what else did she expect a seventeen-year-old boy to do besides eat? Besides *that,* for pete's sake?

"Mama!"

I hugged Charlie and tousled his hair. Thank God the gene for baldness doesn't pass through the father. Even a cue ball has more fuzz clinging to it than Buford.

"What's up, Mama? You want some pizza? The bitch wouldn't let me order extra cheese. Says she's trying to watch her weight."

I accepted dinner from my son. After supper I tousled his hair again. Charlie doesn't mind pizza grease in his hair.

"Honey, Aunt Eulonia died last night. Did you hear?"

He shook his head, tears welling up immediately. "I was at school all day, then football practice. I just got home."

"Look Charlie, I'll tell it to you straight. Anyway, you're going to read about it in the paper. She was murdered."

He sat bolt upright. "No way!"

"Yes, dear, last night. I would have called you then, but I wanted to tell you in person."

He nodded, a far-off look in his eye. Undoubtedly he was remembering some of the good times he had known with his great-aunt. When he was little he used to spend the night at her house, and the two of them would stay up until dawn, playing canasta and making peanut brittle.

"She was one of a kind," I said. "Why would anyone want to kill an old lady like that?"

He looked me in the eyes.

"I know why she was killed, Mama. I know why they killed Aunt Eulonia."

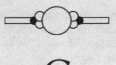

6

"You know who killed Aunt Eulonia?"

"No, but I know *why* she was killed."

Like all teenagers, Charlie lies through his teeth, but he is not given to dramatic statements. He has never felt the need for a spotlight.

"Why?"

He looked me in the eye. "Because of her lace."

Perhaps I had misjudged my son. "Her lace?"

He nodded. "Yeah. Aunt Eulonia had this lace thing—I forget what you call it—that she said was very valuable. That's why she was killed."

I smiled. A full day of school and then football practice. The boy was undoubtedly exhausted.

"Lace isn't that valuable, dear. Sure, if you get some really old stuff, and it's clean and not stained, it's worth something. But not enough to kill for. I mean, who would kill somebody for twenty-five dollars?"

He shook his head. "This was really special. She was going to sell it, you know. At an auction. In New York."

"Sotheby's?"

"Yeah, that sounds like it."

I could feel the hair on the back of my neck stand up. I was on to something.

"Did you see this lace?"

"Un-unh. But she told me about it. She said it was really old. Hundreds of years even. It was made in Italy, or Spain."

"Go on."

He grunted and reached for the last slice of pizza. "That's all I know about it, Mama. Oh, except that if it sold at this place in New York for half of what she thought it would, she was going to retire and take a trip around the world. She wanted to take me with her." His eyes filled with tears. "We were going to Africa first—on a photo safari. When we were all done, we were going to end up in Alaska walking on one of those glaciers."

That sounded like Eulonia Wiggins alright.

"You never mentioned this," I said. I tried not to make it sound like an accusation.

"I wasn't supposed to. Not yet. She wanted me to wait until after the auction. She was afraid talking about it would jinx it. I guess it did." He turned away to wipe his eyes.

I sat quietly until he had composed himself. "Did anyone else know about this?"

He shrugged, the cold pizza hanging from his mouth.

"Do you know where she got it?"

Unlike Peggy, he swallowed before answering. "Some ancestor of ours, I guess. Her grandmother, or somebody. Does that make us Italian or something?"

"Or something," I said. Our family had lived long enough in America to claim a pint or two of just about everybody's blood. Scotch, Irish, English, German, Swedish. French, Catawba Indian, even rumors of an African-American way back when, but as of yet no Italians.

He flashed me a smile. It was like the sun peeking through a stormy sky. "I have always liked pizza. And pasta."

"Me, too."

"I suppose you have to tell the police."

"Yes, dear, I'm afraid I do. I'm sorry."

He nodded. "It's okay. I want whoever did it caught. I want them—Mama, you didn't tell me how she was killed."

He was going to read it in the papers anyway. Maybe see it on TV. "She was strangled. Someone took a bellpull and strangled her."

He took it in. "Well then, I hope whoever killed Aunt Eulonia gets hung. No, I want to hang them myself. *After* I beat the shit out of them."

I did not raise my son to be violent. Football is Buford's influence. Still, if I could catch whoever strangled my aunt, I would call Charlie and have him come over. Together we'd beat the shit out of her murderer.

"The funeral is Thursday at two," I said after a while. "Down in Rock Hill, at Grandma's church. You want to go?"

He looked puzzled. "Why wouldn't I want to go? I'm not a baby, Mama. You going to come to school to pick me up?"

I nodded. "Charlie, did Aunt Eulonia ever give you a key to her house?"

He wiped his nose on his shirt sleeve. Not a baby, but still a boy. "No. You need to get in?"

"I want her to be buried in one of her favorite dresses. Something different than the one—well, you know."

"You won't find what you're looking for," Charlie said. It was uncanny how sometimes that boy could anticipate my next thought.

"Are you sure?"

"Positive. Aunt Eulonia told me she was keeping it somewhere nobody would ever think to look."

"In that old pie cabinet in the basement of her shop where she hides everything else?"

"I don't think so. It was supposed to be someplace really special. She said I wouldn't guess in a million years."

If it was in her safety deposit box then I was a day late and out of luck. It had undoubtedly been impounded that morning.

"Could it be at her house?"

"Beats me. She wouldn't give me any hints. But you can search her house yourself, if you want," he added, ahead of me again.

"What? I can't break in."

He smiled. "I said I didn't *have* a key. I didn't say I didn't know where one was. Try looking in a little clay flower pot tucked behind the azaleas next to the outside faucet. The one in back, near the garage."

Charlie squeezed me hard when I hugged him good-bye. "Love ya," he said.

*   *   *

I couldn't reach Investigator Washburn on the phone. He was off duty, I guess. Probably out gallivanting with women half my age. I was invited to leave a message, but I wasn't about to involve Charlie, not without speaking directly with Blue Eyes first. I left a cryptic message, asking him to call me at his earliest convenience. With any luck he would think I was coming on to him and take a hint. With just about any luck, but not with mine.

To me Charlotte is a big city, so by the time I got to Susan's street on the northeast side, my nerves were as tight as an overdeveloped perm. It didn't help matters any when Susan's building came into view. My daughter, perhaps to spite us, certainly to embarrass her father, chose the worst apartment building in all of Charlotte to call home. Don't get me wrong: the neighborhood itself is fine. It's Susan's building that is guaranteed to give you nightmares. I am convinced that in its better days it served as a training school for slumlords.

A small resident rat, or possibly a large visiting cat, ran out into the street when I opened the lobby door. The combined odors of urine, vomit, and boiled cabbage rolled over me like waves, nearly sweeping me back into the street along with the rat. No wonder the poor thing was in such a hurry.

The fifteen-watt lightbulb in the stairwell was a blessing. The obscene phrases scrawled on the wall were hard to read. Unfortunately I could still make out the crudely sketched body parts—most of which exuded fluids—but someone had kindly scrubbed several feet off the top of a giant, erect penis. I hoped it was Susan.

I had to walk up to the third floor. There was an elevator in the building, but as usual, it was occupied. I don't mean that someone was using it as a means of conveyance. I mean someone was living in it.

There wasn't any lightbulb on Susan's landing, the third, so I felt along the wall counting doors. I would have kicked myself for not bringing a flashlight, but I was still wearing my pointed-toe shoes. I knocked on the third door to the right. After five minutes and sore knuckles someone responded.

"Yeah?" The man who opened it was wearing only gray sweatpants, cut off above the knees. His calves were hairy, his belly was like a sheepskin, and he had very few teeth.

"I'm here to see Susan Timberlake."

He stared at me as if I had spoken in Mandarin Chinese.

"I'm her mother."

The door closed. After five more minutes and a sore right foot it opened again. Susan was standing there, clutching a bathrobe. Apparently she couldn't find the belt.

"Mama!"

"The very one. The same one who carried you through nine long months—during the hottest summer the Carolinas have ever had, mind you—endured seventeen hours of excruciatingly painful labor, sat up with you—"

"Do you want to come in, Mama?" Susan was always more deferential over the phone than in person.

It was a difficult choice. I couldn't figure out which was the frying pan and which was the fire. Foolishly I chose to see what I was getting into.

The apartment looked like it had been stripped. The brand-new sectional sofa Buford had bought for her at Sofas on South was missing. All the furniture was missing. The only thing in the living room was a decrepit mattress on the floor, only half covered by a twisted sheet.

"Susan!"

"Now chill, Mama. Don't get all bent out of shape. It was only stuff."

I took a deep, chilling breath. "Stuff your Daddy paid for. Stuff your roommates—speaking of which, where are they?"

Susan shrugged. It was the first gesture she ever learned.

"I guess Lori's living with her boyfriend. Tanya joined the National Guard, I think."

"What?" I needed to sit down, but I wasn't about to sit down on that mattress. The lobby carpet had less stains on it.

"Mama, these things happen. It just didn't work out rooming with them, that's all. It's no big deal. Everything's fine, honest."

"But you can't live here like this. Not by yourself."

She clutched the robe tighter across her chest. "I'm not alone, Mama. I have Jimmy."

"Jimmy?" Cerebral lightning hit. I wish it had knocked me

brain dead. "*That* was Jimmy? That pathetic old mange bucket was Jimmy?" Fortunately the man in question had retired to another room. Probably the bathroom.

"Mama! I'm not going to talk with you if you're going to say things like that."

I took a deep breath. Somewhere in the universe somebody went without air for a minute.

"Okay. I'm sorry. Now, who is this Jimmy?"

She was studying my face to see if I was really sorry. I thought about Aunt Eulonia's death and the pain it was causing Charlie. It must have worked.

"Mama, Jimmy Grady is the sweetest, kindest man alive. I'm in love with him, Mama. And I know he loves me!"

I kicked my left leg with my pointed right shoe. "How old is he?" I asked calmly.

She was able to look me in the eyes, I'll grant her that. "Thirty-eight."

"Where did you meet him?"

Her gaze wavered slightly. "He's a custodian at school. I mean, he was a custodian there. Last year. It isn't his fault that his wife sued him for child support and he ended up getting fired."

"His wife?"

She nodded. "But he's going to get a divorce. He never even loved her, you know that? He said he knows he couldn't have loved her, because it didn't feel at all like it feels for me. He says he's waited around his whole life for someone like me."

"I bet he has," I muttered. "How many children does your Jimmy have?"

"Five, Mama, but none of them were his fault. His wife kept tricking him into getting her pregnant. She's extremely manipulative."

"Sounds like Jimmy needs to keep his pecker in his pants."

"What?"

"Uh, what I—what did happen to the furniture?" It was a useful tactic, learned from Susan herself. When trapped, change the subject.

"Oh that. Jimmy said it would be a good idea to sell it and

put the money into a better car. I need a good car if I'm going to drive to work every day, not a sofa.''

"I see. But what happened to the car your Daddy gave you?''

"Oh that? Well, you see, Jimmy and his friends were driving around one day, obeying the speed limit and everything, and this old geezer runs a stop sign and totals it.''

That certainly accounted for Jimmy. Thank God Susan wasn't along.

"What about insurance? Didn't you tell your daddy?''

She put her hands on her hips, a gesture learned from me no doubt. ''Well, you know how Daddy's always yapping about high rates and all. I didn't want him to get upset, so I didn't collect.''

"But Susan, dear, you don't have insurance on this *better* car, do you?''

She sighed patiently. "I will, Mama. Just give me time. It's my life, you know, and my car. Daddy didn't have a thing to do with this one.''

She meant her car. I wish I could say the same thing for her life. I don't know what possessed me to marry Buford Timberlake right out of college. Possessed—maybe that was it. I was possessed by something. After all, there was this Haitian girl, into voodoo, who lived right down the hall.

Mama saw straight through to Buford's core. Knowing her, she probably smelled how rotten it was. I was so in love I couldn't smell or see. Of course, comparing Buford with Jimmy was like comparing girdles with peanuts. There wasn't any relationship there at all.

Buford had a college education and a place guaranteed him in law school. Buford had plans. Buford even had some money. Not much, but enough so that I didn't have to work when Susan was born.

What did Jimmy have? He didn't even have a whole pair of jogging pants. I would have to come back to Susan's apartment building in the daytime, with a high-powered flashlight—maybe connected to a high-powered rifle, and do some sleuthing. It was beginning to look like that Haitian girl, the one into voodoo, might be living under Susan's roof.

I kicked myself into consciousness.

"Susan, are you—I mean, is this something more than a platonic relationship?" I am willing, no eager, to talk myself into believing anything that will make life easier for the ones I love. And for me.

Her eyes widened. She was always good at feigning astonishment.

"Mama, no! Of course not! I would never do such a thing. Not without getting married first. Jimmy sleeps out here on the floor. I sleep back there in the bedroom. Mama, really!"

She had thrown me enough scraps to concoct the meal I desperately needed. I was momentarily grateful. It wasn't as late in the game as it could be.

"Well, dear, if you do decide to sleep with him—which I sincerely hope you don't—*please* use protection. Promise me?"

She nodded vigorously. "Oh, I will, Mama. If I ever do, I will. But I won't, so I won't need to."

There was little else to say. I was not emotionally prepared to sit down on Jimmy's mattress and have a pleasant chat. First, I would have to sleep on what I had just seen and heard. Maybe hibernate for a winter or two. Susan should thank her lucky stars that her daddy was too busy, or selfish, to pay her a visit unless forced. I certainly would do nothing to force Buford out there until I had thought things through thoroughly.

I hugged her. She smelled like male sweat.

"Aunt Eulonia's funeral is the day after tomorrow. Two in the afternoon at the Church of Our Savior in Rock Hill."

"Okay. I'll come if the car can make it."

I refrained from asking her if that was the better car Jimmy had talked her into buying. That conversation could wait. It was worth biting a small piece of my tongue off just getting out of there without a major confrontation.

"I love you, Susan."

The quick nod from her was a reciprocal declaration I'm sure.

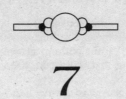

7

I am ashamed to say I hadn't been to Aunt Eulonia's house in over a year. Okay, so it was almost three years, but I had a lot of water rush under my bridge in those three years. Tweetie made a big splash in my life. In fact she almost drowned me. Of course, I can't put all the blame on her— Buford was twice her age and should have known twice as much. Factor in their relative IQs and Tweetie comes out almost innocent.

Don't give me that crap about the home fires being out and that's why Buford went looking. My furnace was roaring when Buford decided to trade it in for a newer model, whose pilot light has yet to be lit. Who knows, maybe Buford couldn't take all that heat. And don't even suggest that the furnace was rusted on the outside and in need of cosmetic repair. I weigh exactly the same as I did the day I was married, and my various parts are within an inch or two of their starting positions. How many other forty-six-year-old women can make the same claim?

So what does Tweetie have that I don't have? Blond hair? Bigger boobs? A firmer butt? I could have bought all those things if I had wanted to be someone other than who I am. The only thing she has, that I can't buy, is a pair of legs that stop at the armpits.

Well, I seem to have digressed, which, in a way, is exactly my point. If Buford's affair makes me this mad now, imagine what it did when I first found out. I didn't know one could hate that much. Or hurt that much. And speaking of pain, I can't begin to describe the depth of the abyss I fell into when Buford won custody of our children. I am still climbing out.

And that's why I hadn't been to Eulonia's in almost three years. I had, however, seen her at Mama's house on holidays, and of course I'd see her professionally from time to time. Like before she dropped out of the Selwyn Avenue Antique Dealers Association.

September in Charlotte is not yet autumn, and the only leaves that have fallen have been whacked out of the trees by errant baseballs and clumsy birds. Aunt Eulonia's street is overgrown to begin with, and I may as well have been bivouacking in the jungles of Southeast Asia. As a woman living alone, I should carry a purse-size flashlight with me at all times—perhaps I do, and just might stumble across it sometime when I have a week to clean out my purse. At any rate, I had a devil of a time trying to find Aunt Eulonia's back faucet, much less a clay pot hidden in the weeds.

"Can I help you?" a man asked.

I jumped at least three feet, which is quite a feat considering the length of my legs. I had once attended a seminar on self-defense for women and had gone away, after a mere two hours, feeling like I could disable Goliath. Now, while I would encourage other women to take similar self-defense courses, I feel that I must warn them about something I didn't learn in my class. It is possible to get so frightened that you wet your pants.

"I'm sorry, I didn't mean to frighten you," the man said.

It took several seconds for my brain to sort through a myriad of quavering stimuli and come to the conclusion that most muggers and rapists are seldom that polite. After a very brief period in which I lay collapsed in a bush (they were not azaleas, but hollies!), and several minutes of the heaviest breathing I had experienced since the advent of Tweetie, I was able to speak.

"Who the hell are you, and what are doing here?"

"Funny, I was about to ask you the same," he said.

"I may be small, but I've been trained in the martial arts," I puffed. "You want a demonstration?"

"That would be very interesting," he said. "I haven't seen

a good demonstration of that since I was in the marines.''

''Move over there to the light, buster, where I can see your face.''

If a bird could bluff to defend her nest, then so could I. Only I didn't have a nest to defend, and unlike a bird I couldn't fly away if the bluff failed. What was I doing? I would have been much better staying in the holly bush. Make him at least get his arms prickled when he tried to get me.

To my astonishment he obediently moved away from the shadows and into the relative light cast by a distant security lamp. The good Lord was right: the light did set me free. The guy might have had a voice like a robust young mugger, but he wasn't a day under ninety. Willard Scott was going to be wishing him happy birthday on national TV before it was time for me to clean the lint out of Aunt Marilyn's dryer again.

''My name is Tony D'Angelo. I'm a neighbor. Who are you?''

''Kimberly McManus,'' I said. For some strange reason it was the first name that popped into my mind. She's a gal who works at Franklin's printing shop down in Rock Hill. But it may as well be her this old codger stalked, rather than me.

''The hell you say. You're Abby Timberlake, aren't you?''

''Who?'' Perhaps I'd found that clay pot after all—hit my head on the damned thing.

''Abby Timberlake. Eulonia's niece.''

''I am not.''

''You weren't looking for this, were you?'' He reached into his pocket and held up something shiny.

''What?''

''Her back door key. The one hidden in the clay pot, back in those nasty hollies. Figured that's what you were looking for.''

''Give me that!'' I charged at him. We were approximately the same height and weight, and except for our ages, evenly matched. I know, he was a male and might still be producing a little testosterone, but he didn't have Buford as an ex-husband. One clear image of Buford and Tweetie doing the unspeakable in my bed, and I had enough adrenaline to run a triathlon.

Fortunately the old coot derailed me by laughing. "Here, you can have it."

"What?"

He gently tossed the key at my feet. "I suppose you have as much right to it as anybody."

I scooped it up, along with a handful of clay. Aunt Eulonia and grass did not get along.

"You're damn right. What were you doing with it?"

"Keeping it safe, that's all. Folks been stopping by, you know. Wanting to get in, but I wouldn't tell them where the key was."

"How did you know where it was?"

He laughed again. If I hadn't seen him, I would have thought he was twenty. "I was the one who suggested she hide it in the holly. Make that burglar work for his take."

"And her, too, then, if she ever needed it," I pointed out wisely.

"Ha. She wouldn't have ever needed that, unless something happened to me first."

"Just what do you mean by that?"

"I have my own key," he said smugly. "Eulonia gave it to me."

"When?" The nerve of my aunt, passing out house keys to every old Tom, Dick, and Harry, and then asking for mine back.

"Hmm, let's see," the old geezer pretended to think. "It was a while back, that's for sure. I think it was the day Nixon resigned from the Presidency."

"Excuse me?"

He was still thinking. "Yeah, it had to be in seventy-three, because I was living in Atlanta in seventy-two. That's when my grandson Cody was born. Wouldn't forget a thing like that now, would I?"

"I'm sure you wouldn't." Maybe I did let a little sarcasm show through, but Aunt Eulonia had no business having a man friend for twenty-three years and not even mentioning him to me.

He took a step forward, but I held my ground. "Look," he said, "it's muggy out here, and there's too many damn mosquitoes. How about we go on inside and continue this conversation there. The power is still on, and so is the air-conditioning.''

Well, slap me silly with a two-by-four and then call me grateful. Talk about nerve! Imagine being invited into your own aunt's home by an ancient neighborhood gigolo. I would have kept my mouth open longer if a mosquito hadn't flown in.

''There's tea in the fridge, already made up,'' he coaxed.

''I beg your pardon!''

''No trouble at all,'' he said. He trotted over to the back door, unlocked it, and then flipped on the porch light. You would have thought he lived there.

''Mr. D'Angelo—''

''Please, call me Tony.'' He had the impudence to usher me inside.

I strode angrily into my aunt's kitchen. There was indeed a pitcher of tea in the fridge, and I made damn sure I was the one to hunt up the glasses and pour it. Then *I* invited the little man to sit at the breakfast room table.

He took the tea without saying thanks. ''It's more comfortable in the den.''

I took off the silk boxing gloves. ''Look, buster, this is my aunt's house, not yours. Stop acting like you own the damn place. I'm inviting you to sit here, in the breakfast room.''

He drained the overly sweet tea in three gulps. He did not sit down. ''Charlie looks exactly like you, you know. Of course he's bigger.''

''Charlie?''

''Your son. Still, Euey and I were worried when he hadn't hit his growth spurt by the end of ninth grade. But he's sure the hell made up for it this year, hasn't he? How much has he grown, anyway? Five inches?''

''Six,'' I said. ''And his sneakers are size thirteen.''

We sat in the den while we polished off the rest of the tea. The man had made his point.

''I can't believe Aunt Eulonia never mentioned you,'' I said. It was a careless thing to say, and I regretted it immediately. I apologized all over myself.

''No need,'' he said, waving a wrinkled hand with enough

liver spots on it to make me dizzy. "Anyway, we've met before. Euey probably talked about me but didn't bother to mention me by name. Thought you knew who she meant."

"We've met?"

He laughed and I closed my eyes. He did sound twenty.

"Remember that time your car wouldn't start, and you didn't belong to Triple A?"

"No."

"Think back. It was a sixty-three Dodge Dart. White. With push-button controls."

This time when my mouth fell open an ice cube fell out. "That was you? How can you remember that far back? I mean, about a car not starting?"

The liver spots danced. "Or how about the time, after Susan was born, when I came over and fixed up a swing seat in that willow oak out back." He sighed. "Actually that one had to come down just this summer, thanks to Hurricane Hugo."

"My God!"

"Yeah, a real shame. Hugo came through six years ago, and still some trees are dying because of it."

"No, I mean, I can't believe how good your memory is. I wish mine were that good. I remember that one of my aunt's neighbors tied up the swing seat, but I didn't remember that it was you. I'm sorry. I don't mean to hurt your feelings."

"Nah. Think nothing of it. My point was, you knew me, you just forgot. Things like that happen."

I took his word for it. I also decided to take advantage of his formidable memory while I had a chance. Before I forgot who he was again.

"Say, Tony, you ever hear my aunt mention something valuable that she planned to auction off through Sotheby's?"

"What kind of thing?" For someone so old, there was a lot of fire in his eyes.

I decided to hold my cards close to my chest. That's far easier for me to do than it is for Tweetie.

"Oh, I don't know. Something very unusual, I guess."

"Ah, that."

"Ah, what?"

He studied me quietly for a moment, the fire in his eyes

dimming. Or perhaps he fell asleep. People his age have been known to do that.

"Euey was always talking about something she'd run across as being a rare find. A 'one-of-a-kind' she called them. Euey had more 'one-of-a-kinds' than a barn full of drunken poker players."

"But I heard this was something really special. Something she wanted to auction off at Sotheby's."

He gave me a pitying look. "I don't mean to speak ill of the dead, especially a dear friend, but look around you. Take a walk through the house. Do you think you'll find anything really valuable here? Or at her shop? Your aunt lived very modestly, you know."

"Yes, but—"

"Who told you about this valuable item? Did she?"

"Who else?"

"She describe it for you?"

"Of course." I'm sure my priest will disagree, but sometimes there is virtue in not telling the truth. "Not telling the truth," as opposed to "lying." There is a difference, you know. One is passive, the other active. One is intended solely to protect yourself or someone else you love. The other is for personal gain.

"Well? You going to tell me about this mysterious thing that's worth a fortune?"

"I can't."

"Why not?"

"I promised Aunt Eulonia I wouldn't."

He stared. There was something not quite right about those bright eyes. Perhaps gramps was overmedicated. I'd read that sometimes blood pressure medicine could produce the same effect.

"Yes, but she's dead," he said in that youthful voice.

"Exactly! I couldn't possibly break my word to a dead woman." I stood up. "If you'll excuse me, I think I'll go look for something nice to have her buried in. A favorite of hers."

He stood up as well. "Mind if I tag along?"

I took a deep breath. "Frankly, I do."

"Oh."

I walked out of the breakfast room, fully expecting him to tag along behind me like a puppy dog, but he didn't. I did need to find something to bury my aunt in, but that could wait. I wanted to see for myself if there was something valuable—something lace—hidden in one of her drawers, or draped over something in her closet.

It is downright weird to walk around in someone's house after they have just died. I think this is especially true if the deceased is a relative. Aunt Eulonia had family photographs covering every available inch of wall space, and in at least half of them I could see my own face grinning out at me. In at least half of those I could see Aunt Eulonia as well. The two of us would always be together in those photographs, but we were never going to be together again in real life. Not close enough so that she would have her arm draped around my shoulder, a bow in my hair thrust up her nose. At least I hoped not.

As familiar as the room was, it seemed strangely different. Something was missing. I turned around in circles a few times, and then it hit me.

"Hey Tony," I called. "Where are those slime-green velvet curtains?"

"Don't know. Maybe at the cleaners."

Hopefully the cleaners would lose them. They were beastly things, refugees from some old movie theater most probably. I was clearly at a genetic disadvantage when it came to decorating.

I wandered into Aunt Eulonia's bedroom, and that's when the heebie-jeebies really began. Besides bathrooms, bedrooms are the most personal, and personalized, rooms in a house. Psychologists and psychiatrists could save their patients thousands of dollars if they analyzed the contents of their bedrooms instead of their minds. Even just a dresser offers enough clues to reconstruct 90 percent of any given human being.

Frankly I did not enjoy rummaging through my aunt's drawers and pawing through her closet, but the job had to be done. And quickly, so that Tony with the bright eyes and phenomenal memory wouldn't become suspicious.

I was disappointed, but not surprised, when my hurried

search turned up not a scrap of lace, except for the crotch on a pair of panties that any decent, God-fearing woman would not have in her house. Especially if she was eighty-six.

"You all right in there?" The fossil with the teenage vocal chords sounded impatient, rather than worried.

"Yeah. Coming."

I snatched a navy blue dress off its hanger and draped it over my arm. I had seen Aunt Eulonia wear that dress several times on special occasions. At least I thought I had. At any rate, it would do nicely.

"She hated that one," the old goat said when I returned. He was standing in the middle of the breakfast room floor, exactly where I had left him.

"Nonsense," I said. "She didn't hate this. She wore it a lot."

"It still has the price tag on it." A surprisingly large, crooked finger swatted at the cardboard strip.

"There, you see," I said, "she didn't hate it. People don't buy clothes they hate."

"I gave it to her last Christmas," he said. "I forgot to remove the tag before I wrapped it. She got a kick out of that. Said she could tell by it how much I thought of her, but I could tell she didn't like it. I offered to take it back, but I wouldn't let me. I said she could always wear it to her funeral. I guess I was right."

I wanted to push the little man right out the back door. Push him off the porch. Maybe he would land in the holly. He was driving me crazy. Not only was he hampering my investigation, but he was showing me up for a fool—a fool who didn't know the first thing about her aunt, her father's only sister.

I sighed and sat down. The navy dress slid through my hands and onto the floor. It had been a very long day.

"What do you suggest then?"

He was gone less than a minute. When he returned it was with a peach suit, a cream blouse, and a pair of black patent leather pumps.

"These were Euey's favorite shoes. She had to wear sneakers to work every day, on account of her bunions, but these were her favorite shoes. Of course you don't need to use any of this stuff. She was your aunt.''

"There's not going to be an open casket," I said.

I took the outfit anyway. May as well bury Aunt Eulonia in something she had once liked. Still, it made me furious to think I was going to bury my aunt in an outfit picked out by a stranger. A man no less.

"The funeral will be at the Episcopal Church of our Savior down in Rock Hill. Noon Thursday.''

It wasn't exactly an invitation, but it was as close as he was going to get. If I had been half the lady Mama raised me to be, I would have given him a hug and offered to drive him there and back. But I couldn't. There was something about the man that didn't seem right. Something that wasn't ringing true but that I couldn't put my finger on. However, to honor Aunt Eulonia's memory I was going to give the old geezer, Tony, or whatever his name was, the benefit of the doubt.

"But I want my aunt's key," I said. There is a limit even to honor.

He fumbled in the right pocket of his baggy pants and fished out a key. I tried it in the door. It fit.

"And now the other one. The one she gave you way back when.''

The eyes shone brightly in the wrinkled face, but his expression barely changed. "It's at home.''

"Then get it," I said calmly.

He mumbled something as he left, but I didn't ask him to repeat it. While he was gone I made a quick trip back into my aunt's bedroom to rehang the navy dress. As far as I could tell everything was just like I had left it.

I went back to the breakfast room, sat down at the table, and laid my head on my arms. Over an hour later I woke up with a stiff neck and a watch indentation in my cheek. The key had not been returned.

8

"**G**o away," I shouted.

The doorbell chimed again. Aunt Marilyn's doorbell is a mini version of London's Big Ben. I found it charming when I first moved in. I am less charmed now.

I squinted at my clock radio. It wasn't yet seven. Since I open my shop at nine, I don't have to get up until seven-thirty. Even eight, if I push it. Anybody who tries to wake me before seven deserves to be appointed a delegate to the International Graffiti Artists Convention in Singapore.

It chimed a third time. Someone was knocking as well.

I pushed Dmitri off my stomach and literally rolled off the bed. Hitting Aunt Marilyn's hardwood floor is the fastest way I know to become fully awake. Sure it hurt, but after a few seconds I was able to struggle into a thick terry robe, one with a belt, and stumbled barefoot to the door.

Mrs. Ferguson was going to get a piece of my mind. Periodically she has the nerve to wake me just to tell me I have placed Aunt Marilyn's plastic trash bin too close to the curb. She is always filled with questions: Who is going to pick up all my trash if some schoolboy tips them over before the garbage men arrive? Do I want to make every dog on the street sick by chewing on my discarded cellophane wrappers? Am I aware that the lid to the bin is warped and that I'm infesting the neighborhood with flies?

Enough is enough. "Look Fergie," I said, before the door

was all the way open, "if you want to be my garbage intermediary—"

Investigator Greg Washburn stood there, tall and handsome, the early morning sun glinting off his thick dark hair. His hands were behind his back.

"You are under arrest for impersonating a crabby homeowner," he said, displaying the full array of piano keys. The sun glinted off them as well.

I grabbed at my robe. I didn't want it tied too tightly.

"I thought you were someone else. What's wrong?"

"I was hoping you'd tell me. I got your message last night, but I thought it was too late to call." He winked. "But I can see that now is probably too early for a visit."

I laughed with strained casualness. "Nah, I've been up for hours reading the paper. Just haven't bothered getting ready for work. Come on in. I'll fix you a cup of coffee."

"Thought you might like this," he said, handing me the morning paper.

I snatched the *Charlotte Observer* from him. I would have beat him over the head with it, except that I like my paper crisp and unwrinkled. Usually, by the time Buford got done with the paper, it looked like it had already been at the bottom of the bird cage.

"I get the Sunday *Times* from New York. It arrives by mail every Tuesday. I save it to read until the next morning." That wasn't so much a lie as it was a minor adjustment of the truth. I do read the *Times* now and then. At the library.

Investigator Washburn was fascinated by Aunt Marilyn's decor.

"Gosh, I haven't seen furniture like this since I was a kid. What is it, Danish modern?"

"Early nineteen-sixties Sears and Roebuck, with just a dash of Montgomery Ward. There are gold veins in the bathroom mirrors you are free to admire."

"Is that coffee table marble? It's so unusual."

"Faux-plastic," I said. "Aunt Marilyn couldn't afford the real thing."

I stopped being bitchy long enough to duck in the kitchen and make him some coffee. The coffeemaker is mine. Every time Aunt Marilyn pops in for one of her visits, I dash into the kitchen and hide it in the wastebasket under the sink. It is the second coffeemaker to reside in this house. The first ended up in the trash bin by the curb and was undoubtedly rescued by Mrs. Ferguson. It had been a hard week.

When I returned with Greg Washburn's coffee I discovered, much to my delight, that Dmitri and Blue Eyes had made friends. That is to say, Dmitri wasn't hissing and lashing out with clawless paws like he used to every time he was within striking distance of Buford. The two handsome males were regarding each other calmly, without any discernible jealousy on either part. It seemed too good to be true.

"I see you've met," I said stupidly. I set the tray down on the coffeetable. "Dmitri is usually shy about company. Especially men. He doesn't seem to like them very much."

"I like cats," Greg Washburn said. "They generally like me back." Somewhere in heaven an angel swooned on my behalf.

While he was sipping his coffee and reading my paper I slipped into the bedroom to dress. It was going to be another scorcher so I was justified in choosing the white sleeveless cotton dress with the deep V neckline. It was certainly not my fault that it fit me like a latex glove. I could have sworn it said a size four, not a two.

I ran a quick comb through my hair, brushed my teeth, flossed, gargled, and touched up my makeup, all in under five minutes, I'm sure. Give or take. It must have taken a few minutes more to spray on some cologne.

He was smiling sheepishly when I returned. "Hope you don't mind that I finished up the coffee. Didn't get a chance to have any before I came over, because I was in a hurry to see what your message was about. Best damn pot of coffee I ever drank."

I smiled bravely. Never apologize, never explain. Some people are just fast coffee drinkers.

"Investigator Washburn—"

He held up a hand. "Please, Officer would be fine."

"Yes, sir. Anyway, I think I may know why my aunt was killed. Not *who* killed her, but *why*."

He pulled the notebook out of his suit pocket. "Go on."

I was very cooperative and told him what Charlie had told me. Every word, to the best of my recollection. He made me repeat everything at least three times. I tried to be patient.

After he had jotted enough notes upon which to base a novel, he focused those deep blues on my cat greens. "Is there anything else you can remember about your conversation with your son that might pertain to this case?"

"No."

"You sure? Anything at all?"

"That's all I know. Do you want to hear it again? I could trot out my college Spanish." Cute as he was, I was starting to get miffed.

"And you had no knowledge about this lace—whatever it is—until last night when your son told you about it?"

I would have whacked him hard with that newspaper, damn the consequences, except that it was spread all over the floor.

"You think I would have involved my son, Charlie, in this if I didn't need to?"

"Ma'am?"

"If I had any knowledge of this lace whatchamacallit, any idea that it was valuable, I would have told you yesterday. I sure as hell wouldn't have held back so that my seventeen-year-old kid had to go through this. You going to ask him to repeat everything three times?"

He looked stunned. "Ma'am?"

"Oops. Sorry," I said. "It's a bad habit of mine, jumping to conclusions before I've had my morning coffee."

"It's all right," he said.

I looked pointedly at the empty pot that he had set on Aunt Marilyn's coffee table. "If you don't mind, I'm going to make some more."

"Please do," he said. "Coffee is one of three things I can never get enough of."

I ignored the twinkle in his eyes. While I was making coffee in the kitchen and zapping up some frozen cinnamon rolls, I heard the front door open and close.

Fine, I thought, run out on me. But you better not be running off to pester Charlie, not without me being there. If you do, so help me, I'll sic Buford on you. Although my ex-husband is the bottom layer of sludge, upon which floats the scum of the earth, he adores his son. And even though Buford Cornelius Timberlake is only an ambulance chaser, he has friends in high places. When Buford bellows, these high placed friends start to tremble. Buford, as I said, is an expert on dirt. He almost always gets his way.

As I was piling the hot rolls on one of Aunt Marilyn's plates I heard the door open and close again.

"Who is it?" To be on the safe side I grabbed the pot of scalding coffee.

"It's only me, ma'am, Greg Washburn."

I took the fresh pot of coffee and the rolls into the living room. Caffeine, sugar, and another, less combative look at Greg Washburn, might yet get the day off to a good start.

"Smells great," he said.

I suddenly remembered a scientific study on odors and male sexual response. In this study the male participants, who had electrodes attached to their penises, were most aroused by the smell of cinnamon. I glanced in the appropriate spot, but everything seemed normal. Perhaps it took time.

There was something else of interest on his lap. He had brought something back inside with him, something in a long plastic bag.

"What's that?"

He handed it to me. "You seen this before? I want you to look at it carefully, but don't open the bag."

I examined the contents of the bag carefully, although I recognized them immediately. It was a bellpull. A nineteenth-century needlepoint bellpull, of exquisite workmanship and design.

My heart pounded. "Is this it? Is this what killed my aunt?"

He nodded. "You recognize it?"

I handed it back carefully. Although it was an instrument of death, it was also the last thing to touch my aunt while she was alive. I felt she was somehow connected to it.

"Yes, I recognize it. It came from a manor house in the north of England. It belonged to a duke or someone. It's a beautiful piece. You see that rooster there, above the crest? That's what makes it so unusual.''

''Is it yours?''

''No!''

''That wasn't an accusation,'' he said quickly. ''Where did you see it?''

''At The Finer Things. It's a shop right next door to mine.''

He flipped over a new page in his notebook. The cinnamon rolls had yet to be touched. ''The owner's name?''

''Wait just one cotton-picking minute,'' I said. ''Just because this pull belonged to someone, doesn't mean they killed my aunt.''

''Of course not.''

''His name is Rob Goldburg. Rob has a bit of a temper, but he's really a decent man. Rob would sooner date a woman than kill one.''

He smiled. ''Mr. Goldburg is not a suspect at this point. I just want to ask him some questions.''

I relaxed a little after my second cup of coffee and two cinnamon rolls. Greg Washburn ate four rolls, but if that study linking male arousal to cinnamon is true, you couldn't prove it by him. Not that I could see. He was completely correct and proper at all times.

''Please, do me a big favor,'' I begged as he stood up to leave.

''Ma'am?''

''Can you run a priors check on a James Grady, age thirty-eight, Caucasian, about five foot ten, looks like something a sewer rat dragged in? I believe he was formerly janitor at UNCC. Now, for some inexplicable reason, he's involved with my daughter.''

I got a glimpse of all eighty-eight piano keys. Well, maybe not that many, but you get the picture.

''Watch a lot of cop shows, do we?''

''It's the only time I actually see them doing anything useful.'' Sometimes a quick retort can head off blushing.

''Well, I can't do anything official, you know. But if I remember, I'll do a little unofficial poking around.''

''Thanks. I'll try to be unofficially grateful. But I've got another favor to ask you. An even bigger one. This one you'll probably say no to.''

''Try me.''

I took a deep breath. ''Promise me that if and when you interrogate my son, I can be there.''

He ran his fingers through thick dark hair. If Buford wanted hair like that, he would have to order it from Japan.

''I might want to *interview* your son, not interrogate him. And yes, you can be there.''

''Thanks!''

I meant it. If Investigator Greg Washburn ever stopped by the Den of Antiquity to shop, I would give him a 10 percent discount on anything not already marked down. If he played his cards right, who knew, someday he might even be able to claim half of the shop as his own. I am all for happy endings.

There was still the problem of the damned camellias to contend with. No sooner did the very attractive last little bit of Investigator Greg Washburn pass out my door, than the phone rang. I know it sounds silly, but there was something about the way it rang just then that sounded urgent.

''I was right,'' Mama said breathlessly. ''You-know-who just pulled in the driveway. You can bet her next stop is Charlotte.''

''Detain her! Please!''

If anyone could detain Aunt Marilyn it was Mama. Back when I was dating Buford, she once detained him for an hour while I washed and dried my hair. The temporary red rinse I'd put in it was just not me. While on the surface Buford and Aunt Marilyn appear to belong to different species, they are both control freaks, and both highly susceptible to flattery.

''I'll see what I can do,'' Mama said. She didn't sound as certain as she once did.

I hung up and began racking my brain. I hadn't even gotten through the first rack when the phone rang. Of course I had to pick it up, what with Charlie involved in a murder case, and Susan living with Charles Manson's identical twin brother.

''Dahling,'' Aunt Marilyn rasped. Fifty-three years of smoking and seventy-two years of trying to sound sexy haven't done her vocal chords any good.

"Aunt Marilyn! What a surprise! What's up in Hilton Head. Or down, I should say."

"Dahling, I'm not in Hilton Head. I'm at your mama's. Just stopped in for a minute to say hi on my way home."

I steadied myself against the kitchen counter. "Which home, dear?"

"Why your home. I mean, my home. The one on Ridgewood. It wouldn't inconvenience you any if I spent some time with you there, would it? Buffy Ledbetter is having her face done and needs me for moral support. Not that I know anything about the procedure, mind you. Still, a friend is a friend, and that's what one needs at a time like that. Or so I imagine."

I politely covered the phone while I guffawed. Aunt Marilyn wouldn't recognize her real face if it jumped out of an old photo album and bit her. If all the stitches that have gone into her face were lined up, they would reach from Charlotte to China and back. The silicone and plastic in those jowls were enough to catapult China into the computer age.

"Well, of course it wouldn't be any bother at all." What else could I say? It was her house. "I'd be delighted to have company."

"That's wonderful, dahling. I'm on my way. See you—"

"But there is something you should know first."

"Yes, dahling?"

"Uh, remember those scraggly junipers you had planted out front?"

There was a pregnant pause. This one was easily long enough to get pregnant during. Especially if Buford was involved.

"What junipers, dahling?"

"The ones on either side of the front door. Well, since they were doing so poorly, I had them removed and—"

"There were no junipers by the front door. Dahling, those were plaster poodles."

"You sure?" Hopefully her memory had started to slip. After all, mine already had, and she was a lot older. I know, it was shameful of me, but I was desperate.

"Positive, dahling. One black, the other white, exactly forty-two inches tall. Eighteen inches at the base. Fifi and

Mimi. I had to special order them from a place called Garden Treasures of the South. They arrived on November seventeen, nineteen forty-eight, the day after you cut your first tooth.''

"Well, in that case, Fifi and Mimi are just fine,'' I said. "Do you mind if I speak to Mama for a moment.''

I begged Mama to stall her. Mama refused to sneak out the side door and stab Aunt Marilyn's tires with a butcher knife, but other than that, she pledged her full cooperation.

While Mama danced jigs to entertain her older sister, or whatever else was necessary, I worked like a damless beaver who has just been handed a forecast calling for drought. Panic can do amazing things to one's adrenaline. Somehow I managed to dig up both camellias, stuff them in leaf bags, and put them in the trunk of the car. How I managed to lug Fifi and Mimi up the basement stairs is beyond my comprehension. The one thing I could not do, however, was replace the two pink plastic flamingos from the backyard. The Charlotte Department of Sanitation had long since laid claim to them. Of course that is only an assumption, but they had yet to show up in Mrs. Ferguson's yard.

Seconds before Aunt Marilyn's car turned left onto Ridgewood, I turned right, going the opposite way. I arrived at my shop only an hour late, sweaty, with dirty fingernails and two camellias suffocating in the trunk.

It was the start of an auspicious day.

9

On any other day it would have knocked my socks off to see a crowd of customers waiting to be let in, but not that day. Given the weather, I had decided to flaunt convention and stay in the white dress I'd put on for Greg. After putting one toe out the door, I had shed my pantyhose faster than a hyperactive snake sheds its skin. In my excitement I had forgotten it was after Labor Day.

"It's not even winter white," I heard a woman mumble. "I mean, there is a correct way, no matter how hot it is."

She had a right to talk. She was wearing a wool skirt, a wool turtleneck sweater, and knee-length leather boots. They were all in shades of brown. Either she had a portable air conditioner hidden in that getup, or she was one of the living dead. Clearly she was not menopausal.

While the crowd surged into my shop—hopefully to make me a rich woman—I struggled with the two camellias. Another five minutes and they would have been compost.

"Can I give you a hand?"

I recognized the voice of Rob Goldburg.

"Sure."

He reached past me and easily lifted one of the plants out of my trunk. "What's this? You offering your customers premiums now?"

"Aunt Marilyn's in town. I escaped by the skin of my teeth."

"Ah yes, the Marilyn Monroe of Hilton Head. How is the old darling?"

"She looked just fine in my rearview mirror. I suppose I will have to find out tonight."

He took the second camellia out. "Say, you got a minute?"

I gestured at the camellias and my shop. A woman was standing on the steps with a silver candelabra in her hand.

"Is this part of a pair?" she called.

I shook my head.

"I know you're busy," Rob said, "but I *have* to talk to you. Maybe between customers?"

He carried the camellias into the relative coolness of my shop. What could I do?

"Shoot," I said. I had just sold the candelabra at 20 percent off the asking price. It was a steal, both for me and the customer. The damned thing had been a wedding present from Buford's mother. Buford, with his eyes full of Tweetie's silicon curves, had never missed it.

"I think I may be in trouble," Rob said, his voice barely above a whisper. "A hell of a lot of trouble."

"Don't tell me you sold yet another original Mona Lisa?"

"This is serious, Timberlake. You know that bellpull everyone's been saying did the old lady in?"

"What about it?"

"I think it belongs to me."

"What?" I tried to sound surprised. It was obvious Greg Washburn was sitting on his information.

I had to interrupt our tête-à-tête to part with a Shaker ladderback chair. I barely broke even on that but consoled myself by remembering the candelabra.

"No," I said to the buyer, a tall gangly woman of indeterminate age, "I don't have any more in stock."

"Well, can you order seven more and have them here by Friday? I'm giving a little informal dinner party for my husband's birthday. Don't you think those would look just darling with bows tied to the top rungs?"

"Just darling," Rob said.

I had to explain to the woman that Shakers were a celibate sect who have virtually died off. Last I heard there were three members left, all of them women, and all around ninety. I doubted very much if they would be able to whip up seven chairs for her dinner party. The woman left with her chair and a promise from me that I would try my level best to convince those lazy Shakers to speed up their production.

"I'm almost positive that bellpull is mine," Rob said, when she was gone.

"What makes you think so? There are oodles of bellpulls in this world."

"With roosters on them? Anita saw *the* bellpull. It had a rooster on it. One I had just like that is missing."

I should have advised him to clean out his cash drawer and hop the first flight to Guadalajara, but I didn't. Rob Goldburg, despite his temper, was an honest man who played by the rules. Besides, he had done nothing wrong. If I believed for one second that it was he who strangled my aunt, I would turn Ron Goldburg into a candidate for the Vienna Boy's Choir. There are certain advantages to being short.

"When did you notice the pull missing?" I shook my head at a customer who was trying to investigate the bagged camellias. They were not for sale.

"I don't know. I'd like to say Monday, after that disastrous breakfast, when I shot off at the mouth. But it may even have been earlier. I've been kind of distracted, you see."

I assumed the distraction was his new partner, whom I had yet to meet. I had seen the guy a couple of times through the window of his shop, and had even waved, but that's as far as I'd taken my southern hospitality. If the Kovels themselves had moved next door, I still would not have found the time and energy to run over with a homemade peach pie.

"Maybe you should take the initiative," I said quickly. The woman dressed like a fall mummy was bearing down on us with a cut glass punch bowl in her woolly arms. "If you contacted the right people with this information, before they contact you, it might go better."

Rob stared under long dark lashes. He has a remarkably handsome face, just shy of being pretty, and it's only because I know he is not interested in women that I resist my temptation to leap on him and declare my eternal love. Let's face it, I am a wanton woman. You would be too if you were in the prime of your life and had not had sex in almost three years.

"What do you mean 'the right people'? Who have you been talking to, Abigail? What's up?"

Mercifully, the blessed woman in the thermal garb came between us with the punch bowl. "How much is this bowl?" she demanded.

She was playing games with me; the price was clearly visible on a card inside it the size of a dinner napkin. I vaguely remembered seeing the woman's face on the society page, something about donating a new wing to some hospital. Even if she were stark naked with a hood over her head I could tell that she had more money than she knew what to do with. Besides the six-carat carbon monstrosity on her wedding finger, she wore an even larger diamond on the middle finger of her right hand. It surprised me that she didn't require a set of luggage wheels just to help tote that thing around.

I would have told her to take her woolly butt to a soup kitchen and serve the homeless, except that I needed extra sales to make up for when I would close the shop for Aunt Eulonia's funeral.

"It's not punch season, dear," I said gently. "One should only drink punch between Memorial Day and Labor Day."

She didn't bat an eye. "I'll give two hundred dollars for this," she had the gall to say.

The bowl was marked at $350. It was deep cut glass, probably with a high lead content. The lead made it sparkle; hopefully it made it toxic as well.

"I can only come down to three and a quarter," I said kindly.

She sniffed. "It isn't worth that. I saw another one at a shop in Pineville that was much more intricate in design. They only wanted three hundred for it. And it had the cups."

I shrugged. "Three and a quarter is the best I can do. Take it or leave it."

She glared at me. "All right, but it's highway robbery. What else do you have that's interesting?"

It was clear this woman was used to shopping in Paris, so I saw it as my duty to my profession to accommodate her.

Rudeness doesn't come easy to me, mind you, but I did my level best. Five thousand dollars later I helped her carry things out to the car. I would have licked those knee-high boots if she'd asked me.

Rob was still waiting for me by the register, sitting on a Victorian side chair that had a SOLD sign on it. Tension showed in his gray eyes. "Well?"

"Sorry," I said, "but a buck is a buck. This is a business. You know how it is. Hey, you ever see that Money Mummy before? She looks awfully familiar."

He shrugged. "Who have you been talking to, Abigail? Not the police?"

"Not exactly. Investigator Greg Washburn, homicide division. He was over at my place this morning. Showed me the pull. I thought I recognized it, and so I told him."

He stood up. Like most everyone else he towered over me. "Told him what?"

"I told him that I recognized the pull as coming from your shop. I also told him that I knew you didn't do it. That you couldn't."

"Damn!" Rob pounded a fist on my glass register counter. Fortunately he hit a wood panel.

I gave him Greg Washburn's phone number. "He's a decent guy. Call him, Rob. It's the wisest thing to do."

"Oh shit!" Rob said, and left my shop.

For some strange reason business was so good that day that my fingers suffered register burn. Who would have guessed that half of Charlotte, and their Yankee cousins, would be out shopping for antiques on the hottest September day in decades? I stayed so busy that I didn't remember, much less worry about, Aunt Marilyn's presence in town. Not until she showed up at my register, a brass towel rack in hand.

"What is this?"

I looked up from stuffing money in the drawer. "Uh, looks like a towel rack—Aunt Marilyn! How good to see you!"

There she stood atop her six-inch heels, as big as life and twice as awesome. In the summertime Aunt Marilyn dons puffy little sundresses and combs the sidewalks, looking for

cold air registers to inflate her skirts. Mama and I have re-
peatedly tried to convince her that upper arms are usually best
kept covered by the time one cashes their first Social Security
check. But summer was officially over and Aunt Marilyn, who
is more correct than I, was wearing a crimson taffeta cocktail
dress. The mini feather boa around her neck was her one con-
cession to the daylight hours. As usual the platinum hair was
sprayed into hard perfection. I have long ago concluded that
my aunt need never fear meteors or other heavenly debris.

I ran around the counter and embraced her tightly, her arms
pinned to her sides. "What a wonderful surprise," I said, spit-
ting out the boa between words.

She gave me two little air pecks and pushed me to arm's
length—heaven forbid I should bend her hair or dislocate the
mole on her left cheek. She held up the towel rack again.

"What is this, dahling, and what is it doing in my house?"

"It's a towel rack, of course."

"I know what it is, dahling. I want to know what it was
doing in my bathroom."

I willed myself to be calm. It was a doable thing. Aunt
Marilyn was merely a pain in the side compared to Buford.
But enough was enough. The platinum terror had to be stopped
before either I or my camellias died.

"I slipped while reaching for a bath towel," I said. "Unfortunately I grabbed the cheap, plastic rack you have in there,
and it broke. I fell, bumping my head, spraining my wrist, and
bruising two knees. I had to close down my shop for a day
just to find something that looked vaguely like the piece of
junk that was in there before.

"Since there were no bones broken, and I didn't require
stitches, I didn't have a doctor bill to send you. However, I
was sore for weeks and undoubtedly lost customers because I
wasn't able to get around very well. But of course I would
never sue a flesh-and-blood relative, now would I?"

Aunt Marilyn lit a cigarette and blew a perfect smoke ring
through bright red lips. "Dahling, you simply must take better
care of yourself. Why, I tell you what. This evening when you
get off work I'll have a nice little supper waiting for you.

Things I brought up fresh from the coast. How does she-crab soup and shrimp gumbo sound?''

It sounded superb. I had been so busy I hadn't had a bite to eat since the futile cinnamon rolls that morning. I had never seen Aunt Marilyn so docile. I should have thought of threatening her with a lawsuit two years ago. After all, I had been married to the king of ambulance chasers. Foolishly I decided to push the envelope.

''Supper sounds great, Aunt Marilyn. Then after supper, if it's still light, you can help me plant my camellia bushes.''

She teetered on the six-inch heels. ''I beg your pardon?''

I pointed to the bagged plants. ''I thought they would look great where Mimi and Fifi are now. We could move those plaster mutts over a couple of feet—''

Aunt Marilyn gasped, sucking in a generous chunk of boa. I hastened to extract it before she choked. Two aunts dead in one week by strangulation would be hard to explain to Greg Washburn. Especially if one of them asphyxiated in my shop.

I patted her back to get her breathing again. ''There, there, dear. If you insist, I can plant my camellias somewhere else. Maybe up by the front of the driveway.''

I wouldn't be a southern lady if I repeated what Aunt Marilyn said next—when she could get her voice back. I bet the real Marilyn Monroe didn't talk like that. Hilton Head is just too close to Parris Island, I suppose. My guess, based on the words I heard, is that Aunt Marilyn regularly entertains marines. She sure didn't hear language like that growing up in Rock Hill.

''But the neighbors all love my camellias,'' I said calmly. ''Even Mrs. Ferguson loves them. When she saw mine she went out and bought four just like them for herself. She said they're the prettiest camellias she's ever seen.''

The boa bobbed dangerously close to my aunt's open mouth. Even I would never gasp like that in public.

''Then again, what does Mrs. Ferguson know?'' I said helpfully.

''Out!''

''Why, that's exactly what I said to those pink flamingos,

dear. Haven't you had a chance to glance at the backyard yet?''

"Out!"

It was the only word she could say for the next few minutes. When she could finally manage a multiple word vocabulary, she made it crystal clear that I, my cat Dmitri, and what few belongings I had in her house, were never welcome there again. Not unless I got down on my hands and knees and begged her forgiveness. This dictum inspired a few choice words of my own, which I will spare you.

"And I don't allow smoking in my shop!" I shouted as the last of her boa drifted through the door.

It was too late. My favorite aunt—my only aunt, now that Eulonia Wiggins was dead—had just shut the door on me. Figuratively, that is. I was no longer welcome on Ridgewood Avenue. Thank the good Lord I had most of my stuff stored at Mama's.

"What do you mean I can't spend the night?"

Mama paused a long time. Long enough for me to hear a stifled giggle.

"Abigail, dear, you know you're always welcome in my home. I want you to think of it as your home, too, but not tonight. I have plans."

"I'll watch TV with you, Mama. I'll even watch those in-fomercials you like so much. How about it?"

"Sorry, dear, but not tonight."

"Can I at least drop off Dmitri? Aunt Marilyn has threatened to run him through her neighbor's composter if I don't have him out of there by eight."

Somebody giggled again, and it sure didn't sound like Mama. Neither did Mama, for that matter.

"I told you, Abby, tonight's not good. Try calling a vet."

"Is your bridge club there? Is it that Dot McElveen who hates cats? No problem, Mama. I'll just sneak off to the guest room with Dmitri before anyone sees him, turn the TV on low, and you won't hear a peep out of us."

There were two distinct giggles this time. One Mama's, one belonging to somebody else.

"It isn't bridge, dear. It's other plans."

I sighed sympathetically. "Mama, you shouldn't allow the Werrels to impose on you like that. They can afford a sitter. Maybe two. Just because—"

"I'm not baby-sitting," Mama said. There was a bounce in her voice I hadn't heard in years. Maybe since Daddy died.

"Good, Mama, then I'll be right over after work."

"Really dear, I'd rather be alone tonight."

"No you wouldn't, Mama. You've never liked living alone. Listen, I'll stop in at the Bojangles on Cherry Road, and then the video store—"

"Show up at the door and I'll break both your legs with a rolling pin," Mama cooed. She sounded half serious.

"Excuse me?"

"Abby dear, I have a date."

I nearly dropped the phone. "With a man?"

Some of the giggles turned into guffaws. They were definitely manly.

"Mama! What's going on there?"

"Oh, nothing dear. Nothing that concerns you."

"If it concerns you, Mama, it concerns me." There is nothing wrong in recycling someone's words right back at them if you get the chance. I'm sure it must irritate the heck out of them. I know it does when it happens to me.

"This doesn't concern you, dear. Bye."

I called her right back, but the phone just rang and rang. I was stunned. Mama—to whom I had spent nine of the best months of my life hooked up by an umbilical cord—had just unplugged that other most important cord, cutting me loose for the second time. Against my will I had been born again.

Even worse, Mama—*my* Mama—was having, or about to have, sex!

10

Mama could have her disgusting roll in the hay. Aunt Marilyn could keep her precious Fifi and Mimi right where they were. It didn't matter one whit to me what they did, because I had friends. The kind of friends who invite you to dinner on the spur of the moment.

"This is Bob Steuben," Rob said, as I was locking up my shop.

I introduced myself to a pale, spindly man, possibly in his late thirties. He had mousy brown hair and a very small, narrow face. His eyes were set suspiciously close. His mouth was a thin gray line. Frankly, it looked like the good Lord had made him out of leftovers and run out of material when he came to the face.

"Pleased to meet you," Bob said, his secret revealed. He had a voice that could calm the Bosphorus Straits. "Rob told me all about you. You two set the date yet?"

"Excuse me?"

"He's kidding." Rob read the question in my eyes. "Yes, Abby, I made the call. You were right. This Washburn guy sounds okay. He said I did the right thing by calling. I feel a lot better now. Thanks."

"Good enough for me to invite you two out for some dinner? Maybe smoke a tobaccoless peace pipe and call a truce."

Rob and Bob exchanged glances.

"I had a great day at the shop," I hurried to say. "This is my treat."

"Well, uh—"

"Please. I need the company. Auntie Dearest kicked me out."

"She didn't!" Rob said with just the right amount of sympathy. "The camellias? Or was it the pink flamingos?"

"I'll tell you all about it at dinner," I said for Bob's benefit.

They exchanged glances again. They must have been meaningful glances because they'd made a decision.

"Bob's a hell of a cook," Rob said. "You're invited to our place for supper."

Of course I said yes. My Mama didn't raise any fools. Never mind the money I would save on dinner. I'd known Rob for seven or eight years, been friends with him for half of that, and had yet to be invited to his inner sanctum. From what I heard through the grapevine, Rob Goldburg's decor made Versailles seem shabby.

"I have to pick up my cat, Dmitri, first," I explained. "Auntie Dearest said she would turn him into a hand muff if I didn't pick him up by eight, and she means that literally. The only reason she let me keep him there was because she had a cat named DeMaggio when she first bought that damn house, and Dmitri looks just like him."

The shared glances showed terror. "Does he shred?" Rob asked.

I shrugged in my nonchalant way. "All cats shed, dear. Even we shed, you know."

"He said *shred*," Bob boomed. "We just bought a silk Chinese Aubusson carpet over the weekend. We'd like it to last until next weekend if possible."

I smiled sweetly, since beguiling wouldn't work with those two. "Dmitri is declawed. Both front and back. He's strictly an indoor cat."

"I guess then it would be all right," Rob said. He looked at his partner for confirmation, and got it. Reluctantly.

"And if he even starts to throw up a hair ball, I'll whisk him off into the kitchen," I said sensibly. "You do have linoleum in there, don't you?"

They shook their heads no. They didn't have to do it so vigorously, however. If I was going to make it to dinner at the highly coveted and much touted table of Rob Goldburg, I was going to have to find some other kind soul to take my precious lambkins for the evening.

Tony D'Angelo took forever to open his door.

"Yes?"

"It's me, Abby. Remember?"

"Cara mia!" he cried in that boyish voice.

He would have hugged me, had I let him. But for all his warmth, he didn't invite me inside. Perhaps he too had a sex partner stashed in the boudoir. The way my luck had been running, it was probably Mama. I shouldn't have given her call forwarding for her birthday.

"Tony, I have a big favor to ask you."

"Ask!" He sounded eager to lay down his life for me, anything but ask me inside where it was twenty degrees cooler.

I pointed to the car, which I had carefully parked in the shade. "I need a temporary home for my cat, Dmitri. He's really sweet, honest. He's been declawed, neutered—"

"No problem! I love cats. Leave him here as long as you want."

It had been too easy. Suspiciously easy. Maybe Mama really was inside flagrantly flaunting her delicto. I said good-bye and drove off before I was given a chance to discover what was wrong with that picture.

I should have at least asked him why he hadn't returned with my aunt's key the night before.

I wasn't disappointed. Bob lives in South Park and owns a fairly modest house by neighborhood standards. Inside is what makes the difference. From the hand-painted Chinese wallpaper in the foyer to the Regency carved and gilded beech armchairs, everything was exquisite. It was perhaps a little overdone for my taste, but a refreshing change from Aunt Marilyn's fifties modern and Mama's Victorian hand-me-downs.

The food was something else. Something else that I could not identify. Frankly I couldn't tell if it was chicken or beef, but I didn't want to be boorish and ask.

"I've never had anything to compare with this," I said,

after I had safely eaten most of it. Generally that is a safe statement when one needs to say something but still be kind.

Bob beamed, his narrow face widening. "Ostrich en cassoulet."

"He's kidding again, right?"

Rob looked at Bob fondly. "Not this time. Bob was so happy to find that a few people down here actually raise the damned things. Thought he was moving to the sticks."

I swallowed hard, willing my throat muscles to keep it all down.

"So, you're from New York?"

"Nope. Outer Mongolia. My father was a yurt merchant."

"Bob!"

"Okay, Toledo originally. But I've lived in Manhattan the last twenty years."

I nodded. A voice like that might move to Manhattan, but it sure wasn't born there.

"Welcome to the South," I drawled. "I hope you like it here."

The Rob-Bobs exchanged meaningful glances. It was getting to be too much on a queasy stomach. The ostrich was having a hard time staying down. Much to my relief the doorbell rang.

"Officer Washburn!" I could hear the shock in Rob's voice. "Come in. We were just eating dinner."

Greg Washburn mumbled something, and Rob mumbled back. They were in the foyer and we couldn't see them, but we didn't have to know that our evening had taken a turn for the worse. Bob Steuben regarded me somberly. A cock might as well have crowed three times.

They stepped quietly into the dining room. Both of them averted their eyes from me.

"Well, it appears there has been a slight change of plans. My dessert tonight is going to be courtesy of the county." He spoke calmly, almost nonchalantly. I knew it was for Bob's benefit. If I'd been alone he would have sworn.

"What the hell?" Bob boomed. So much for the mousy appearance.

Greg stiffened. "I have a warrant for the arrest of one Robert David Goldburg for the murder of Eulonia Wiggins. I have read him his rights and he has agreed to come peacefully.''

I stood up. "Officer, you've arrested the wrong person.'' I know, that was a cliché, but I was in shock and had a stomach full of ostrich.

The blue eyes bored through me. "This is police business, Ms. Timberlake.''

I steadied myself on the chair. "Well it's my business, too. I'm the one who told you that the bellpull belonged to Rob. I also told you that he didn't do it. Besides, he has alibis.''

"Who?'' I never knew blue could be so cold.

"Well, like Bob here, for instance. He's Rob's partner now.''

"Actually Bob had Monday afternoon off,'' Rob said in a stupid display of honesty. "He had to change his driver's license and do some other errands. I was running the shop alone.''

"But you had customers!'' I practically screamed.

"Yeah, some. But it was a pretty slow day for me. Everyone was down at your shop.'' He laughed weakly.

Greg Washburn had the nerve to dismiss me by turning slightly away. His body language was deafening.

"I'm taking Mr. Goldburg down to the precinct house with me,'' he said to Bob. "You can follow if you want, but there isn't any point as far as I can see. The bail hearing won't be until tomorrow morning, and since this is a capital offense, I wouldn't count on your friend walking anytime soon. My advice is that you get a good night's sleep and call the best lawyer you know in the morning.''

"Call your lawyer now,'' I said.

Greg Washburn turned his back. Bob Steuben looked helplessly from Rob to me.

"Call him,'' I said.

For the first time since I've known him, Rob Goldburg seemed helpless. "I don't know any criminal lawyers. Not personally. And Bob has just moved here.''

"Then call Clay Timberlake,'' I said.

"What?'' Rob's jaw dropped almost to his chest. Even Greg Washburn was surprised enough to turn my way.

"Okay, so Clay is Buford's brother, but he's also the best criminal lawyer in Charlotte. Maybe even in the state."

Rob stared for a minute, thinking. In the meantime I stared at Greg Washburn. He was the Judas, not me. Maybe he felt a little guilty; I could swear I saw him blink. Then again, one of those long, thick lashes, come loose, might have been the problem.

"Abigail, you're serious? Clayton Timberlake, the timber snake?"

I nodded vigorously. "I don't have to like him to know he's good. And he's the best."

"The best is probably more than I can afford," Rob said. Not that it mattered. Rob made a fair living from his shop, but he had a rich, widowed mother who doted on him. F. Lee Bailey or Clayton Timberlake? It was merely a matter of convenience.

"Excuse me," Bob said, in that rich vibrating voice. "I'm new here, and I don't know all the players, but I do know that you, Abigail, and your ex-husband don't get along at all. What makes you think your husband's brother is going to want to be Rob's lawyer, given the fact that you two are friends? How am I supposed to talk him into that?"

"Look, I'll call him for you," I said. "I've had a lot of experience handling snakes. After all, I was part of that family for eighteen years."

Bob studied his partner's face.

"All right," Rob said at last. "Abby, give it a shot." He turned to Bob. "It's not Abigail's fault. It really isn't."

Bob Steuben shrugged.

"I mean it, Dinky. Do what Abigail says, I trust her on this."

"Yeah right," Bob said.

I didn't blame him for being skeptical. I should have kept my mouth shut about that bellpull. But oh no, once again I made the mistake of thinking that truth and reason added up to justice. Boy, was I ever wrong. Surely, somewhere, there was a math class for the dangerously naive. Before I opened my mouth again, on any issue more important than which way to hang a roll of toilet paper, I was going to have to take that class. As it was, I was a menace to myself and to my friends. And now the Rob-Bobs were counting on me.

But "Dinky"? That had been my pet name for Buford!

I wouldn't mind having the weight of the world placed on my shoulders now and then if I wasn't already so damn short. As it was, I had to stand on tiptoe to dial Rob's wall phone.

"Hello, Timberlake residence. Marsha Timberlake speaking."

"Shit," I said, and then remembered to cover the mouthpiece.

Marsha Timberlake, Buford's sister-in-law, is one of those people born with a recessed left ear and an indentation in her left jaw. It would be a simple matter to graft a telephone receiver to her head. Outpatient surgery at the most. Marsha can, and does, talk for hours without feeling any ill effects. No cauliflower ear for her. At any rate, I hadn't expected Marsha to answer. She does, after all, have a seventeen-year-old daughter who was born with the same cranial deformity. Need I say more?

"Who is this," Marsha demanded, "and what did you say?"

There was plenty of time for me to think. Marsha does not hang up on callers, even if they've already hung up on her. Not unless call waiting patches in a new victim.

"It's me, Abby," I said finally. "I was telling my dog to sit."

"You don't have a dog, Abigail. You don't even have custody of your children anymore. Speaking of which, how are they, dear? Did you know that my little Dorothy was elected to vice president of the senior class? Of course that shouldn't come as much of a surprise, not when you recall that our dear, dear Redmund was class president three times when he was in high school. Now take our Scarlet, she's still just in seventh grade, but—"

"I have a cat, Dmitri," I said. "Anyway, I want to speak to Clay. Is he there?"

"Clay?"

"Yes, dear, the man you're married to. Is he allowed on the phone?"

"Ha, very funny, Abigail. Of course Clay is allowed on the phone. But why would he want to speak to you?"

"Because it involves money, dear."

Marsha severed the phone from her head. For her, money doesn't speak, it shouts. She has a larger shoe collection than Imelda Marcos. I mean, not only are her feet much larger, but so is the number of shoes in her collection. I bet her shoes are more expensive, too. Marsha once showed me a pair of Italian heels, made from the skin of an unborn albino calf, which were studded with small but VVSI (very very small inclusion) diamonds. Throw in a matching handbag and you have half the national debt.

Clay has no phone skills. "Go to hell, Abigail. For the last time, I'm not going to take your case against my brother."

I took a deep breath for my children's sake. Clay might have been the one to tempt Eve with the apple, but he was still my children's uncle. Charlie, at least, adored him.

"Clay, dear, I am no longer trying to sue Buford for custody of the kids. Susan is nineteen, and Charlie will be eighteen before we know it. This is a different matter altogether. This client can pay."

Robert David Goldburg had a lawyer.

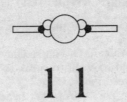

11

Bob Steuben's need for company outweighed his resentment toward me. He allowed me to help him clear the table, and when I made a halfhearted attempt to leave, he stopped me promptly.

"That's a real Queen Anne," he said pointing to the sofa, "so it doesn't unfold into a bed. But if you don't mind sleeping on it, we have some fresh sheets and pillows in the hall closet."

I didn't mind. It would serve Aunt Marilyn right if I didn't come home that night, my tail between my legs, dragging my camellias behind me. She would undoubtedly call Mama to ask if I was there, which would, in turn, serve Mama right. Imagine having sex so close to seventy! And only sixteen years after Daddy died.

After Rob made his one allotted call to Bob, who in turn called Rob's mother, I monopolized the horn. My first victim was Peggy Redfern.

"Hrrun?" Peggy was eating again, so at least *she* wasn't having sex.

"Peggy, dear, I'm afraid I have some bad news. Rob Goldburg's been arrested for my aunt's murder."

She gasped appropriately.

"Of course he didn't do it, dear. And that's why I'm calling. I thought some of us could meet tomorrow morning at Denny's again. If we put our heads together, maybe we can come up with proof he didn't do it."

Peggy took another bite of something. "Whangwha?"

I waited patiently for her to swallow. "Seven-thirty then?"

"Abby!"

I hung up before she could protest further, and dialed Gretchen Miller. As long as there was food in the picture, Peggy Redfern would be there.

"Abigail? Do you know what time it is?"

"Nine or thereabouts.

"Eight fifty-eight to be precise. Do you realize that *Masterpiece Theatre* starts in just two minutes?"

I spoke rapidly. "Rob Goldburg was just arrested and I think we all need to get together tomorrow morning at Denny's and see what we can do for him since he's obviously not guilty."

Gretchen is a fast listener. "What is so obvious?"

"The man is a talking teddy bear, Gretch. He might growl, but he doesn't have claws."

"Well, I don't know if I can make this breakfast, Abigail. I always watch *Good Morning America* before I go into work, and tomorrow Charles Gibson is interviewing Sir David Frost."

"You have a VCR, don't you? So, see you there?"

"Oops, have to run now. *Masterpiece Theatre* just started." She hung up.

I took that as a yes and called Wynnell Crawford.

Wynnell was undoubtedly busy sewing herself another pitiful outfit when I called. She didn't stop. I could hear that Singer humming away the whole time. Please don't misunderstand me. There is nothing wrong in wearing homemade clothing. But Wynnell, who can afford as many store-bought clothes as she wants, can't sew two consecutive stitches in a straight line. What's more, she chooses the gaudiest material I have ever seen. Bright oranges, iridescent greens, pulsating purples, all mixed together in one fabric. At any rate, her clothes are forever falling apart, shedding whole sections like a giant molting parrot. Women in some bars get paid for what she does unintentionally.

"Abigail, what do you mean he's innocent? He's living

with a Yankee now, isn't he? Some fellow named Sherman.''

''Yes, Bob is from Ohio, but his last name is Steuben, not Sherman.''

''Abigail, dear, didn't your mother teach you anything? You can't trust Yankees. Any Yankee south of the line is out to get something from us. Even tourist Yankees want what we have—our sun, our mountains, our water, our golf courses. But do you think any of them hung around when Hurricane Hugo blew through in 1988? Do you think any of them would be willing to subject themselves to the New Heritage Festival of Lights tour come December?''

I listened to her thread a new bobbin while I composed myself. ''Wynnell, dear, Bob Steuben hasn't been arrested, Rob Goldburg has. And Rob Goldburg's great-granddaddy fought in the War Between The States. On *our* side.''

I heard a scissors snipping several times. Perhaps she was making threatening gestures.

''Well, this Sherman guy is probably one of them—what do they call them—hit men. You know, one of those Mafia boys they send down here from up North. Does he have any scars that you can see?''

I dug around in the bottom of my psyche for a scrap of patience my kids had yet to use up. ''Tell you what, dear. I'll invite him to that breakfast, too. Then you can take a good look at him. If he seems at all greedy, shifty, or threatening, I'll personally drive him back to Ohio.''

That satisfied her. That and a promise that I would display at least one Confederate flag somewhere in my shop. Well, I am a proud southerner, but I don't want to offend anyone. I do display the Stars and Bars—on an inside wall of my storage closet. Only those coming out of the closet get to see it.

Herr Major was a harder sell.

''There's no way in hell I'm going to come to that damn breakfast. The guy is as guilty as—''

''Hitler?''

''The Führer was only exercising the will of the German people, you know. He had no choice.''

''Bullshit,'' I said. ''That demon knew exactly what he was

doing, and I hope he's burning in hell. If I could, I'd throw his pajamas down in after him. Might make the fire burn hotter.''

The Major sputtered around for a while, which wasn't half as pleasing as Wynnell's sewing machine. Finally he said words that I couldn't repeat to Mama (although now that she'd become a sex fiend, her standards may have dropped). Still, they were terrible words.

''What?'' I gasped. ''You think Rob Goldburg's kind can't be trusted?''

''Get a grip on it, girlie. I'm not talking about his bloodlines. I'm talking about you-know-what.''

''Well!'' So it was gays who got his goat.

''Those folks are the slipperiest, slimiest, most conniving sons of bitches. Hell, they're capable of anything.''

''Takes one to know one,'' I said. Very few other sayings ring as true now as they did in the third grade.

He had the affront to laugh off my accusation.

''Well, if the truth hurts,'' I said, skipping up to the fifth-grade level.

He laughed again. ''You don't really think I'm one of them, do you?''

''It has occurred to me,'' I said. ''Among other things.'' There was little need to worry about the Major's feelings. If elephants had hide that thick they wouldn't be facing extinction.

''Come on, now! Me?'' He sounded almost flattered.

''If the shoe fits,'' I said, trotting out an adult axiom.

There was silence on his end. I preferred it to sputtering, but it still wasn't as soothing as the purr of Wynnell's Singer.

''So you really think I'm an antiques expert?'' he asked at last. ''A bona fide expert, eh?''

''What?''

''Say, as much of an expert as Goldburg?''

''I beg your pardon?''

There was an odd sound. Possibly a stifled sob, which I prefer not to think about. ''You don't know just how much this means to me, Abigail. I always thought you looked down on me because I sold military antiques. That you thought my merchandise was somehow inferior.''

''Well, I—''

''But that's what I've been trying to tell you and the rest of this bunch all along. I mean, just because I don't sell Louis the fifteenth this, or Louis the sixteenth that, doesn't mean I don't know my antiques. It just means that I have chosen to narrow the scope of my shop down. It certainly doesn't mean that I'm not an authority on antiques in general.''

I was beginning to see the dawn. ''Certainly not.''

He took a deep breath. ''Well, I'm glad that's all been cleared up.''

''Glad enough to come to breakfast?''

''What the hell—why not? We experts need to stick together. Right?''

''Like grease on Teflon,'' I said, and hung up.

Anita Morgan must have been praying. ''Amen,'' she said after the eighth ring.

''Anita, dear, don't you have any customers?''

My concern was genuine. Anita's shop, The Purple Rose, sells middle-of-the-road antiques, some very fine estate jewelry, and a good deal of religion. Anita's customers are always complaining that they find religious tracts tucked in the nooks and crannies of her furniture pieces. Consequently she gets few repeat customers. This doesn't seem to bother the poor dear, who simply gets down on her knees and prays for more customers.

Now, none of this would be any of my business except that Anita has been thinking lately of switching over entirely to estate jewelry. This is where she gets her only repeat customers. Of course the reason for that is most jewelry items are too small to have pamphlets wadded up inside them. Again, I would be perfectly content to stay out of this matter if it were not for the fact that Anita wants to call the new shop Gems for Jesus.

''Well, I'm never alone, if that's what you mean,'' Anita said in response to my question. ''The Lord is always right here in the shop with me.'' She laughed perfunctorily. ''You might say he's my best customer.''

"But does he pay cash?"

"Abigail! That isn't funny!"

"Sorry, dear. I couldn't help myself. Listen, why I called is because I wanted to invite you to breakfast tomorrow morning at Denny's. Same time as on Monday, same crowd."

There was a moment of silence. Perhaps she was praying for patience. Although she is the president of our little association, Anita Morgan disapproves of our breakfast meetings. Apparently they cut into her early morning personal devotions. Anita has made sure that we all understand the spiritual hardship one morning a month has inflicted on her soul.

"Abby, what is the reason for this?"

"Rob Goldburg has been arrested, dear. I want us all to put our heads together and see what we can do for him."

There was another moment of silence, during which I prayed for the grace to hold my tongue, and to respond graciously to what was undoubtedly about to happen next. Anita has made it clear that she believes Rob Goldburg is going to burn forever in the fires of hell because of his lifestyle. Of course it's nothing personal, or so she would have you believe. It was God who made the rules, not she.

At the same time, Anita is very much a southern lady and would never confront Rob, or any other sinner, directly to their face. The wadded-up tracts are about as direct as she gets, *except* that she has been known to bend my ear from time to time. I am ashamed to confess that I have given the woman an audience, but only because she was such a good listener when Buford first took up with Tweetie. And it didn't hurt that Anita assigned the two of them to eternal flames as well. Adulterers rank down there on a par with homosexuals, or so says Anita. According to her, God agrees.

Anita coughed. "Abby, this could be the Lord's judgment on his life, you know."

"Could be, dear. It could also be that he was framed by that bellpull. Anyway, if you don't want to come for his sake, come for ours. We need you to say grace."

"Well—"

"His new friend, Bob Steuben, is going to be there. Look at this as a perfect opportunity to witness."

"Yes, but—"

"Besides, I wanted to go over some hymn selections with you. For Aunt Eulonia's funeral. You are going to sing at her funeral, aren't you?"

That was like asking a six-year-old if he was going to eat his Halloween candy. It was also a tremendous sacrifice on my part, and on the part of anyone attending my aunt's funeral. Anita Morgan claims to be in her church choir, but I don't see how that's possible. Even Mother Teresa would be tempted to throw an old shoe at Anita if she sang outside the nun's window on a moonless night. But as bad as she sounds, Anita Morgan must be given an A for enthusiasm and willingness to perform at the drop of a hat.

"Is this going to be at your Episcopal church, Abby?"

"Yes, dear, the one down in Rock Hill."

I could hear her catch her breath. The way she smoked, she may have been gasping for it.

"Would it be an Episcopal hymn?"

Mama and I had already gone over the congregational hymns with the priest and the musical director. Nothing had been said about a visiting soloist, but I assumed that neither of them would object. At least not until they heard Anita. However, I had no idea how they would feel about her singing a hymn that was not in our hymnal.

"Of course, dear," I said just to be on the safe side.

She sighed deeply. "Well, in that case, I just don't know. Y'all's hymns tend to be kinda—well, you know—"

"Dignified?"

"Uh—"

"Staid?"

"Uh—"

"Boring?"

"Yeah, that's it. And I mean it in the nicest way."

"Of course, dear. Look, why don't you pick one of our hymns, and if you're willing to sing a cappella, then liven it up however you want to. Okay?"

"I don't know, Abigail. The truth is, the Lord might not approve of me singing an Episcopal hymn."

"Then sing anything you want!"

I was going to owe our music director big-time for that. It's bad enough that I talked Mama into singing in the choir after Daddy died. At the time I thought of it as a perfect way to get her back out into the world, at least on choir practice nights and Sunday mornings. Of course back then it never occurred to me that my Mama would feel so comfortable in the world that she would bring six feet of it home with her to bed. But anyway, at least Mama gives to the church, and rather generously I might add. I was going to have to donate rather generously myself to the organ fund if I expected to show my face around there again after the funeral.

"Does it matter what key I sing in?" It was sweet of her to be concerned.

"Any," I said. "Just try to stay on it."

I don't think she heard me. She had already begun a rousing rendition of "Bringing in the Sheaves."

Through my front window I saw three cats make a beeline for The Purple Rose. One of their number was either in excruciating pain or it was time for a roll in the hay.

12

I slept very well on that authentic Queen Anne couch. Probably better than the old gal had herself. I am not used to having someone else around, and it was a real treat to feel safe. There is definitely something to be said for sleeping with both eyes closed.

I was determined to get to Denny's early to grab a table in the nonsmoking section. Anita is the only one of our number who still puffs, but because she belongs to a strict religious denomination that views cigarettes as "tools of the devil," she doesn't dare complain. I know, it is probably unfair of me to take advantage of her in that way, but so be it. Besides, she's not going to be able to smoke at those celestial breakfasts she's always raving about, so she might as well get used to it.

Bob wanted to go uptown first, on the off chance he would be permitted to see Rob, so I drove to the restaurant alone. Before leaving, I made Bob promise to stop by Denny's for at least a token appearance so that I could properly introduce him. It was in his own best interest to do so, but the poor man was practically a basket case, and I wasn't going to count on him. Just seeing him was enough to reclaim half my night's sound sleep.

Much to my surprise, the nonsmoking room at Denny's was virtually empty. The only other folks were a family of Yankee tourists from Wisconsin. They were big, blond, and underbred, all in obscenely good health. They had expansive gestures and loud voices, and there was nowhere in the room that was free of their presence. It was the Northern occupation all over again. I briefly considered moving to the other room. However, when one is trying to do a little detecting, it is helpful to be able to see.

"What is this 'grits' thing?" the mother asked.

She pronounced grits in one syllable, and it grated on me something awful.

"That's what they call cream of wheat down here," the father said.

"I want the kids to have that," the mother said. "And ask the waitress for milk to go with it."

"The milk might cost extra," the father said. "There are some cheap pancake breakfasts on the children's menu."

"Pancakes, pancakes," the children chorused. They were probably preschoolers, but they were about my height. Mama should have sent me up north for my wonder years.

The parents dutifully returned to the menu.

"Well, I don't know," the mother said. "They can get pancakes back home. Aren't we here for the cultural experience, John?"

"You bet," the father agreed. "And I'm going to try the biscuits and gravy."

The mother smiled victoriously. "That settles it then, biscuits for us. Hot cereal for them."

The children wailed, giving credence to that obscure theory that it really was Yankee preschoolers who gave forth with the infamous rebel yells during the War Between the States.

Their waitress arrived at the same time Wynnell arrived at my table.

"Y'all ready to order now?" the waitress asked pleasantly.

"We all is," the father said. He laughed, as if he had just said something funny.

"Damn Yankees," Wynnell snarled. Of course being a southern lady, Wynnell snarled discreetly.

The waitress, a mere child herself, waited patiently while the father nudged the mother, priming her for his next funny remark.

"They all," he pointed to the children, "will be having the grits. We all," he gestured at his wife and then himself, "will be having the biscuits with sausage gravy. That isn't too spicy, is it?"

"Sir?"

"On account of John's heart," the wife said. She spoke loud and slow, as if the waitress had a hearing problem, "The doctor says he has to avoid spicy foreign foods."

"Ma'am?"

The father belched good-naturedly. "Spice. That's what it does to me. This stuff isn't spicy, is it? You know, hot?"

The waitress shrugged. "I don't think it is."

The wife nodded sagely. "That means it's hot," she translated. "Well, in that case, we'll be having the grits, too. And toast please."

"Yes, ma'am."

"Oh, does cinnamon on the toast cost extra?"

"No, ma'am. What would y'all like to drink?"

The wife whispered to her husband, who shook his head. She whispered again, as loud as a choir of snakes.

"Is the water here safe to drink?" he asked obediently.

"That does it," Wynnell said.

She stood up and would have charged the Yankee pestilence had I not grabbed a fold of her outer garment. As I should well have expected, a piece about the size of a pillow case tore loose.

"Now look what you've done!"

I looked. The swatch of fabric was in my hand, but Wynnell's outfit looked no different.

"Oh, you've ruined it," Wynnell wailed, oblivious of the Yankees. "Now I'm going to have to go home and change."

I tried to pat the fabric back in place. There was no telling where it came from. Wynnell sews free-form.

"Not there, you idiot," she snapped. It is hard being a southern lady when one's ensemble is in shreds.

"Hey, hey, what have we here?" the Major asked. It must have been his military training, but I hadn't heard as much as a sole scuff against the floor.

"Sit," I hissed to Wynnell. "No one will notice anything."

She sat, the severed material draped across her lap like an

oversize napkin. I hoped my other guests didn't request napkins to match their outfits.

Gretchen showed up at 7:30 on the dot, as I expected her to. The woman has a thing about punctuality. She claims—and I believe her—to have given birth to all four of her children on their respective due dates, as determined by her doctor months in advance. Furthermore, all four children were born at precisely 10 A.M. All this from a woman who refuses to wear a watch.

"You know of course that Joan Lunden is interviewing the three tenors at seven-forty-six."

"No ma'am," I said.

Gretchen shoved her glasses back up into place. "Of course, I'm taping the show, but I would rather watch it live. You know, Abigail, I really don't see why I'm needed here. I didn't make any threats against Rob Silverburg, now did I?"

"No ma'am, and that's Goldburg, not Silverburg."

Peggy's iridescent blue eye shadow preceded her into the room, providing a much needed diversion. She was chewing something. The woman eats three square meals a day, plus innumerable "pre" and "post" meals. It isn't humanly possible to be that horny. Neither is it possible to eat that much and not be any fatter than she is. The woman is either an alien from another solar system or a bulimic sex addict. If you knew Peggy, you'd vote for the former.

"Is that friend of Rob Goldburg's here yet?"

I ducked a shower of crumbs. "No, but he'll be coming later on."

"Good, maybe then there's time."

"For what, dear?"

She glanced hungrily over at the Wisconsin family who were being served their toast and one-syllable grits.

"To vote Rob out of the association, that's what."

"Peggy!"

"Well, it's embarrassing, Abby. Having one of our members up on murder charges. What do I say to customers?"

"He didn't do it, Peggy! That's why we're all here. To find a way to prove he didn't."

"Still, in the meantime, we should vote him out. I'm sure we all feel that way. Don't we, Major?"

The Major sidled up to Peggy. "Yes?"

He has been trying halfheartedly to woo Peggy for as long as I've known them, but she isn't the slightest bit interested. Apparently their chemistry just isn't right for each other. It is a real shame, too, because I can see a lot of good coming from that union. Peggy could finally give up food, and with any luck, the Führer's pajamas would be retired. Personally, I think it's worth a shot.

"Tell Abigail what you told me," Peggy said.

The Major stepped forward and squared his shoulders. "We don't want an accused murderer in our little group. That's what I said."

I glared up at him. "Why the hell not? Won't he give you exclusive rights to his pajamas?"

"Very funny," the Major said, and then stepped wisely back out of kicking range.

"Gretchen, do you feel this way, too?"

Gretchen nodded and mumbled something about the three tenors and Joan Lunden getting it on. I made a mental note to ask her for details later.

"How about you, Wynnell?"

"Well, Abby—"

I couldn't believe my eyes and ears. Everyone was deserting the cause before the breakfast had even begun. Even before Anita, our most conservative member, had arrived.

"Do y'all really feel this way?"

Wynnell, Gretchen, and the Major nodded. Even the Brady Bunch from Wisconsin nodded, although it was none of their damn business.

There was the staccato rap of machine-gun fire in the doorway, and I ducked behind Peggy. The Major, who has been properly trained in these matters, hit the deck. Peggy and Wynnell are much braver than I, and didn't budge. Either that, or they recognized the sound of Anita coughing.

Sure enough, there she was, standing in the doorway, a vision of holiness. Anita wears modest, wrist-length sleeves, even in summer, and her skirts are what Rob calls "muddraggers.'' She never wears any jewelry because it is somehow inherently sinful. However, I must say that the Holy Roller hairdo she sports is actually rather becoming on her. The woman is a very pale, natural blond, with no discernible lashes or brows. It is my personal opinion that she would benefit enormously from a little makeup, but who am I to judge? Besides, the tobacco stains on her teeth do supply a little contrast.

''Oh there you are, dear!'' Peggy ran up to Anita and gave her a quick hug.

Anita smiled. ''Are we all here?''

''All except for Bob Steuben, our newest member,'' I said cheerfully.

Anita frowned. ''You didn't tell her, then?''

'' 'Course I did,'' Peggy said, ''she just—''

I snatched a piece of cinnamon toast from the tourists' table and crammed it in Peggy's mouth. They were too busy complaining about the butter in their cereal to notice.

''Let's all take a seat, shall we?'' I asked brightly. ''We have a lot to cover this morning.'' Whatever my colleagues had decided didn't count, not until they had heard me out.

We were able to order and listen to Anita say grace before returning to the subject of Rob Goldburg.

''Amen,'' I chanted. I gently tapped my water glass. ''Now, folks, about Rob Goldburg. Here's what I had in mind. Of course—''

''Anita is our president,'' Gretchen said. She looked at me over the tops of enormous round frames. ''Shouldn't she be calling this meeting to order?''

I smiled sweetly. ''Yes, dear, but I called this meeting.''

''Are you paying for our breakfasts?'' Peggy asked.

''Hey, no fair! Not unless she does something about my dress first!'' Wynnell turned to me and gave me a world-class withering look.

''You may rummage through my sewing scrap bag,'' I said generously. ''Take whatever you want, but not that square of cotton paisley. I'm saving that for a halter top.''

It was like telling a child they could have all the candy in a candy shop except one particular chocolate bar. Of course, I was one step ahead of Wynnell.

"That's the hot-pink material with the yellow paisleys, isn't it? Why can't I have that?"

I sighed deeply. "All right, dear, you can have the paisley piece, but you owe me one."

Wynnell nodded happily.

"Well, are you paying for breakfast, or not?" Peggy demanded.

"Okay, okay. But you can't change your order." Believe it or not it was a happy compromise for both of us.

I tapped on my glass again. The Yankee children tapped on theirs, but I ignored them.

"Does anybody know what time it is?" I asked.

"It is exactly seven-forty-six," Gretchen said wistfully. "Right now the three tenors are on Joan Lunden having a good time."

"I think you misspoke, dear. Anyway, it's time we banded together to protect ourselves and our reputations."

"By ousting Rob Goldburg, right?" Anita started to reach into her purse but stopped. The cigarette would have to wait for a private moment.

"Wrong," I said. "Even if we oust Rob, and he is found guilty, our reputation is going to suffer. We will have had a murderer among our group. It will always be a scandal. Not only is no one going to want to buy my aunt's shop, but no one will buy his, either. We will have two shops sitting empty on our street.

"But on the other hand, if we help prove him innocent— which I believe he is—our little group has nothing to be ashamed of. Besides, once the police are convinced that Rob didn't murder my aunt, then they can start looking for the real killer. He may kill again, you know."

"Not likely," Anita said. "Now that he's in jail."

I thought of borrowing one of Wynnell's withering looks but wisely opted for the candy approach.

"My aunt had many friends, dear. From what I hear that church is going to be packed for her funeral."

Anita's eyes glazed over in anticipation of her Rock Hill

debut. Her lips moved, but she said nothing. Perhaps she was mouthing the words of the hymn she would sing.

"Now, back to what we can do to help Rob out," I said firmly.

"Hmm, hmm." The Major outlined his abbreviated mustache with a pudgy finger. "Not so fast there, girlie. There is just one thing wrong with your little scheme."

"Yeth?" It is hard to enunciate clearly while biting one's tongue.

"Well, what's wrong is that Gretchen here saw Rob Goldburg enter your aunt's shop the evening she was killed. Just minutes before, as a matter of fact."

13

"What?"

Even the Yankee dawdlers jumped.

"Tell her, Gretchen."

Everyone was nodding like a rear window full of plastic puppies. Poor Gretchen had no choice but to come clean.

"It was six-sixteen, time for the local weather, not that I had a television on, mind you. I don't keep a TV in my shop."

"No need," I said sweetly. "Please, go on."

Gretchen glanced at the Major, who was nodding more vigorously than the rest of the puppies. She pushed her glasses back into place, probably to protect her from my wrath.

"Well, I was just locking the front door, when I saw Rob Goldburg doing the same thing. Only he got done first. I waved at him, but I guess he didn't see me, 'cause he trotted right on over to poor Eulonia's place."

"Did you see him go inside?"

"No, but I'm sure he did. I know he was parked in the other direction, right in front of me, and when I got to the car, he was nowhere to be seen, but his car was still there."

"What does that prove?" I tried not to sound too triumphant.

Gretchen squirmed. She has a short, plump torso, with only the hint of a neck. When she squirms her whole body is put into motion.

"Well, at exactly six-nineteen, just in time for the sports roundup, I drove up the street, past Eulonia's shop, and there was no Rob. So he must have gone inside."

"I see."

She smiled and nodded, along with the rest of the rear-window pups.

"So, you're saying that you saw Rob head off in the direction of my aunt's shop, but you turned away before you saw him go in. Later when you didn't see him on the street, you *assumed* he was inside? Killing her?"

This time Gretchen glanced at Anita, who was busily studying the Yankee dawdlers. Perhaps she could sense their souls were ripe for saving.

"Well, he didn't evaporate into thin air," Gretchen wailed.

"Yes, he did."

The bobbing heads all froze and then pivoted in unison to gape at the speaker, who was male.

"Ah, Bob, just in time," I said, pushing my chair back. The hug I gave him was for my colleagues' benefit just as much as it was for his.

"What the devil is going on?" the Major bellowed.

I introduced Bob Steuben. When I mentioned that he was from Toledo, the Yankees became agitated. Perhaps they thought Bob was going to be our next course.

The Major was the first to recover. "Now tell me, boy, what you meant when you said he evaporated into thin air?"

Bob smiled bravely. "He didn't exactly evaporate, but he didn't go into Miss Wiggins's shop. I can vouch for that."

Gretchen peered over her lenses. Clearly she found the man less intimidating than yours truly. I didn't know whether or not to be flattered.

"But I saw him head that way, and then three minutes later he wasn't there. How do you explain that?"

"Easy. I picked him up. I drove past y'all's shop while y'all was locking up, and parked down the street a short way. Rob was headed for my car when you last saw him."

"The subject of *y'all* is always plural," Peggy said generously. Perhaps she hadn't heard that Bob was gay.

"Well, that explains it," Gretchen said. She sounded relieved. I knew it was important for her to be believed, no matter what the outcome.

A couple of the heads nodded; Wynnell's did not. "You have any kin that fought in *the* war?"

Bob turned and regarded her pleasantly. "Yes, as a matter of fact, my dad fought in the war."

"Which side?"

"Ours, of course."

Wynnell looked like she'd been slapped. "That ain't so funny to some of us. Some of us still take it pretty serious, you know."

Bob looked about as confused as a palmetto in a snowstorm. "My dad took it very seriously. He was wounded in the Battle of the Bulge. He would have died, but a German medic saved his life."

I couldn't help but laugh hysterically. "I'm sorry," I said between gasps. "You were talking about World War II, but Wynnell was talking about the Civil War!"

"The War Between the States," the Major corrected me.

"The War of Northern Aggression," Wynnell snapped.

"Speaking of saved," Anita said, "Are you?"

"I beg your pardon?"

"If you died today, do you know where your soul will go?"

I turned to Anita. "Is that a threat, dear?"

Anita glared at me through lashless lids. "If Rob Goldburg had been saved, he wouldn't have killed your aunt. Jesus would have stopped him."

"Rob is Jewish, dear," I said wearily. "Maybe he has a different take on things."

"Jesus saves, Moses invests," Bob said lightly.

Anita was not amused. "You haven't answered my question."

Bob shrugged. I could see he was losing patience with us. If he enlisted the Yankee dawdlers, it could be a fair fight.

"Well?"

"I was raised Presbyterian. Any other personal questions?"

"Northern Presbyterian, or southern?"

The Major cleared his throat. "What I want to know is, did you serve in the army? The United States Army?"

"No, I did not. They were no longer drafting when I turned eighteen."

"You could have enlisted. I did. It's a patriotic man's duty, if you ask me."

"There are other ways of showing your patriotism," Bob said. He looked like he was about to bolt.

"Pledging to PBS is just one way of showing your patriotism," Gretchen said.

"Bullshit!" The Major pounded the table and sent Denny's cutlery flying for the second time that week. "PBS is commie crap."

"My singles group is planning a trip to Russia next month," Peggy said generously. "I'm sure there is still time to sign up. I hear that old icons are a bargain. You can pick up some authentic Byzantine pieces for a fraction of what you'd have to pay for them in New York."

"Really?" Bob actually seemed interested.

"Of course the trip itself is rather expensive. It's much cheaper if you choose double accommodations. I signed up for a single, but I'd be willing to share, if you want."

"I bet you would," the Major said. The mustache twitched like a mouse in heat.

"Hey, how far is it to Disney World?" the Yankee husband called from his table.

"Three thousand miles and you're going the wrong way," Wynnell said with a straight face.

Actually, with Wynnell it's very hard to tell if she's smiling. You could grow okra in those furrows and never even see it. Maybe even a little cotton.

"That does it, Wilbur," the Yankee wife shouted. "We're turning around right after breakfast and heading home. Back to where people are polite."

It was time to wrest control of my meeting, so I tapped loudly on my water glass. Everyone but Wynnell gave me their attention, so I whistled Dixie. Just the first few bars.

"Look folks, we have gotten way off the subject here. We're supposed to be helping our friend and colleague, Rob. Not giving Bob here the third degree."

"Rob may be y'all's friend, but he isn't mine," Anita said. "The Bible warns us not to be unequally yoked with sinners.

Some of y'all may want to share Rob's yoke, but don't count me in.''

The Major squared his shoulders. "Hey, what's that supposed to mean?"

I banged on my water glass. One of the copycat Yankee children banged on a plate with a fork, and the din was horrible. Neither Mama nor Daddy Yankee made a move to correct the child, proving Wynnell's often expressed opinion that proper etiquette is solely a southern virtue.

I ignored the child's noise and smiled sweetly at my guests. "Remember just who is picking up the check."

"I sure as hell am not!"

I dropped my fork on my plate and made more noise than the Yankee child. There, in the doorway of the nonsmoking section, stood my ex-husband Buford Timberlake. On each arm was a woman, and neither of them was Tweetie.

The woman on his left was at least six feet tall, with bottle black hair, and hips still quivering from liposuction. The woman on his right was of average height, with auburn hair, but she was definitely not built for speed. If those boobs didn't have their own zip codes, then she had to be in violation of some federal statute. Perhaps that's why she was having breakfast with a lawyer.

"Why, if it isn't that rat, Buford," I sang out. "I'm telling Tweetie."

I know, it was childish of me, but I couldn't help it. Also, I will admit to feeling a certain kinship with the woman. Perhaps hell has no fury like a woman scorned, but there are few bonds so easily formed as those between two scorned women.

Buford, as ever, was without a conscience. He didn't even have the decency to blush.

"Not that it's any of your goddamn business, but this is a business breakfast."

"Ah, yes, monkey business."

He disengaged his right arm from the mammary monster, so that he could gesticulate. "You're one to talk, Abb. Where the hell did you spend last night? I called over at Marilyn's a dozen times. The old biddy is so pissed at me she can't see straight. She tried to tell me that you weren't there and she didn't expect to see you. Something about you two having it out over plaster poodles and pink flamingos. Claims you defaced her property. Is that true?''

''In a pig's ear.''

''Well, where the hell were you? I called your Mama's, but you weren't there either. At least that's what some guy said when he answered the phone.'' He chuckled. ''Your Mama been getting it on, Abb?''

''Leave Mama out of this!''

It was bad enough that Mama broke the seventh commandment, but to flaunt it publicly by not answering her own phone was unspeakably bad manners. I was going to have to do a thorough examination of my own wood pile. It was undoubtedly chock full of Yankees.

''Abigail spent the night with me,'' Bob said gallantly. To his credit he said it in a low, booming voice that I hardly recognized.

''What the hell did you say?'' Buford bellowed.

Anita gasped.

Wynnell frowned.

The Major snorted.

Peggy's blue lids fluttered.

Gretchen glanced at her bare wrist. ''It's eight thirty-seven. Spencer Christian will just be wrapping up the morning weather. Since most of us will be opening our shops in just twenty-three minutes, I move that we adjourn this breakfast so we can get to work.''

''I second the motion,'' Wynnell said. ''All in favor say 'aye.' ''

The chorus of ''ayes'' was deafening. Even the Yankees voted to end my breakfast, but that didn't surprise me. What surprised me was Bob Steuben. Here I was, shelling out good money for a breakfast, during which we were supposed to come up with proof of his partner's innocence, and he was folding. Fleeing from the table like a startled rabbit. Perhaps it was the sight of Buford with a bimbo on each elbow he found intimidating. Boy, would I set him straight. Buford Timberlake was no macho man. As near as I can remember, the only thing on Buford that consistently went up was his blood pressure.

It did no good for me to protest the straw vote. I was chewing at the time, and by the time I had politely swallowed, all of my ungrateful guests had fled. Not one left even so much as a quarter for their tip. Wynnell, at least, left a piece of bacon behind. It was nice and limp, and I would have to remember to thank her for it—maybe when I returned the swatch of fabric she'd left behind as well.

"Can I take y'all's picture?" the Yankee husband asked on his way out. "*Gone with the Wind* is my wife's favorite movie."

He had to be talking to me. Scarlet might have been a little taller than I, but she certainly wasn't six feet. And she most certainly didn't have hooters that hid her view of her shoes.

"Okay, but I charge five bucks for a solo shot," I drawled. "Each additional face in the pose is another two bucks."

The Yankee brushed rudely past me. "Not you. Him!"

"Excuse me?"

"Well, I know he doesn't look the part, but you did call him Rhett Butler, didn't you?"

"I did not!"

The Yankee husband looked helplessly at his wife.

"I heard her," the Yankee wife said. She glared at me, daring me to contradict her.

"Well—"

"Since we decided not to go on to Disney World, we have to get photos of something." The Yankee husband snapped his flash into place. "So, it may as well be a man named Rhett Butler."

I decided not to spoil their trip. If they wanted to think that 'rat Buford' and Rhett Butler sounded alike, that was fine with me.

"Great, take his picture," I said agreeably. "But you pay me. I'm his agent."

They left Denny's quite happily, I assure you. After apologizing for Wynnell's rude exaggeration, I informed them that Disney World was only a few more exits down the interstate. Of course, that wasn't quite true, but we do have Carowinds, a wonderful amusement park of our own that straddles the border of the Carolinas. Anyone who took a picture of my ex-husband as a vacation trophy would certainly not notice the difference.

Buford stashed his bimbos in a booth and caught me just as I was exiting the front door. I mean that only figuratively; by now the man knows better than to lay a finger on me. Spilling pennies on the sidewalk is not the only thing guaranteed to bring him to his knees.

"What the hell is wrong with Susan's apartment?"

"Susan's apartment?"

"Susan, our daughter. Her apartment."

"Her apartment?"

"What the hell are you, some goddamn echo machine?"

I smiled sweetly. "What makes you think something is wrong with her apartment?"

"I tried calling her last night, looking for you. Some guy answered. Said he was a janitor, and that Susan couldn't come to the phone. Something about a leak. When I called again no one answered. What's going on?"

Clearly Buford didn't have a clue, and that put me between a rock and a hard place. Should I tell on my daughter and risk losing her trust, or did I owe it to her father, scurrilous as he was, to let him know what was going on in our daughter's life? At any rate, Buford's money was the only thing I could think of that could possibly get Susan back on track again.

"Susan has dropped out of school, lost her female roommates, and is now living with an ex-janitor old enough to be her father. A male janitor. That's what's going on."

Buford's jaw dropped to tripping level. I will admit that I felt sorry for him. I mean, up until Tweetie came along, we were in that parenting thing together.

"What?"

"Maybe it's not as bad as it seems," I said quickly. "After all, she's found herself a job behind the cosmetics counter at Belk's. And at least now with a man living there, we don't have to be so concerned for her safety." After all, Buford had yet to see Susan's apartment, so he didn't know how important that consideration was.

"How old did you say this creep is?"

"Thirty-eight."

"His name?"

"James Grady. She calls him Jimmy. Buford—"

It was too late. I thought of calling Susan and warning her, but reluctantly decided against it. There would be no stopping Buford. Sooner or later he would catch up with her, and it was better that the confrontation happen at her apartment, than at Belk's. Besides, having Grady there would deflect most of Buford's ire. Perhaps, even, the two men would punch each other out.

I quit daydreaming and went back inside Denny's. The two bimbos were sprawled quietly in the booth, as complacent as two cows chewing their cud. They sat up at attention when I approached them.

"Rhett Butler had an emergency," I kindly informed them. "He said to go on home."

"But he didn't pay us," the tall one whined.

"Yeah, he owes us twenty bucks." The shorter one had been resting her breasts on the plastic seat, and there were two damp ovals where she had lain.

"Then I guess I'll have to pay y'all."

I dumped the contents of my change purse on the floor in front of their table. The last I saw of them they were down on their knees picking up pennies. It was worth every one.

14

Greg Washburn was waiting for me when I got to the shop. He looked as cool as a cucumber and as dry as toast. I would have eaten him, had I not just had breakfast.

"He didn't do it," I said, "and I have proof."

He smiled. "Tell me."

Before I could open my mouth, the fall mummy came between us. This time she was dressed in a mohair sweater and a long suede skirt. I could only hope that her blood had been replaced with Freon.

"That's better," she said.

"Excuse me?"

"Your dress. You're wearing black. It's a little severe, but it's more in keeping with the season."

I smiled patiently. "I'm going to a funeral this afternoon, dear."

"I want a refund," she said, switching gears faster than a race car driver on a hilly track.

"What?"

"I want a refund on that punch bowl. It broke when I got it home."

"How?"

"I dropped it trying to get it out of the car." She had the nerve to look me in the eye.

"I'm sorry, dear, but glass breaks, you know."

"A good quality cut glass punch bowl wouldn't have broken. And that's what I thought you were selling. Since you obviously weren't, I want my money back."

She was able to say all that without batting an eyelash. Clearly the woman had a future in politics. Or perhaps she already was in politics, which would explain how she could afford my prices.

I trotted out my sweetest smile. "Bring in all the pieces, and I'll give you back your money."

She laughed prematurely. "Honey, I don't think you heard me. It hit the driveway. Kaboom! It's in a million pieces now—in a Dumpster."

I nodded sympathetically. "I did hear you, dear, but I don't think you heard me. You can have your money back when I get my punch bowl back."

I turned back to Greg. "He did *not* go into my aunt's shop just before the murder, like Gretchen said he did. I mean, I assume she got around to telling you that story, too."

He appeared startled. "She took back her story?"

"Yes, she had to. That's because I found an alibi for Rob."

"Rob Goldburg?" It was the mohair monster. For one, brief, sinful moment I felt like taking a match to her sweater.

"This is a private matter," I said through gritted teeth.

She pushed me rudely aside. "I know all about Robby's arrest," she said to Greg. "And I agree with her, he didn't do it. He couldn't have, because he was with me."

Greg stared at her expectantly. I stifled a snicker.

"Who are you?" he asked.

She tossed her bleached mane imperiously. "Cozette Ballard, but my friends call me Cozy."

"Address?" To Greg's credit, he didn't miss a beat.

She gave him one of Charlotte's poshest addresses.

"Phone number, please?"

Cozy looked at me and I turned discreetly away. It was all pretty stupid, considering she had given me her unlisted number the day before when she charged the punch bowl.

"When was he with you?"

"Late Monday afternoon, of course. From about four to six."

"Where were you, and what were you doing?"

"Why, shopping of course. In Robby's shop. *He's* got the

ood pieces on this street.''

I forgave her. "You see?" I cried. "Here's another alibi. And Bob Steuben got back from doing his errands at six-sixteen. Just ask Gretchen. That leaves only sixteen minutes!"

Greg took a small notebook out of his shirt pocket and started scribbling in it, but he didn't take his eyes off Cozy. For all we knew he really was scribbling.

"How can you be sure of that time frame?"

Cozy's smile was testimony that at least one Charlotte orthodontist was able to send his children to college.

"That's easy," she said. "I had lunch with a girlfriend who had a hair appointment at two. I dropped her off and then wandered over here, because it's only a few blocks away. I was supposed to pick her up in an hour, but the next thing I knew it was six o'clock. My friend Mignon had to take a cab home. She hasn't spoken to me since."

Greg shook his head stubbornly. "Sixteen minutes is plenty of time to walk from his shop to your aunt's, do what he's accused of, and then drive off with this Bob Steuben. And anyway, Gretchen Miller didn't see Bob Steuben pick up the suspect. We have only his word for it that it happened."

"He has a point," mohair said.

I shoved her gently aside, forcing Greg to look at me. "Right, and I suppose that even if Gretchen did see Bob pick him up, that wouldn't count, either, because Bob is probably a suspect, too."

Greg looked over my head. "Did you buy anything at Mr. Goldburg's shop, Miss—"

"Cozy Ballard," she said with a straight face. "And yes, I bought a pair of Regency carved and gilded beech armchairs."

"How much did you pay for them?" I asked. I knew the chairs: they were the most expensive things in Rob's shop.

"Thirty-two thousand even," she said.

Greg gasped. "No wonder he calls his place The Finer Things."

"That was a steal, you know," I told him. "A pair just like that sold for almost forty-seven thousand dollars at an auction in New York about six years ago."

Cozy looked pleased. Greg looked mortified.

"Well, New York is a major antiques center," I explained
"and a lot of people with money—wait a minute! If Coz
here bought those chairs, Rob couldn't help but remember it
Only he said Monday was a slow day."

Greg frowned.

"Well, I was the only customer in the shop at the time,'
Cozy said.

My mouth had already helped put my friend behind bars.
needed to change the subject before it convicted him.

"I just got in an empire chest with corner columns and a
overhanging top drawer. You want first crack at that? I'm will
ing to knock ten percent off."

Cozy cooed happily and trotted off in the direction
pointed.

"Look," I said to Greg, taking care not to do any lookin
myself, "Rob Goldburg is innocent. I just *know* he is. H
doesn't have it in him. He's all bark but no bite. The Major
however, is quite capable of biting"

"Do you have any proof?"

"No."

I could feel him staring at me. "Until there's been a tria
and a verdict handed in, the only way you can know Rob'
innocent is if you did it yourself."

I braved the blues and stared right back at him. "See here
buster, this afternoon is my aunt's funeral. The last thing
need today is to listen to crap like that."

He appeared stunned. "Sorry," he said. I could tell h
meant it.

Never let a man off easy, Mama keeps telling me, but ther
again, what does she know? She's had Daddy on a pedesta
ever since he was killed—until last night when she allowe
some man to push Daddy off the pedestal so that he coul
crawl into bed with her.

"She was my only aunt on my daddy's side," I said. The
sniffle would have sounded phony to a woman, but Greg
Washburn was far from that.

"Hey, I said I was sorry. But it's my job to consider every
one a suspect until the real killer gets put away. Any clues
no matter how slim, have to be followed up on."

"Did you test the bellpull for sweat?" I asked.

Dmitri had that same expression once when he accidentally ran into a mirror. "Say what?"

"It was ninety-five degrees on Monday and as humid as the inside of a goldfish bowl. If Rob killed my aunt, like you claim—dashed off there, because he only had sixteen minutes—his hands would have been sweaty. Some of that sweat should have come off on the bellpull. You test it for sweat."

"Hmm," was all he said. His daddy must have taught him not to go easy on women. I mean, he could have thanked me for the suggestion.

"Well, have it tested," I said graciously. "In the meantime, what's the scoop on Jimmy Grady?"

He sighed. "You're not going to like this, and there's no way to sugarcoat it."

I braced myself against a walnut highboy. "I already don't like it. Now give it to me straight."

"James Robert Grady has a rap sheet that would reach from here to Raleigh. Most of it petty stuff, but a few more serious."

"Like what?"

"Stealing money from newspaper machines."

"Tell me the serious stuff."

He looked away. "I shouldn't be telling you any of this, you know."

"I know, now tell me."

"Grady was convicted on car theft in Georgia eighteen years ago. Served just over five years in Atlanta."

I knew he was holding back. "I said to give it to me straight."

He took a deep breath. "He was convicted of being an accessory after the fact in a murder case. One involving the stolen car."

I leaned back against the highboy. "Tell me *everything*."

It was an ugly story about one of Grady's buddies in a small Georgia town who beat up his wife and then intentionally killed her when she threatened to go to the police. The buddy needed a car to leave town in, but he didn't have one, so Grady stole one for him. Apparently Grady's bulb was dimmer than December sunshine in Alaska because the car he stole belonged to the mayor and had city plates.

"Shit," I said. The tears were splashing off my cheeks and I was out of tissues.

Greg took a step forward. If I would have moved at all, he would have hugged me.

"Hey, good luck with your daughter. I mean it."

I turned away. It was my fault Susan was living with scum like that. If I had only been more—whatever it was Buford really needed—he wouldn't have dumped me for Tweetie, and we would have stayed together as a family. Sure, Susan would still be in college, but she wouldn't be in college with something to prove. Our divorce had put a chip on her shoulder that was never there when she was growing up. It had to be my fault, because up until Buford found Tweetie, everything was peachy-keen. I swear it was.

Greg cleared his throat. "Uh, there's one more little thing I found out, but it can wait until later."

I whirled. "What? Tell me now, damn it!"

"It seems that James Robert Grady is not thirty-eight. He's fifty-two."

I felt like laughing. What difference did it make now if he was sixty-two? The man was a convicted criminal. He had aided and abetted a wife-killer. At least if he was sixty-two he would be ten years closer to the grave.

"Thanks," I remembered to say.

Greg touched my shoulder briefly. "Hey, I'm sorry what I said before. I really am. Just between you and me—unofficially of course—I know you had nothing to do with your aunt's death. Sometimes I just get carried away in my professional capacity.

"Anyway, I have to be going now. I'm sure the lab checked that pull for everything under the sun, but I'll check on it just to make sure."

I nodded.

When he was gone I wandered over to Cozy, who was sniffing around the chest like a hound over fresh coon prints. So far she was my only customer, and I needed her to help take my mind off things.

"Well, am I ever glad you found this first," I gushed. "A piece this fine deserves an informed and astute buyer."

Cozy beamed. "Make that twenty percent off and I'll take it."

I snapped my fingers. "Lord Almighty! I plum forgot. There's this gentleman up on Lake Norman who won the New York lottery last year. This is his first house and he doesn't have a clue how to decorate. Still, he wants to do it by himself. The real kicker is he can't bear to part with all the Kmart stuff he already owns. Can you believe that?"

She shuddered.

"Anyway, the guy is loaded and asked me to keep an eye out for any really special pieces. So, if it's all the same to you, I'll just save this for him."

I reached for the price tag but she snatched it away from me.

"I'll pay your asking price."

I scratched my head. "Well, that would be more than fair, I'm sure. In retrospect, however, I priced this item far too low. My customer on Lake Norman has virtually unlimited resources and told me that money would be no object. Plus, he specifically asked for an antique chest upon which to display his lava lamp collection."

She blanched. "Lava lamps?"

"Lava lamps *and* pet rocks. The Cabbage Patch dolls he'll store inside the drawers."

I sold the chest to her for twice the ticket price, which made us both happy campers.

I closed my shop at noon and stopped in at The Finer Things before heading down to Rock Hill and the funeral. Poor Bob Steuben looked like he had just come from a funeral. I swear he had been crying.

"It's not bad news, is it?" I asked gently.

He turned away and pulled a handkerchief out of his pocket. If there had been any wild geese flying over the shop they would have undoubtedly landed and made a courtesy call.

"There isn't any news," he said finally. "That's the trouble."

"No news is good news," I said. "Before you know it, things will be looking up. In the meantime, I'm here for you."

For the sake of my children I learned how to force cheer the last two years of my marriage. Believe me, it can be done, no matter what the circumstances, if you're willing to put up with a little facial pain. As for the trite platitudes, I come by them naturally.

He turned, smiling weakly. "Thanks. This is going to sound selfish, but I feel kind of vulnerable. I don't really know anyone in Charlotte, except for Rob. I don't have any friends "

"Nonsense, dear, you know me. Count me as your friend."

"Thanks again."

Before he kissed my feet I changed the subject. "So Bob, I hear Rob sold that pair of Regency carved and gilded beech armchairs."

He drew a blank.

"They were over there, next to that mahogany secretary."

"They still are."

I looked in the direction I was pointing. Indeed they were there, exactly as I had last seen them. The one abutting the secretary still had the same silk tapestry draped elegantly over its left arm.

"Rob didn't sell them?"

I should have just asked him which way was up. He would have been less confused.

"Monday afternoon? To a lady who looks like a woolly worm?"

"I'm sorry, I'm just not in the mood for jokes," he said. He looked like he was about to cry again.

I apologized for my insensitivity and hurried out before my tongue and my curiosity got me into any more trouble that day. I had a funeral to attend, and that was going to take my full attention.

As I was pulling out of my parking spot a Lincoln Towncar nearly swiped my left front fender. Not only did the driver of the car not slow down, but in a very un-Charlottean manner, she gave me a private viewing of her middle finger. I recognized the rock on it as belonging to the woolly worm.

15

I was shocked to see Mama in pink.

"For a funeral?"

"Black is only for funerals in movies anymore," she said. "Mafia movies. Look around you when you get to church; people will be wearing all colors."

"But pink isn't even a fall color."

"Who cares," Mama said blithely. "Pink is my color."

I stared at her and would have driven off the road if it hadn't been for a couple of plastic garbage bins set too close to the curb. For the first time in sixteen years, Mama wasn't wearing pearls.

"They make me look old," Mama said, after I'd turned around twice and been talked out of it once.

"But you are—*mature*."

"You turn this car around this very minute and I'll give you the damn things."

I made a U-turn on Charlotte Avenue in front of the Y, setting a bad example for any truant kids that may have been lurking about. Mama's pearls were eight-millimeter beauties that Daddy got her for their twenty-fifth wedding anniversary. I had a feeling that if I didn't claim them quick someone was going to go home from a garage sale very happy.

"Tell me about him," I said.

"Who?"

"Mama!"

"All right. He's sweet, he's gentle, and he makes me laugh

115

a lot. And not that it's any of your business, but he's exactly my age. Well, two days younger in fact.''

"Does he have a name?''

She *giggled*. "Of course he has a name, but I'm not ready to tell you that yet.''

"What do you mean, you're not ready? You're ready to wear pink to a funeral and give away your pearls, but you can't tell me the name of your boyfriend?''

She giggled again. "Boyfriend. What a silly word.''

"Mama, is he somebody I know?''

"Maybe, maybe not.''

"That's a yes, I take it.''

"Take it any way you want, dear, but I'm not telling you his name.''

I gave up on trying to force it out of her and concentrated instead on finding a parking spot. Funerals in Rock Hill are always well attended; they outrank even weddings in popularity. Although a lot of the folk were coming to see my aunt off—she had been born and raised here, after all—there were undoubtedly a large number of more casual drop-ins. Until Rock Hill Cable adds AMC to their lineup, this will continue to be the norm.

Not only was the church parking lot full, but the nearby city lot was surprisingly full as well. We had to park all the way over by McCrory's department store. Thankfully, southern girls never sweat, and they rarely perspire. They merely dew. And dew I did. By the time we stepped inside the church, thanks to my black dress and the blazing sun, I was drenched with dew.

The Episcopal Church of Our Savior is the epitome of what every church should look like. Every church with good taste, that is. It is brick on the outside and dark wood and stained glass on the inside. It is also fifty degrees cooler on the inside during the summer, even in the narthex. My dew dissipated rapidly.

"Lord have mercy,'' Mama said, with justified concern. "You're shaking like a paint-can mixer.''

"Maybe she sees a ghost,'' Wynnell said. She was standing

there looking lost in a fuschia chiffon muumuu. There is no end to that woman's talent.

"I do not see a ghost. I'm just evaporating."

Wynnell wisely went on into the nave to look for a seat before I dematerialized in front of her eyes. I peeked through the doors before they closed behind Wynnell; Mama was right. I was the only one there dressed in black and not wearing a tie. At least three women, and one man, were wearing bright red.

"This isn't Mary Magdalene's funeral," I wailed. "Aunt Eulonia always wore navy dresses and opaque stockings."

"Times have changed," Mama said, tugging at the bodice of her pink dress to reveal a little more cleavage.

It was time to go in. Susan was a no-show, but Charlie was waiting for us just inside the nave. I had volunteered to drive him down, but for some odd reason Tweetie had decided to be a sweetie pie and drive him down herself.

"I'll sit with her in the back," Charlie whispered.

"He doesn't want to sit up front close to the coffin," Tweetie said. "Loss of a loved one is a difficult thing to process at that age."

She might well know, since she wasn't that much older than Charlie. Still, I made a mental note to ask her where and when she got her degree in psychology.

Mama, sensing my anger, grabbed my hand and practically pulled me along with her. At one point, as we were walking down the aisle, Mama hesitated slightly, and I thought I saw her winking at someone. I glanced around surreptitiously, but was unable to pick a black suit out from amidst the sea of color. No doubt her gentleman was the one in red.

The dew had pretty much dried by the time I took my seat at the front of the church, just in front of Anita Morgan, who was there with her husband, Brandt. As is our custom in the Episcopal Church, I immediately knelt for a moment of silent prayer. When I sat back up Anita poked me in the ribs.

"You sure this is the right church, Abigail?"

"Yes, dear. There's my aunt."

I nodded to the coffin which had been placed at the transom of the nave. As per our tradition it was covered with a simple green pall. Coincidentally, that shade of green matched Anita's dress perfectly.

"Will they be opening the casket?"

"No, dear."

"Told you," she said to Brandt. She sounded mighty relieved.

Brandt whispered something and Anita poked me again. "You *sure* this is the right place?"

"She's sure," Mama said, somewhat annoyed.

"But there was a man in a gown, back there."

"That was our priest, Father Pridgin."

"Then you're right, she's Catholic," Anita told Brandt.

I let her think we were Catholic. It made no difference to me. Not unless I planned to get married again, which I didn't. As an Episcopalian I am allowed to remarry and participate fully in my church. As a woman, having been married to Buford Timberlake, I was unlikely to exercise that option.

In all respects it was a normal and dignified Episcopal funeral except for two things. The first was Anita's a cappella solo.

"What on earth is she going up there for?" Mama demanded. "It isn't Communion yet."

"Anita has kindly volunteered to sing."

"Is she any good?"

"Remember when Cousin Grazier sang at her own birthday party in Savannah?"

"Three of her neighbors called the SPCA!"

"Only two did, Mama. The third called nine-one-one."

"Has our music director heard this woman sing?"

I patted Mama reassuringly. "Don't worry, the organ fund will be getting a hefty donation this year."

"Shhhh!" At least Anita had a loyal husband.

I had to admire that woman's confidence. She gave Aunt Eulonia's coffin wide berth but then hopped up the first set of altar steps and strode boldly up to the lay reader's microphone. You would have thought she had years of show biz experience.

"I'll be singing 'When the Roll Is Called Up Yonder,' "

she practically shouted. "Y'all feel free to join in any time. Clap if you want."

There was a stunned silence. Not only do we Episcopalians not know that song, but we are genetically incapable of clapping in church, except for at the end of the annual parish meetings. The last time someone clapped during a song, it was revealed that she was an undercover Methodist with no plans to convert. We Episcopalians proudly bear the label God's Frozen Chosen.

If Anita had sung *after* Communion, I would have accused her of drugging the wine. There is no other explanation for why the congregation not only clapped and sang their way through that rollicking song, but a couple in the back actually did a little soft-shoe—discreetly, of course, behind their pew.

"Lord have mercy!" I shouted to Mama above the din. "This is worse than today's rock 'n' roll."

"When the roll, when the roll," Mama echoed, her hands a mere blur.

It was utterly disgraceful. Mama has been a member of Our Savior's choir since 1947. She has been an Episcopalian since birth. I have a sneaking suspicion she is even a closet Republican, and here she was bouncing up and down like a kid on a pogo stick.

I was the only one there, I am sure, who saw Aunt Eulonia's coffin shudder. It lasted for a full three seconds. Undoubtedly my poor aunt was turning over, and her not even in her grave yet.

I was in a daze the rest of the service and didn't hear one word of Father Pridgin's undoubtedly good sermon. However, I came sharply out of my stress-induced coma as Mama and I made our exit in advance of the mob. Far more powerful than a shot of adrenaline would have been was the sight of Tony D'Angelo in a maroon sports coat standing among the mourners. I swear he was smiling.

It would only be a slight exaggeration to say that everyone in Rock Hill with chewing teeth attended the actual burial, but maybe it only felt that way. By three-thirty area thermometers read 105 degrees, a record for the day. Factoring in the body heat of the crowd, I'd say it felt like at least 120. It was a wonder only three people collapsed from heat exhaustion during the brief interment service.

"Maybe the gates of hell are open," someone whispered in passing.

I turned to identify the speaker, but they had undoubtedly lost themselves in the throng. No one I knew would speak ill of the dead that way.

After the interment, about fifty invited folk gathered at Mama's for a light supper and some fond reminiscences. This was very generous on Mama's part since she was not blood kin to Aunt Eulonia and was never particularly fond of the woman. I have never understand why, exactly, but ever since Daddy passed Mama and Aunt Eulonia couldn't be bothered to give each other the time of day. Up until then, if memory serves me right, they were at least cordial.

I was even more impressed by Mama's generosity when I discovered that she had invited all the Selwyn Avenue antique dealers, even Rob Goldburg. The rest of the folks were Aunt Eulonia's friends, people from church who knew her, or local bigwigs. Mama is, after all, an unabashed social climber. Fortunately, she is blissfully unaware that you don't have to accomplish much to be a bigwig in Rock Hill. That is how I explained the presence of the Rock Hill man who made national news by finding a human finger in a can of luncheon meat.

Of course, I couldn't explain the presence of my Aunt Marilyn. Sure, she knew Aunt Eulonia, but she despised her for being too pedestrian. As far as I know, Eulonia Wiggins was the only woman to tell Aunt Marilyn to her face—and live—that she didn't believe the Norma Jean story. Besides the fact that the two women had maintained a hostile relationship for almost forty years, there was the matter of blood loyalty to consider. My blood. Granted, Aunt Marilyn is my mother's blood sister, but my blood came from Mama herself. She had no business inviting the woman who threw me out on the street.

In order to act like the lady Mama raised me to be, I studiously avoided Aunt Marilyn. It wasn't easy. At one point

Aunt Marilyn charged in my direction, like a bull at a red flag. This was one of those rare times when being small has its advantages, and I was able to duck behind Peggy Redfern and squat on the floor beneath a food-laden table. Peggy didn't seem at all surprised at my action. Perhaps she finds herself in need of refuge under furniture from time to time.

"The shredded pork barbecue is to die for," she said blithely.

"Hand me a plate, will you? I haven't had a bite to eat since breakfast."

"Ah, breakfast. It didn't turn out quite like you hoped, did it, Abigail?"

"What do you mean?"

She handed me a plate with a paltry amount of pork and without a bun. At least there was a fork included.

"Well, you were expecting one of us to crack and confess to your aunt's murder, weren't you?"

I popped the pork into my mouth before answering. Peggy, of all people, would understand.

"I didn't expect any such thing. I merely wanted us to put our heads together and get Rob Goldburg off the hook."

"I'd like to get him on my hook," Peggy said, "if he wasn't gay, of course. Do you think I could straighten him out?"

"I don't think so, dear. Besides, I thought you wanted to kick him out of our association because you were convinced he was a murderer."

"What?"

"At breakfast this morning you said he was an embarrassment to the group. You were worried about what your customers would say."

"Oh that! I didn't really mean it. I just said that to make the Major happy."

"Excuse me? Since when do you care about what the Major feels?"

"Since he made an offer to buy my shop."

"Say what?"

For the first time in her life, Peggy decided to chew thoroughly and swallow before speaking.

"Well," she said at last, "he made me an offer I couldn't refuse."

"Why?"

"Because he wants to expand his shop, that's why. He plans to connect my shop to his with an annex and call it Major Calloway's Military Antique Emporium. Personally, I don't think it's a catchy name. What do you think, Abigail?"

"I think you should rustle up some more pork for me, dear. I need a moment to absorb the shock."

My plate came back with another scanty serving.

"Well?"

"Couldn't you at least have added some potato salad?" I try not to whine, but from the sea of legs around me it was obvious that the table still held some bounty.

"Abigail! Do you want to talk about food or the Major's offer?"

I put my empty plate down. "Spill it, dear. About the offer, I mean."

"Well, I was just as surprised as you are, of course. But it seems that the Major has been thinking about this for some time. Done a little market research even. Anyway, the offer he made was almost double what I paid for my shop five years ago. How can I pass that up?"

I pantomimed stabbing Peggy's toes with my fork. A glob of barbecue landed on the floor within reach and I stabbed it instead.

"You mean you haven't accepted his offer yet?"

"Well, I did want to think about it a day or two first. You know, scout around and see if there were any other antique stores that I could buy at a good price. I mean, why not have my cake and eat it, too?"

"Why not, indeed. So tell me, dear, when did the Major make you this lucrative offer?"

"Tuesday, I think it was. Yeah, that's it. I remember because I was in a hurry to get to the dry cleaners after work, and wouldn't you know, that's when the Major stopped by. We talked until seven, and I never did pick up my clothes."

"You talked until six fifty-six."

There was no mistaking Gretchen's precise enunciation. "Gretchen honey, is that you?"

"Abigail, you can come on out now. Your aunt with the blond wig left three and a half minutes ago."

I scooted out and stood up with as much dignity as the situation permitted. If Father Pridgin hadn't been glancing in my direction right then, I might even have preserved my reputation as a deeply serious, religious woman.

"Hey!" I said when I saw Peggy's plate. "You've been holding out on me."

She covered her barbecue protectively with her right hand and dodged into the crowd.

"I hope she chokes."

"Careful," Gretchen said. "Peggy said something similar about your aunt, and here we all are. At her wake."

I smiled tolerantly. "This isn't a wake, dear. Wakes are—"

Gretchen was gone. In fact, I didn't see either woman for the rest of the day. As for the Major and Wynnell, I avoided them as much as possible. Anita had become something of a celebrity, and although I avoided her presence, I couldn't escape her altogether. She was all anyone wanted to talk about. Thanks to her performance, she was now a bigwig in Rock Hill and would undoubtedly be invited to all the parties.

"And to think she was right here in my very own home," Mama said, as we were cleaning up afterward.

"Wow."

Mama's fingers drummed at her throat, where her pearls had been.

"Mama, what's wrong?"

"I guess it's just nerves leftover from having a star in the house."

"Anita is not a star!"

"You've always been quick to turn jealous, Abigail."

I took a deep breath. "Mama, may I stay here tonight?"

"Well—"

"Please? You're always saying that I should consider your house my second home."

"Yes, dear, but—"

"I have no place else to go," I wailed.

I suppose I could have foisted myself on Bob again, or one of my unsuspecting friends, but mothers are meant to be there when you need them, aren't they? At least that's the job description that came with my title.

Mama glanced at her watch and then the phone. "Excuse me, dear."

She ducked into her bedroom and closed the door. When she returned a few minutes later, she was carrying her purse and wearing a goofy smile.

"Are we going someplace, Mama?"

"Not you dear—me. Now listen up. The clean towels are still in the laundry room, and you might have to get a new bar of soap out for the shower. And I'm afraid there isn't any milk in the house, except for what's left in the creamers. Bye."

The screen door slammed behind her.

"Mama!"

"Don't wait up," she yelled over her shoulder.

16

I will confess to tippling Mama's wine, but I maintain that I was stone sober when I drove to work the next morning. Still, I had a hard time believing my eyes when I got there just a few minutes after nine. Susan has never voluntarily gotten up before noon in her life, except for the day she moved out of Buford's house. Considering all the makeup she was wearing this morning, she must have gotten up before the birds.

"How dare you, Mama!" she said, proving that she was capable of speech before lunch.

"Sorry, dear, I would have gotten to work on time, except there was an accident on I-77 just north of Carowinds."

"That's not what I mean, and you know it. You told Daddy on me, didn't you?"

"Well, dear—"

"Mama! How could you?"

"You see, dear—"

"Did you know that Daddy cut me off? He said he's not paying another red cent until I kick Jimmy out and move into what he calls a decent place. Can you imagine that?"

"In my fondest dreams."

"But that's not all! He said that if I go back to boring old school he'll buy me a brand-new Porsche."

"Why, the nerve of that man!"

Buford didn't care if I was driving around in a bucket of bolts held together by rust, but he was willing to pay the price of a small house to rescue his teenage daughter from sin. Not that she didn't need rescuing, mind you, but he could have tried first with a cheaper car.

"What does Daddy think I am, a whore? Does he think I'm so greedy and shallow that he can buy me off with things? Doesn't he believe my love for Jimmy is real?"

I nodded up and down and from side to side. Susan could interpret as she wished.

"That's what I told him, Mama. I told him that Jimmy Grady is the only man I'll ever love and that *nothing* Daddy offers is going to come between us."

I unlocked the shop, but Susan declined to go in. I suppose she thought it would be easier to escape if things got uncomfortable, if she were out in the open. I raised a smart child.

"What did he say?"

"He said that if I don't accept his offer, he's going to find someone who will, and that person will break both Jimmy's legs and ship him back to Puerto Rico where he came from."

"Jimmy's from Puerto Rico?"

"No, Mama! You know how Daddy talks when he gets angry."

I did, and nodded sympathetically. "Sweetie, it's beastly hot out here. Why don't you come in for a second."

"I can't, Mama."

"I have some Pepsi in the minifridge. And a Snickers bar."

A breakfast like that was too hard to pass up, and Susan trotted in expectantly behind me. She smelled it first.

"Oh gross!" She pulled her T-shirt up to cover her nose.

I gagged politely into my hands.

"Mama! What is it?"

It was something in the mail that was piled up beneath the door slot. I get tons of the stuff every afternoon, mostly catalogs and auction announcements but occasionally a bit of personal mail as well. The big bubble-lined envelope with the blue crayon address scrawled on it was definitely personal.

"You aren't going to open it, are you?" Susan made no attempt to distance herself from it.

I answered her by finding two plastic memo clips and clamping one tightly over my nose. Susan refused hers. The envelope was easy enough to open with my desk scissors, but there was no need to open the newspaper package inside. By then the smell of dead fish was too strong to be stopped by a nose clamp.

There was a folded sheet of white paper attached to the newspaper with a small strip of masking tape along the spine. The words SORRY CHARLIE were scrawled on the outside in green crayon, and the words IT'S YOUR TURN NEXT on the inside in red. Despite a love of color, the author of this greeting card was not going to get a job at Hallmark.

I began to shake, faster and harder than any paint mixer I'd seen. A whirling dervish wouldn't have been able to keep up with me. It took me several minutes before I had a grip on myself. Someone had just threatened my son, and if that someone was the same person who'd taken a bellpull to my aunt's neck, they meant business.

"Oh, Mama, you can't possibly take this seriously," Susan said. I suppose she was trying to be helpful in her own way.

"You bet I do."

I called Charlie, but of course he was at school. Tweetie assured me that he was fine. She, however, had broken a nail *and* found two new spider veins. "But who would want to kill Charlie?" Susan demanded. "For all you know, the little creep himself sent you this."

"Shut up, dear." I said it gently.

Susan wisely obeyed. The young adapt remarkably well to odors. While Susan drank her Pepsi and ate her Snickers, I disposed of the bubble envelope. I may have small lungs, but I was able to hold my breath until after Flipper was in the trash bin outside and I was back in the shop with the air conditioner cranked up to max. I was still shaking slightly when I called Greg. To my astonishment I reached him directly.

"I'm at my shop," I said, without introducing myself. "Someone has just threatened my son."

"Be there," Greg said, and hung up.

"Susan, put the CLOSED sign back on the door."

She obeyed twice in a row.

"Now, dear, I wasn't going to say anything to you before, but I have to now. Do you think you can take it in the right way?"

"Mama!"

"It's about your Jimmy."

She snatched up the black, fist-size purse she carries with her, regardless of the season, and headed for the door.

"I'm not *even* going to listen to this shit. It's none of your damned business if Jimmy is older than me, and just for the record, he didn't steal anything from UNCC. That's not why he was fired."

"I don't care about his age either, dear."

She stopped halfway to the door. "What then?"

"I care about the fact that he was proven guilty of aiding and abetting a murder."

"What?"

"A friend's wife. In Georgia. Investigator Washburn can fill you in on the details when he gets here."

Susan took a defiant step backward toward the door. "Oh, so now you've had him investigated?"

"Did you know he served six years in prison for that?"

"Then he paid his debt to society!"

When someone is barely three times more than six, how do you make them understand that a life is worth much more than a half a dozen years behind bars?

"Susie, listen to me, please. People don't change that easily."

She stared at me, and to my surprise I could see the anger ebbing away. "Mama, did Daddy ever hit you?"

I wanted to say yes. Buford had done everything but *hit* me. Bruises, at least, you can prove.

"No dear." My heart pounded. "Does Jimmy hit you?"

She turned half away. "That's why I couldn't come to Eulonia's funeral. It was too sore to put makeup on then."

"Oh, baby!"

I tried to hug her, not so much for her sake, but for mine. I needed to reassure myself that my baby was okay. Susan, however, has never been demonstrative and is an expert at eluding my arms.

"Mama?"

"Yes, dear?"

"Would you choose a hot-red Porsche or baby blue?"

"Definitely red, dear."

"Yeah, I think red, too."

I didn't need the hug so bad anymore.

"You what?" Greg was flailing those handsome arms around like a traffic cop at rush hour. Apparently I had screwed up somehow.

"That stinking fish is in the garbage bin out back where it belongs."

"That stinking fish is police evidence."

Greg came back five minutes later, and if it hadn't been for the times I'd seen, and smelled, him prior to that, I wouldn't have let him in the door.

"The rest room is off the back of the storage room, and feel free to use those little soaps shaped like roses."

He was barely out of sight when the front door opened and the woolly worm wiggled in. This time she was wearing an orange silk jumpsuit, zippered to the neck, and a pair of black snakeskin miniboots. At least the reptile was out of its misery.

"You spin your own cocoon, dear?"

"I beg your pardon?"

"I said I'm glad to see you back so soon, dear."

"Yes, well, actually I came back yesterday afternoon, but there was a sign on the door saying you had gone to a family funeral."

"There's a sign on the door right now, I believe. It says I'm closed."

"The door was unlocked."

"Yes, well, that's an oversight. Now, if you'll excuse me—"

She put an icy hand on my arm. "Everything all right?"

"No dear, of course not. My aunt is still quite dead, I assure you."

She didn't have the courtesy to blush. "I mean, are you doing okay?"

I gave her a Susan-approved stare.

"Well, ask a silly question, I guess. Anyway, I'd like to look around for a while, if you don't mind."

There's a secret to not blinking, and maybe someday I'll share it with you.

"I just love that secretary I bought from you."

"As well as the Regency chairs you bought from Rob Goldburg?"

"I hate picking favorites. They're both to die for."

"Excuse me?"

She paled against the orange. "I'm sorry, bad choice of words. You have my condolences."

I put my hands on my hips like a good Yankee housewife. "Come off it, lady. You didn't buy Rob's chairs. They're still in his shop. I saw them for myself."

"But I *did* buy them. I bought them and then returned them. You can ask Robby."

I wish I'd taken the time to tease my hair that morning or at least put on heels. It's hard to look threatening and up at the same time.

"Either you tell me what's really going on, or I'm going to call the police."

I must have been more intimidating than I thought, at least far more intimidating than I'd hoped to be. Cozy Wozy fled the shop like a coon with a pack of hound dogs on its tail.

"Like I said before, everyone is a suspect when it comes to that fish," Greg said. "So you're right: she might be the one who sent it."

"Which might also make her my aunt's killer?"

"Look, officially we have our suspect. Unofficially it isn't over until the fat lady sings. But if this woman is guilty, you've probably scared her off for good."

It wasn't what I wanted to hear. "I was just postulating. You know, brainstorming. She's probably just a memsahib."

"An Indian?"

"A rich, bored housewife. It's hard to fill up one's day entirely with lunches and phone calls."

"So she shops for thrills?"

"Thank God for her kind."

"Well, if you give me her credit card number—"

"She pays cash!"

Greg laughed. "That might be un-American, but so far it isn't illegal. Still, there's something about that woman that bothers me."

"You and me both!"

"I mean from a professional point of view."

I am much smarter than I look. "Hey, you don't suppose she's from New York?"

"You mean a tourist?"

"You have to admit it; she doesn't sound like a native Carolinian. But I was thinking more of a visitor than a tourist. Someone who came down to snoop."

"About the lace thing?"

"Exactly." I was on a roll. "Come to think of it, she didn't set foot in here until after my aunt was murdered. Now suddenly she's a regular."

He shrugged.

"What's that supposed to mean?"

He shrugged again.

"Well?" I felt like grabbing him and shaking him, but decided to wait until we found ourselves in more favorable circumstances.

"Look, I've been in this business a long time. If I've learned anything, it's not to take anyone or anything at face value. Jumping to conclusions might be a great form of exercise, but it doesn't solve crimes."

"You sure jumped to conclusions about Rob Goldburg." Chalk one up to me.

"You're wrong."

"Excuse me?"

"I wasn't jumping to conclusions about Mr. Goldburg; I was simply following procedure. We had circumstantial evidence, and pretty convincing evidence at that. You're the one who concluded he was innocent."

"I didn't conclude anything. I *know* Rob is innocent. Wait a minute, what do you mean 'had' evidence?"

How could such a handsome man look so goofy when he grinned?

"You mean he's out?"

"The lab report came back first thing this morning. You

were right about one thing: someone did sweat on the bellpull, and it wasn't Rob Goldburg. Not recently at any rate.''

I was so excited I had to catch my breath. ''You know who?''

He laughed. ''You made a good suggestion, and we took it. But we can't work miracles. I've told you everything I can at this point.''

''You know more?''

It wasn't any use pestering him for information. Maybe if I had been six inches taller and a blond. Boobs might have helped.

In the end I had to settle for a promise of timely updates on the case. Even as he promised, I realized that we were probably not envisioning the same timetable. He was undoubtedly two time zones behind me, but what choice did I have?

''I'm going to see what I can scare up on this woman,'' he said casually. ''It shouldn't be that hard to track her down. In the meantime, we'll have someone keep an eye out on Charlie. So don't worry.''

''Do you ask chickens not to cluck?''

''I realize this note seems ominous, but I don't think it's directed at Charlie.''

''Who then?''

''You.''

God gave us attached tongues on purpose. Still, I came awfully close to swallowing mine. When I thought Charlie was in danger I didn't feel scared, I felt angry. I would have fought a tiger with my bare hands—and quite possibly torn it limb from limb—in order to protect my child.

Now suddenly I felt vulnerable. Thanks to Tweetie and four pounds of silicone I was alone in the world. Even Mama was too occupied with her mysterious giggler to come to my aid.

''Me?''

''You.''

''You can't be serious. Why would anyone want to kill me?''

''To make you back off. Whoever killed your aunt wants

you to stop playing private eye. And I agree with them. You should leave that up to us.''

''Just what am I supposed to do when my aunt is murdered and a friend thrown in jail? Sit around and twiddle my thumbs?''

''In law enforcement we work as a team.''

I ignored the twinkle in his eye. ''So?''

''So, you let us investigate the suspects, and you concentrate on what you know best. You find out anything more about that antique lace your aunt supposedly had?''

My face burned. I'd been far too busy planning a funeral and trying to clear a friend, not to mention being evicted, to give the lace much more thought. Fortunately I had learned from my teenage children that the best way to defend oneself is to counterattack.

''She didn't supposedly have it—she *did* have it. Charlie wouldn't lie. Not about something like that.''

He nodded. ''Find out what you can. It's always better to have someone working on each end of a case. Maybe we'll meet in the middle.''

''Any bets that the middle is wearing a silk orange jumpsuit and snakeskin boots?''

He chuckled. ''I don't suppose you remember details, other than her clothes?''

''Hey, you've seen her, too, so don't ask me to describe her to a police artist. I might not be kind.''

''How old would you put her at? Thirty-five?''

I do not bray like a donkey when I laugh, no matter what Buford says.

''Forty?''

''That woman was born when God was young,'' I said kindly.

''She was blond, I remember that.''

''Miss Clairol number seventy-four. I hear it covers gray the best.''

''About average height for a woman.''

''Average is relative.''

''One hundred and thirty pounds?''

"Without her hips, maybe."

"Well, I've gotta run. Remember, I'll investigate the people, you stick to the lace. Got it?"

"Got it," I said.

I locked the door behind him and turned the sign around. It was time to go to work.

17

Rob's bear hug left me smelling like cologne for the rest of the day.

"Sorry," he said, "but I didn't have time to shower, and you know how jails smell."

"Actually, I don't."

"Right. Anyway, Bob here told me how you went to bat for me."

"It was nothing."

"Taking on the entire association single-handedly is not nothing. I don't know how I can ever thank you."

"Another night's lodging?"

The Rob-Bobs exchanged nervous glances.

"Okay, dinner again sometime," I said charitably. "Maybe something with *four* feet."

"Deal!" Bob boomed. That man really ought to consider broadcasting.

"In the meantime, I have a small favor to ask."

"Anything. Except a bed for tonight." Rob laughed.

"What do you know about lace?"

I swear both men blushed just a little.

"What kind of lace?"

"Old lace. Antique lace."

Bob stepped forward. "Most of it is crap, from a collector's point of view. Machine-made stuff less than a hundred years old. You can buy it anywhere for a couple of dollars. Hell, most of the time it's even cheaper than the new stuff."

I shook my head vigorously. "This isn't what I have in

mind. The lace I'm talking about is handmade and *old*."

Rob chuckled. "How old is old?"

"Four hundred years. Maybe more."

They whistled in unison. Bob is a better whistler, too.

"So, what do you know about that kind of thing?"

"That it's more common than you might think," Bob said. "It was made for people to wear—rich people, granted—but there were a lot of them, even back then, and they wore a lot of the stuff. I read someplace that King Henry the third had state robes trimmed with four thousand yards of pure gold lace. Sometimes even horses wore lace back then.

"However, most of it was made with natural fibers that deteriorate with time. As a consequence most lace from that period shows up as scraps and isn't worth all that much."

"But what if one came across a piece of lace that old in mint condition. Say a fancy neck ruff, or a pair of sleeve ruffs?"

"You're talking big bucks then. Is this lace yours?"

"How big is big?"

"That all depends. There are other factors besides age and condition."

"Like provenance?"

"Exactly. History means a lot to some collectors. I know a dentist from New Jersey who paid a hundred and fifty thousand dollars for one of Charlemagne's teeth."

"You're kidding!"

"He's kidding," Rob said. "But seriously, people do pay a lot extra for lace if there's a story attached, and, of course, depending on whether or not it is point."

"Point?"

"The term used to mean needle lace, as opposed to bobbin lace, but now it can mean either thing if it is of exceptional quality and design. Old Venice point generally brings the highest prices."

"I see. Okay, let's say the lace has no known history, but it's point lace. And the best. How much then?"

Bob scratched his head. "That's like trying to guess what's behind door number one."

"Please guess. It's important."

"Maybe forty, at the right auction."

"Forty dollars?"

Both men laughed. "Forty thousand. If it was an exceptional piece."

I felt lightheaded and braced myself against a French highboy. "And if it was worn by some king, maybe even the Pope? How much then?"

"Up to ten times that, *depending*. Look, you know this business. This isn't a supermarket where you've got fairly standard prices for standard items that everyone has to have."

"I get it."

"But do you have it?" Rob asked. "You still haven't answered that."

"Not yet. Oh, by the way, did a blond woman come in this morning who was wearing an orange silk jumpsuit and black snakeskin boots?"

"Mother's here?" Bob asked.

"He's kidding," Rob said. "What about this woman?"

"She said you sold her your Regency chairs. Did you?"

"No, the chairs are right there."

"I can see that. However, she said she bought them and returned them. According to her she bought them Monday afternoon, just prior to my aunt's murder. For some strange reason she claims to be your alibi."

Bob glanced at Rob, who looked away. Too casually, if you ask me.

"The world is full of lunatics," Rob said. "People who get vicarious pleasure from associating themselves with tragedy. Isn't that right, Bob?"

Bob nodded vigorously. "I know a woman in Manhattan who hangs around the emergency rooms of hospitals squirting ketchup on herself. They call her Bloody Mary. And she's a stockbroker with a six-figure income."

"How *is* Mary?" Rob asked.

"Fine, now that Letterman has shown an interest in her shtick."

"Very funny, guys. I'd love to hang around all morning and chat, but some of us have more important things to do. If you see the woman in the orange silk jumpsuit—she also likes to wear woolly things—give Greg Washburn a call.''

"Why? Is she in some kind of trouble?" Again, Rob sounded about as casual as Mama did when she first tried to talk to me about sex.

"Let's just say something is rotten in Denmark, and I think it's fish."

"Rotten fish can taste surprisingly good," Bob said. "In Iceland they bury shark on the beach for a month and then dig it up and serve it for dinner. They consider it a delicacy. It's kind of hard to find in this country, but it's worth the search."

"He isn't kidding," Rob said. "It smells worse than hell, but it tastes kind of sweet. Like Thai fish sauce."

I glared at them, wishing them both a mild case of diarrhea. "The fish I'm talking about wasn't shark, and it wasn't buried for a month. It was stuck through my mail slot."

"Ooh."

"With a threatening note."

"What did it say?"

"It threatened my Charlie, that's what."

"Whoa," Rob said. "Why would anyone do that?"

"Apparently they don't like me looking for my aunt's killer."

"That's heavy stuff," Rob said. "Did you see the woman in orange deliver the fish?"

"No. She'd be orange juice if I had."

"Ah, so then it could have been anybody."

"Absolutely anybody," Bob agreed.

Rob practically waved a fistful of papers in my face. "Well, I'd love to chat, but I have a whole lot of catching up to do."

"Ditto," Bob said.

I couldn't get anything else out of either of them, not even a dinner invitation for that night. I would have bet Buford's bank account that they both knew the lady in orange, but unless I could find a way to tie them down and insert flaming bamboo slivers under their fingernails, they weren't going to squeal.

It was time to pay my respects to the Major. His shop was directly across the street from mine, and if anyone had seen the blond pumpkin slip something through my door slot, it was him. Besides, someone had to put a stop to his expansionist plans. Our block was supposed to be populated by genuine antique stores selling upscale merchandise. The last thing we needed in our midst was a paramilitary store frequented by tattooed men with no necks. Since no one else in the association had the gumption to stop him, it was up to me. And stop him I would, no matter what it took.

The Major was in a good mood. Either he'd finally gotten Peggy into bed or he'd sold Hitler's pajamas. I'd forgotten to look at the dummy in the window when I went in. Not that it mattered, however, because the dummy came bounding over to meet me at the door.

"That guy just bought them," he bubbled. I've seen percolators with less verve.

"Bought what?"

"The Führer's nightwear."

"You're kidding! Adolph's pj's finally sold?"

"For my asking price, too, if you can imagine that."

It was hard to imagine. The proud new owner of the Führer's flannels didn't look like he had two nickels to rub together. If he did, he surely didn't have a place to keep them. The man was naked except for a pair of very brief spandex shorts and flip-flops.

Call me old-fashioned, but I didn't count the rings through both nipples, and the three in his nose, as clothes. Nor did I consider the thirty-some wire hoops in his ears anything but ornamentation. As for the large zirconia stud on his tongue, it undoubtedly spent as much time inside as it does out. Clothes, by my definition, are external things.

"The poor fellow could use a pair of pajamas," I said kindly.

"The diamond is real," the Major said smugly. "The 'poor' fellow is Malcolm Deiter the third. He could buy all of Selwyn Ave, and half of South Park Mall if he wanted to, and not miss a buck."

I couldn't help but stare. Malcolm Deiter the third went to high school with me in Rock Hill. M. D. Three, as we called him, was the poorest boy I knew. Since his career aspirations never went beyond changing tires at a hole-in-the-wall garage, M. D. Three remained poor.

It was only recently that he had the good fortune of spilling a bowl of chili on his crotch while dining out at a fast-food restaurant. I never did learn how Buford found out about it, but it was the best thing that ever happened to Malcolm. Just the week before I'd read in the beauty parlor that M. D. Three was well on his way to becoming one of the richest men in the Carolinas. *If* he made it through all the appeals, then Buford would be very rich as well. No doubt then he could buy himself an entire flock of Tweetie birds. I, however, would remain poor, unless I spilled a bowl of chili on my crotch. Given my sex life over the past three years, it was an option I might do well to consider.

"It's rude to stare," the Major said needlessly.

"Some folks would say the same thing about public nakedness."

"Mr. Dieter is not naked. He's wearing shorts. After all, it is almost ninety degrees out there."

"Ninety-two. We're looking to set a record. Incidentally, do you know a blond woman who dresses just the opposite from Malcolm?"

"You mean no jewelry?"

"No, I mean too many clothes. This morning she was wearing an orange silk jumpsuit and black boots. She is maybe fifty and has bleached blond hair."

"Nope."

"Wednesday she was wearing—"

"I don't keep track of my customers' clothes, Abigail."

"Well, maybe you should. That," I pointed to Malcolm, "has got to be against the law."

I spoke softly, but Malcolm had good ears. "So sue me," he said.

"I just might do that, M. D. Three."

"Abby!"

The man came straight at me, arms open and rings clanking. I'm sure he meant to hug me, but I stepped deftly behind the Major.

"Long time no see, M. D. Three."

"Abby, you hear about my case?"

The Major is on the plump side, and I made no attempt to look around him. I am not a fan of punctured body parts. When I first got my ears pierced, it was all I could do to look at myself in the mirror. As for a close view of pierced nipples—I would rather eat ostrich again.

"I heard," I said. "Maybe if you wore clothes the chili wouldn't have burned you."

Fortunately the man has a short attention span. "Hey, you got any S.S. uniforms the same size?"

The Major pointed to several racks in the back, and Malcolm trotted off happily.

"So Major, have you seen the woman I was describing, or not."

"Not. Most of my customers are men, and the women who come in are with them. You know—"

"Tweetie birds."

"What?"

"Young women. Very young women."

"No, bald."

"Bald young women?"

"That's right. It's a free country, girlie."

"You mean skinheads? White supremacists, that kind of thing?"

"I don't ask them their politics."

"And they obviously don't need to ask yours."

"You have a problem with that, girlie?"

"Yes, as a matter of fact I do."

He drew back. I wouldn't go so far as to say he clicked his heels together, but he puffed his pudgy little chest out and stood at attention.

"My politics is none of your damn business."

"You are quite right. However, as a fellow member of the association, your expansion plans are. How come you didn't bring them up at our last meeting?"

He deflated. "Peggy tell you about this?"

"Yes. And frankly, Major, I think you're going to have a

hard time getting us to agree to it, much less the zoning board.''

''Why the hell is that?''

''Well, for one thing, you don't sell real antiques.''

He looked stunned. ''You said before that I did.''

''Well, I lied then.''

''The hell you say! What's that?'' He pointed to a German helmet, circa World War I.

''An old hat, Major, but not an antique. According to the bylaws of the association an antique must be a minimum of one hundred years old, and at any one time, over fifty percent of our stock must be antiques.''

''Screw the bylaws.''

''Be my guest, Major, but then I'm afraid you are going to have to relocate.''

''What the hell are you talking about?''

I smiled calmly. ''May I remind you that this is primarily a residential neighborhood, and that it was the association that pressed for the zoning variance. Now, if you were to expand your shop further, you would be flaunting your violation of the current ordinances. In other words, Major, someone might notice that you aren't selling proper antiques.''

''The hell I'm not! I've got a musket over there from the War Between the States.''

''One musket does not a majority make.''

''Get the hell out of my shop, girlie!''

I took a step back. It was not a retreat, mind you. I simply don't like hostile breath in my face.

''I hear there's going to be a military antiques show for dealers only in Atlanta next month. You might want to pop over there and buy some inventory,'' I suggested kindly.

''Get out, bitch!''

I got.

18

"You didn't!" Peggy's screaming voice does not flatter her.

"It is clearly against the bylaws, dear. Besides, the zoning board would never allow it."

"He was offering me twice what I paid for my shop. *Twice,* Abigail. I could have retired from this business and gotten into something else."

"What's this about retirement, Peggy? You were talking about stashing half the money and buying a shop somewhere else."

"It's about options, Abigail, and you just took them away!"

"Sorry, dear, but he never would have gotten away with it. Besides, you don't really want to see this block turned into a little Berlin, do you?"

"But I wanted to go to Alaska," Peggy wailed.

I tugged at my blouse, which was plastered to my chest with dew. The woman was on to something. September in Alaska had to be cooler than this.

"There are antique shops in Alaska?"

"Options, you ninny!"

"Anita has a cousin who works for a travel agency, dear. Maybe she can get a special discount for your cruise. Maybe you still can go."

The blue eye shadow multiplied, which meant Peggy was looking at me through half closed eyes. Susan often does that when she's annoyed.

"You don't get it, do you? I didn't want to go to Alaska

on a cruise; I wanted the option of moving there.''

''You're kidding!''

''I've never been more serious in my life. Do you know what the ratio of men to women is up there?''

''But it's so cold!''

''A good man can take care of that, or have you forgotten?''

I shrugged off her nastiness. There was no point in telling her that a bowl of chili could do the same, since she would just as soon eat it.

''They don't have grits there, you know. Or collards. Or blacked-eyed peas and corn bread. And they've probably never even heard of boiled peanuts. Why, you probably can't find a decent glass of sweet tea in the whole state.''

''Oh, Abigail, you're so mean! It's still such a long way to lunch.''

''And don't forget Carolina peaches. On a hot day like to-day you won't be able to stop at a roadside stand and bite into a fresh peach and feel that sweet cool juice dribbling down your chin.''

''There won't be any hot days in Alaska! And now, thanks to you, there won't be any Alaskan days at all. Do you realize that you have just ruined my life?''

''It isn't me, dear. It's the zoning board.''

''Of course, you could fix that, you know.''

''Excuse me?''

To her credit she attempted a sweet smile. ''*You* could buy my shop, Abigail. You could pay me what the Major was willing to pay.''

''Me?''

''Now that you've inherited your aunt's shop and her house, you're rich.''

''I am not rich! No longer desperate, maybe, but not rich. Besides, that's only assuming I'm going to inherit. For all I know, I may not even be in her will.''

''You and Toy are her closest living relatives, aren't you? And from what I understand, Toy is somewhat estranged from the family.''

''Right, but until I see the will, I'm not taking anything for granted.''

"Why not?"

I shrugged. "Ask Gretchen. According to her, a woman she saw on *Geraldo* had fifteen children that nobody, herself included, was aware of."

"I saw that, too," Peggy said thoughtfully, "but it was all baloney. There's no way a woman who looked like that could get pregnant fifteen times."

"Just the same, it's always possible that there is someone out there to contest the will, or that Aunt Eulonia left all her money to charity."

Peggy nodded. "Or three-legged cats."

"Excuse me?"

"I saw it on a talk show. A California billionaire left his entire fortune to build an international home for three-legged cats. The will stood."

"My aunt was afraid of cats."

"Well, in that case, what *are* you going to do with your aunt's shop, Abigail?"

"I don't know—sell it I guess. I haven't had time to even think about it."

"Well, maybe you should give it some thought. I mean, you want to make sure you sell it to a legitimate antique dealer, or the zoning board might come down on *you*."

"Is this some kind of a threat, dear?"

The little brass bell above her door announced a customer, and she responded like a bass fisherman to a tug on the line. Being small is advantageous when it comes to overcoming inertia, and I was able to grab her skirt before she got away.

"Please, Peggy, I have a very important question to ask you, and it will take only three seconds."

"One, two, three."

"Have you seen a woman in a silk orange jumpsuit and black boots? I mean, today?"

"You mean Penny?"

"Penny?"

"A terrible bleach job and not enough makeup?"

"That could be her!"

"If that's the one, her name is Penny. I don't know her last name though."

The customer was still casually scanning the place. It was far too early to pounce on her, and Peggy knew it. Premature pounces are guaranteed to scare away the fish. They have to see and taste the bait before you try and reel them in.

"Is Penny a customer?"

"She's been in once or twice lately, but she didn't buy anything. We have the same aerobics instructor."

"You take aerobics?" I didn't mean it to sound like it did.

There was an explosion of blue. "Just because I have a little extra padding doesn't mean that I'm not in great shape. This is a well-toned body you're looking at—not all hard and angular like Jane Fonda's. Men find me comfortable."

"I'm sure they do, dear. I wish I had a body like yours." It was one of the hardest lies I've had to tell. My kids would have been proud of me.

Peggy gave me the once-over. "For starters, you'd have to eat more. Your boobs are too small and your hipbones jut out like fins on an old Buick. But you realize, of course, that if you put on the pounds, you're going to have to do some toning. Men like padding, not flab. Of course there's nothing we can do about your height."

I swallowed my pride. "Where and when does your aerobics class meet?"

"My aerobics class is full, but there's millions of others. Just look them up in your phone book, or call the Y."

"I'm sure not all aerobics classes are the same, dear. Maybe your instructor could recommend a good one. For beginners, I mean."

"No, he can't."

"Excuse me?"

"Now that I'm not going to Alaska, Joe is mine."

Morning had broken, even if it had taken a little longer than the first morning.

"Not to worry, dear. I'm already spoken for."

The blue disappeared entirely. It was a wonder her eyes didn't fall out.

"You?"

"Yes, I am finally in a relationship, as we say these days."

"You?"

I bit my tongue and counted to three. "Yes, I was married, you know. At least once in my life a man has found me desirable."

"And dumped you," she said cruelly.

I forgave her for Charlie's sake. "But now that's all behind me. The new man in my life has scruples."

"Don't tell me the man is Investigator What's-His-Name. Somebody Sideburns."

"That's Washburn, dear. So, are you going to give me the dope on your aerobics class? If not for me, then do it for Greg. I'm afraid he likes comfortable women, too."

"How do you know he does? Did he say so?"

The customer had begun to circle a Federal sofa like a shark around a bleeding swimmer. I had to act fast.

"Because he mentioned you, dear. He referred to you as 'an extremely attractive woman.' "

"Well, Penny and I are in separate classes, but if you hurry you might catch her. If I remember correctly, her class meets Friday mornings about this time."

I trust Peggy was able to reel in her customers as easily as that.

Jumping Joe's House of Aerobics is one of Charlotte's best-kept secrets. I mean that literally. It took me an hour to find the place which, as it turned out, was just over a mile away. Peggy neglected to tell me that Joe's studio is his garage and that his office is his living room. She also neglected to describe Joe.

"Jumping Joe," he said, opening the door. "How can I be of service?"

I looked slowly up, past a few low clouds, to one of the homeliest faces God has put on this good earth. Only a blind mother could love a face like that. Just about everyone, however, could appreciate Joe's body—himself included. Perhaps that is why he was wearing the skimpiest denim shorts I had ever seen on a man. These were so frayed around the legs that in some places there was too much fray and not enough fabric, if you know what I mean. I looked down again. It was hard not to stare.

"Is this Jumping Joe's House of Aerobics?" I asked foolishly.

"Sure thing, babe."

"It is?"

"Low on frills, high on thrills. That's my motto, babe. How can I be of service?"

I took a deep breath. Unless it's Sonny Bono, I'm not too fond of men calling me "babe."

"I'd like to ask you a few questions about your studio. But you can go ahead and get dressed first."

"I am dressed."

I can remember when it was acceptable only for women to parade around in public half naked. If you ask me, the world has already gone to hell in a handbasket.

"Perhaps I could ask them here."

"Suit yourself, babe, but it's thirty degrees cooler in there."

I reluctantly jumped into the handbasket headed for hell. It had to be at least twenty degrees cooler in hell than on the sidewalk.

He pushed a stack of pizza boxes off the couch and sat down. "Let's have a seat at my desk, babe."

Call me old-fashioned, but a beer-can-covered coffee table is not what comes to mind when I think of a desk. Still, it was a handy thing to have between us.

"I'd just as soon stand, thanks. I've been sitting all day."

"No prob, babe." His mocking did nothing to improve his face. "So, you're interested in taking one of my classes?"

"Yes, the one Penny is in."

"Who?"

"You know, Penny. Blond hair, about this tall. Likes to sweat."

"Ah yes, blond Penny. Sorry babe, but that class is full."

I stared dejectedly at the floor. "That's too bad. I don't always have a car, and Penny said I could hitch rides with her."

"Blond Penny said that?"

"Her very words."

"I see. Jumping Joe's is a private establishment, and I don't advertise much. How'd you hear about me in the first place, babe?''

"Penny told me, of course. She said your classes were just what I needed."

He picked a beer-stained tablet off the table and flipped a few pages.

"Well, well, lookee here. I seem to have an opening after all. You want to start today?"

"What time today?"

"How about now?" He stood up and started around the table.

I edged to the door. "I'm afraid I left my aerobics clothes at home."

"No problem, babe. Clothing is optional. Didn't Penny tell you that?"

"Penny is a woman of few words."

"That's because there isn't any goddamn Penny." In one step he blocked off my exit. "Now, why the hell are you really here?"

"This woman named Penny bought a large piece from my shop, and I lost her address before I could get it delivered. All I want is her address, honest.''

"Drop the phony act, babe. You're here for the same reason every other babe shows up. Aerobics, right?"

"Right!"

"A little special one-on-one aerobics, right?" His leer actually improved his looks.

"Wrong!"

"Come on, babe, my rates are really reasonable."

"Look here, buster, I'm not in the least bit interested in whatever it is you're selling. Now get out of my way, or you'll be sorry."

He didn't budge.

I was trapped but not entirely helpless. There are certain advantages to being short. What may be too high for some women to kick, was perfect punching height for me, especially on a man that tall. I had never done that before and hope I never have to do it again, but I was glad to do it this time. Jumping Joe, incidentally, does live up to his name.

*   *   *

An ambulance was just pulling away from in front of the Major's shop when I returned. Three squad cars had traffic blocked off on that side of the street, and a rope barrier prevented any pedestrians from getting within yards of the shop. Despite the heat a small crowd still lingered across the street, right outside my shop door. Had I still been open, it might have been a good day for business after all.

I spotted Peggy at the edge of the crowd and tapped her on the shoulder.

"What happened?"

She whirled, nearly knocking another woman over.

"As if you didn't know!"

"The Major have a heart attack?"

"Someone tried to strangle him," she hissed. "With their bare hands. If it wasn't for that new fella, Bob, the Major would be dead."

"What did Bob do?"

"He gave the Major CPR until the medics could arrive."

"Who would try and kill the Major?"

"Don't you play games with me, Abigail. Give me one good reason why I shouldn't turn you in."

"For what?"

"For trying to strangle him, that's what!"

I had to laugh. "Me?" I held up my hands. "Do you honestly think I could manage that?"

She scowled, obliterating her blue. "Well, you did go to see him this morning, didn't you?"

"Yes, but I saw you, too, and you look just fine to me."

That woman can turn on a dime. "Well, thank you," she said patting her hair. "Some folks wilt in the heat, but some of us just get ripe."

"Then you obviously don't need to go to Alaska," I said generously.

She accepted her compliment with a smile. "You didn't find Penny at the aerobics school, did you?"

It was my turn to scowl. "I did not! What I found was a gigolo in a pigpen."

"Joe is not a gigolo! He's a sexual addict with financial problems."

"Hey, wait one minute. How did you know Penny wasn't there?"

"Because she came into my shop a few minutes after you left. She said she was on her way to the mountains for the weekend."

"Did she say where?"

"Some place called Mossy Lodge. It's near Grandfather Mountain, I think. It sounded expensive."

I practically ran. There was a lot I had to do if I was going to spend the weekend in the mountains as well.

19

"I don't want to go away for the weekend," Mama said. "We can get back in time for church Sunday morning, I promise. They can count on you for the choir."

"I don't want to go!" Mama brought the bowl of chicken salad down on the table with considerable force.

I stared at this woman who used to be my mother. Gone were the pearls, the full skirts, and the gingham aprons. Dangling earrings, a tank top, and blue jeans were not adequate replacements by any means. Not for somebody's mother!

"Where have you taken her?" I wailed.

Mama gave me the fish-eye and refilled my tea.

"I've got a life now, Abigail. It's time you realize it."

"Does this life have a name, Mama? Why won't you tell me who he is?"

"All in good time, Abby."

The doorbell rang—croaked was more like it. Mama's doorbell sounds like the time I accidentally stepped on a toad in the dark.

"Maybe you can get him to install a new one," I said, hopping up.

"Maybe we'll just disconnect it and not answer the door," Mama said to my back.

I ignored her.

"Yes?"

There was a man at the door—about my age—who looked familiar, although I couldn't place a name. Perhaps he was long lost kin come to claim my inheritance.

"Hello, Abigail. May I come in?"

This person was not too lost to know my name. It could only mean one thing.

"Mama, you're robbing the cradle!"

The man smiled nervously. "I'm Breck Whitehead, the probate lawyer for your aunt's estate."

"You sure? You look awfully familiar."

"We go to the same church. You sit two pews behind me and three people to the left."

"Of course. Please, come in."

I should have known. In Rock Hill you can live your entire life and have it populated solely by the Episcopal church. Want to speak to a teacher? We have tons of those. How about a college professor? Would half the congregation please step forward. Need a dentist? Will a pair of them do? Gynecologist? We have at least three of those. Oh, it's a brain surgeon you need? Why didn't you say so. She sits four pews behind me, next to the family of research engineers. Just behind the architect. At the Episcopal Church of Our Savior we even have a crazy woman mystery writer with frizzed-out blond hair who claims she was raised among a tribe of headhunters in the Belgian Congo. She's not exactly another Sue Grafton, but you have to give her credit for her imagination.

Breck Whitehead obediently followed me into Mama's parlor for a private conference. I was beginning to remember something about him. He was a year behind me in high school, but we attended the same youth group at church. Slow Breck, we called him then. No one from that group could ever totally forget the night Breck Whitehead threw up on the roller coaster on our annual outing to Myrtle Beach, try as we might. He was sitting in the first car and it was a windy night. At least two of the kids changed denominations after that.

"Your aunt was a very generous woman," Breck said, digging through his briefcase.

I breathed a sigh of relief. "Yes, family was always very important to her."

He looked down at me through the bottoms of his bifocals. "I beg your pardon?"

I smiled warmly. "I was her closest living relative, you know. Except for my brother, Toy."

He gave me an odd look. "Shall we begin."

"Begin away," I said, perhaps too gaily.

"I, Eulonia Louise Wiggins, being of sound mind and body do, on this—"

"Skip the preamble, Breck."

Breck took his bifocals off and leaned back in one of Mama's Victorian armchairs.

"She didn't leave you the house. Or the store."

"Not Toy!"

"No, Toy and you fare the same, I'm afraid."

"Then I don't understand. There must be some mistake."

"Like I said before, your aunt was a very generous person. Ten—no eleven, years ago she deeded her house over to a charitable foundation. The same with her store."

"But that's impossible! She was living in that house until the day she died, and running the store. You've misunderstood something in those papers."

I tried to snatch the sheath from him, but Breck was a lot faster than he used to be. After the roller coaster incident he learned to dodge punches pretty well.

"It's all clearly spelled out here, Abigail. Your aunt deeded her real estate holdings to this foundation with a stipulation that she be allowed to live in the house until her death. And now she's dead."

"No shit, Sherlock!" I apologize, but one can't be a lady all the time. "What the hell is this foundation?"

Breck cleared his throat and swallowed. "The Society for the Reestablishment and Preservation of the Carolina Parakeet."

"What!"

"The Carolina parakeet was a little bird that went extinct—"

"I know about the damned parakeet—we studied it in school—and that's my point. It's extinct."

"Not according to the society. Some hunters in the low country supposedly spotted a pair of them in a swamp in the early sixties, and ever since then a few faithful believers have dedicated themselves to verifying this report and setting up a preserve in preparation for that day.''

"But that's crazy! That should be against the law."

"Believing in something is not against the law, Abigail," he said solemnly.

"But fleecing people is. You can bet your sweet bippy I'm going to contest this will."

"I'm afraid it won't do you any good. It's already a fait accompli."

"English please, Breck."

"Although it mentions your aunt deeding away her property in this document, it isn't part of this will. That she did over a decade ago when she was of sound mind and body, so it's a separate issue. What's in this will is a brief discussion of what she left you."

"Her savings? Stocks and bonds?"

Breck shook his head while I prayed he wouldn't get motion sickness.

"Your aunt had no savings. Like I said, she was very generous—always giving things away."

"She was cuckoo."

"If that's the case, I wouldn't spread it around. Someone might contest her actual will." In retrospect, I missed the sarcasm.

"Contest away," I said blithely. "Nothing shared is zero, right?"

He smiled, triumphantly. "In this case it's more like two pairs of green velvet curtains."

"What?"

"That's what it says. You want to see for yourself?" He thrust the document in my face, bending an eyelash and nearly giving me a paper cut on the lip.

"Well, I was right, then, after all," I said. I was trying to sound smug, but it is hard to do when you've just had a house and a shop taken away from you.

"How so?"

"The aforementioned curtains—monstrous, ugly things, anyway, are at the cleaners. And I have no idea which one. Not that it makes a difference, mind you."

"Then sign here." He shoved a pen at me.

"Hold it, Breck. It may not be in that will, but my aunt was supposed to have left me some valuable antique lace, and I want to know where it is."

He stared at me. I stared right back, willing him to remember that the night he threw up on the roller coaster I was one of very few kids who didn't make fun of him all the way home from Myrtle Beach. And, if memory serves me right, I gave him some tissues to clean up with. My kindness had to count for something.

"That, I'm afraid, I can't say. Among her effects, I suppose."

"What about her effects?"

"Lawyer talk for personal possessions."

"I know what 'effects' are. I want to know who gets them." If I sounded crass, so be it.

"Why, you and Toy share in those equally, as well. I was just coming to that."

I breathed a huge sigh of relief. "For a minute I thought they were going to the birds. You know, someone from the society was going to haul everything down to the swamp and scatter it about."

He gave me a pained smile. "To the contrary. You will be responsible for removing your aunt's effects yourself. You have until three weeks from today."

"I see. Does that include the furniture?"

He consulted the papers again. "It does not. Apparently that has all been donated as well."

"To that damn bunch of bird-watchers?"

He barely nodded and stood. He was about to bolt, now that the dirty deed had been done.

I grabbed his arm. "Look, Slow Breck, just tell me who the hell the chief bird-watcher is, and you're out of here."

"A Charlotte gentleman by the name of Tony D'Angelo."

I slammed the door behind Breck and stormed into the kitchen. "Mama, I am about to commit murder!"

"Slow Breck get on your nerves again, dear?" Mama has a memory like an elephant.

"It's this man named Tony D'Angelo up in Charlotte. I'm going to wring his scrawny neck." I snatched my purse off the counter.

"But you can't," Mama said. It was as close to shouting as I've heard Mama get since I graduated from high school.

"Excuse me?"

"I mean, you shouldn't be talking like that. Not with poor Eulonia fresh in the grave."

"Well, I didn't mean it literally. Not about the strangling. But I may well do this man some bodily harm."

"No, you won't."

"I sure as hell will, Mama. I'm driving up there this very minute. The old geezer is not going to get away with it."

"What exactly do you plan to do to him?"

Of course, I hadn't thought it through, so my answer was perhaps a trifle unrefined.

"I'll whip the shit out of him, that's what. Just because he's eighty something doesn't mean I'm going to take it easy on him."

"He isn't over eighty, and he could whip the shit out of you with one hand tied behind his back." Mama sounded almost proud.

"What?"

"Tony is my age. I told you that before. He just has bad skin."

"What?" Not only had she lost her pearls, but her marbles as well.

"Tony D'Angelo is my boyfriend."

"What?" It may have been only a coincidence that one of Mama's best wine goblets shattered at that very moment.

"Abigail, calm down, please. I was going to tell you, I really was. It was just taking me a while to work up to it."

"Mama!"

"Abigail, Tony and I love each other very much. We've been in love for some time now, but it's only been just recently that—"

"I can't hear you!" Actually, I could. Even though my hands were clamped tightly over my ears.

"Abby, honey, I am a red-blooded woman with certain *needs*."

"You *need* to get your head examined," I screamed. I swear, even in the worst of my teenage years, I treated Mama better than that.

Mama, to my surprise, was getting calmer by the second.

"I'm sort of glad it's all come out, you know. I didn't want to keep secrets from you."

"You mean like Tony is keeping from you?"

"What do you mean?"

I had a chance to spare Mama some pain—maybe—but I was still so riled up my head was swimming. I know, there is no excuse for abuse, but I want you to understand that I didn't really mean to hurt Mama.

"I suppose you don't know that your precious Tony was two-timing you."

Mama laughed, the laugh of innocence about to take the plunge. "Abby, darling, not every man is a Buford."

"That's right, Mama. Buford discarded me when he found his new toy, but Tony—" I had to stop and catch my breath. It was too horrible to contemplate.

"Tony what? Honey, that man is the salt of the earth."

I shook my head vigorously. It was a good thing Breck was no longer around to watch.

"Mama, Tony D'Angelo is the slime at the bottom of a stock pond. He was two-timing with you. You weren't even his number-one choice."

Mama's otherwise porcelain complexion had turned gray.

"What are you saying? Do you have any proof?"

"I got it from the horse's mouth himself, Mama."

"You know Tony?"

"Unfortunately, yes. He's boarding Dmitri for me."

"How did you meet him?"

"The question isn't how, but where. I met him at Aunt Eulonia's house. In the bushes, the night after she was killed."

"The bushes! Abigail!"

"No, Mama, I'm not the other woman! Aunt Eulonia was."

Despite my sense of betrayal and anger, I hurt for Mama then.

"Are you trying to tell me that my Tony was having an affair with Eulonia?"

"Yes, and no, Mama. He wasn't exactly having an affair; it was a long-term relationship. Apparently it lasted many years. He was having the affair with you."

"Oh shit," Mama said, "shit." Even the best-bred southern women have their breaking point.

"Mama, surely you knew that Tony was living across the street from Aunt Euey."

"Of course, that's how we got to know each other, but that doesn't necessarily mean anything. I'm not involved with Bubba Bussey next door."

"But there had to be signs, Mama. Something over the years."

Mama was sitting with her hands clasped, her eyes closed.

"I first really remember meeting Tony the year after your Daddy died. I was just coming out of my grief. Not looking for a man, mind you, but opening up to life again. It was a hot day, like today, and there he was mowing his lawn, and without a shirt. In those days, gentlemen did not go without shirts. Not in public, not in the South."

"Times have changed rapidly, Mama, that's for sure."

"Something in me turned over then, Abigail. Like an engine turning over, but not catching. Still, it made me feel alive again. That was the beginning.

"We gradually became friends. I'd drop by Eulonia's and there he'd be, out in his yard, or fixing something for her—" She stopped and opened her eyes. "That son of a bitch!"

"You go, girl!"

"Are you *sure* of this, Abby?"

"As sure as I am that the Carolina Panthers will win their division this year."

That didn't stop Mama. "Well hell, Abby, what are we waiting for? Let's go kick some ass."

"Sure thing, Mama, but now that we're together on this, I think we need to strategize."

"What do you mean?"

"Well, like they say, you catch more flies with honey than with vinegar."

Mama frowned. "You're not planning to throw yourself at him, too, are you?"

I tried not to laugh too long.

"Mama, please. Don't make me sick. What I mean is, we have to think this through carefully first. Maybe there is a way to get my property back."

"Oh yes, I forgot. Dmitri."

"Yes, Dmitri, too. But I meant other property."

"You didn't store your clothes there as well, did you? Oh Abby, I'm so sorry I didn't let you—"

"Mama, it's much bigger than that. Tony is walking away with Aunt Euey's house, shop, and furniture. All I get is navy dresses, her underwear, and those awful green drapes."

"What?" The second goblet shattered safely within the confines of the hutch.

I nodded.

"But he can't! How!"

"You ever heard of the Society for the Reestablishment and Protection of the Carolina Parakeet?"

Mama's gray paled to light ash. "Yes."

"You have?"

"Your aunt mentioned it a couple of times. Years ago. She was thinking of donating some money to it. You don't mean . . ." Mama was definitely a quicker study than I.

"Lock, stock, and barrel. Breck Whitehead says it's legal."

Mama was on her feet and raring to go. I made her drink a glass of ice water first. It served as chaser for half a Valium.

20

Mama stalled. I don't mean she delayed. I mean my Mama stalled like an old car on a cold day.

"I can't go anywhere like this, Abby."

"Like what, Mama? You look great."

"Can't you do some shopping? Give me an hour or so to fix myself up?"

"Mama, you're dumping the bastard, remember? You don't want to fix yourself up. You want to fix yourself down."

"Abby!" she wailed.

I took off for an hour. First I headed over to Glencairn Gardens and wandered around the lily pools and old camellias which have grown into full-sized trees. Then I browsed through Upcountry Antiques and the Woodbin.

I got back to find Mama standing on her front porch, her car keys in her hand. She'd been shopping, too.

"Mama!" I shrieked.

She clutched the new strand of pearls around her neck, looking for all the world like Donna Reed again.

"We all have to deal with tragedy in our own way. Didn't I teach you that, dear?"

"You did, Mama, but—"

"Then hush, dear. I'm on my way over to Tony's alone. When I get back I don't ever want to hear his name again. Is that clear?"

"Yes ma'am, but I want to come with you. It's my inheritance he stole."

Mama smoothed her full skirt over the layered crinolines. "He stole worse from me, dear."

"Worse than a house and a shop?"

"He stole my self-respect."

"I understand, Mama. But you're not going over there alone. What if he gets nasty?"

She ignored me. I made an attempt to physically restrain her, but Mama deftly sidestepped me and beat me to her car. After forty-some years doing housework in her spike heels, Mama can walk across gravel in those things and not teeter.

"Be sure and bring back Dmitri!" I yelled to the sound of her spinning tires.

Depression makes even stranger bedfellows than politics. Fortunately Wynnell Crawford and I were not in bed, but merely sitting on an Empire sofa tucked away in one of the many wooden coves of her overstocked shop.

"What else would you expect from a Yankee?" she asked matter-of-factly.

"Tony D'Angelo is not a Yankee. He's from Atlanta."

"You sure?"

"Well, I haven't seen his birth certificate. Then again, I haven't seen yours, either."

"Well, I never!"

"Give it a rest, Wynnell. Not all Yankees are evil, and we southerners have our share, that's for sure. This Tony D'Angelo is a slime-sucking, shit-eating, son of a bitch bastard, if you'll pardon my French. Cheating on Aunt Eulonia with Mama, and betraying them both!"

She nodded sympathetically. "Cheating is about the worst thing a man can do, if you ask me. Ranks right up there with murder. If my Eddy ever cheated on me, I'd find my biggest, sharpest kitchen knife . . ." Her voiced trailed off, and I had visions of Eddy doing the talk-show circuit and maybe even writing a book.

"Mama will give him hell, you can count on that. You should have seen her peel out of the driveway."

"Must have been a sight, all right, and I hope she does give him hell."

It might only have been the size of my thumbnail, but a red flag went up nonetheless. Wynnell Crawford does not agree with you twice in a row, not unless there is a decade stuck in there.

"What is it you want, Wynnell?"

"Nothing, why?"

"Cut to the chase, Wynnell. I know you want something."

"If I help you find what you're looking for, Abigail, can I have a piece?"

"Excuse me?"

"The lace. I just want a small piece. The size of a walnut will do."

It took me a minute to pick my jaw up from the floor. "What lace?"

"Oh, don't be coy, Abigail. The antique lace your Aunt Eulonia inherited from her mother's family. We all know about it."

"Who is we?"

She waved an arm. "We, in the association."

"Everyone?"

"Well, maybe not everyone. But Heather and Anita do, I know that. And I think the Major was there that day."

"What day? When?"

"If I tell you, then will you give me a piece?"

For both our sakes, I sat on my hands. "Spill it, Wynnell."

"Okay, okay. It was no big deal. A couple of us were sitting around after a meeting and Eulonia mentioned the lace. I can't remember all the details now, except that it was Venetian and very old. Fourteenth century, I think.

"Somebody—it might have been Heather—wanted to know how lace could get to be that old and not fall apart. How could it, Abigail?"

"Beats me, since lace wasn't even around then. You just added two hundred years to my aunt's lace, dear."

Wynnell didn't bat an eyelash. Sometimes I think she's half cat; the woman has never been wrong in her life.

"So, you going to give me a piece of it?"

"Whatever for?"

"Oh, didn't I tell you? My Catherine and her Jimmy have

finally set the date. It's going to be Valentine's Day. I thought the lace would the perfect contribution to the 'something old' department.''

I freed one of my hands. ''Wynnell, dear, you have an entire store filled with antiques at your disposal. Why do you want to cut up a four-hundred-year-old neck ruff?''

She rolled her eyes, which looks defiant on a teenager, but somehow deviant on someone the shady side of fifty.

''Catherine can't wear a credenza when she walks down the aisle.''

Actually, Catherine could, but I am far too polite to point that out. Besides, I wasn't through with Wynnell yet.

''I'll think about it,'' I said. ''Did you happen to see a woman in a silk orange jumpsuit and black boots enter my shop this morning? Or leave it?''

''Was she a Yankee?''

''Wynnell!''

''To tell you the truth, Abigail, the only customers I've had all day were this morning, and they kept me jumping. We wouldn't even be sitting on this sofa if it weren't for them. They bought the love seat I had on top of it.''

You see what I mean about that woman's tendency to stack? If we were in California her shop would be in violation of several codes, I'm sure.

''Well, her name is Penny. She loves to wear hot clothes, even in this weather—''

''Then she is a Yankee. Did you look at her eyes?''

''What's that got to do with anything? You can't tell a Yankee by their eyes.''

Wynnell nodded vigorously. ''Oh yes, you can. It has to do with the lack of sunshine they have up north. When they come down here they're always squinting. Haven't you noticed that?''

''She was wearing sunglasses, dear.''

Wynnell smiled knowingly. One day I was going to have to call her bluff and show up at her shop with a pillowcase full of Confederate dollars. Nobody minds Ulysses S. Grant, squinty eyes and all, on Union money. Wynnell included.

"Who'd your Mama take with her when she went to break it off with her boyfriend?"

"Nobody that I know of. Mama likes to operate on her own."

"Your Mama went to see him *alone*?"

"There's no stopping a Wiggins," I said proudly. "Even one by marriage."

Wynnell's eyes were as big as magnolia blossoms. "This guy might. He could hurt your Mama, or worse. You thought about that?"

"Hurt Mama?"

Wynnell grabbed my wrist and squeezed it tightly with a bony hand. The woman might consider a career arm-wrestling in bars.

"It could have been this Tony guy who killed Eulonia, you know."

"What makes you say that?"

"To get at her estate early. No offense, Abigail, but that woman might have hung on until the Lord comes back the way she was going."

She had a point. I'm not claiming royal blood, but I am suggesting that the Queen Mother has a little Wiggins in her. When allowed to die naturally (something Daddy and Aunt Eulonia never got to experience) a Wiggins can outlive some landscape trees.

"May I use your phone?"

"If I can have a piece of that lace."

"Your granny was a Yankee whore who came South with Sherman's troops," I said calmly.

I went next door and used Heather's phone.

The phone was still warm in its cradle when Heather pounced on me like a teenager at a dessert bar. "What was that all about?"

I had neither the energy nor time to fill the woman in. It would take an hour just to get the time and dates down to her satisfaction.

"Mama's having a little problem with her boyfriend," I said.

"Was that the police you called?"

"Just a friend, dear. It really isn't all that serious."

In the meantime, Tony with the young voice and old face could be wrapping Mama up in butcher paper for next year's tetrazzini. There was no time for small talk.

"You see a silk pumpkin with black boots anytime this morning, Heather?"

She stole a glance at her watchless wrist. "At nine thirty-six she entered your shop, and left precisely at nine-forty-two."

"She did?"

"I don't make mistakes."

"That was rhetorical, dear. Do you know this woman?"

"No."

"You've never seen her before?"

"I didn't say that. I saw her enter your shop on Wednesday morning at—"

"But you don't know her name? Where she lives, that sort of thing?"

"She lives in Charlotte, at least in Mecklenburg County."

"How do you know that?"

"The inspection sticker on her car."

"You've seen her car?"

Heather sighed patiently. I know I tax her sometimes.

"Not many customers walk here from their homes."

"Do you remember her license number?" I asked hopefully. Given it was Heather, she probably had a printout of the woman's vital statistics.

"Nope. I'm afraid I can't help you there."

"Why not?"

"She didn't have a license with numbers. She had one of those personalized tags."

"So?"

Heather turned the color of a Yankee at Myrtle Beach. "I don't *do* words, only numbers."

"What?"

Tears welled up and appeared enormous behind the Coke-bottle glasses. "It's been that way ever since I can remember.

"Why even on my first day of first grade, September sixth, nineteen—"

"You don't even have an impression what her license plate read?" I didn't mean to be rude, but my Mama's life was at stake.

"She needs to have her oil changed on October fifteenth, unless she puts another three thousand miles on it first," she said helpfully.

I thanked Heather and boogied on out of there. I forgot to ask her if she had indeed heard about the lace. Live and learn, Mama likes to say. Sometimes, however, you don't get to do both.

"It was my day off," Greg said nonchalantly. "I was just heading back from a little boating when I got your call. Came as soon as I could."

I looked him up and down. Several times. The man should boat more often. He was wearing a white polo shirt and white shorts—not Bermudas, but sexy short shorts, like European men wear. Either his tan had gotten darker, or his blue eyes brighter, and he smelled like sun, wind, and just the right amount of testosterone.

"It's that gray house there. The one with the beige car in front of it. That's my mother's car. She's been in there for at least an hour. What are you going to do?"

He smiled, confirming the tan theory. Teeth that white could damage retinae if viewed too closely.

"I'm going to walk up there and ring the doorbell."

"What? He could be armed and dangerous?"

"Would you prefer that I call the SWAT team?"

"Yes."

I was serious. I read the papers. I know that even old men, with skin like starved elephants, are capable of heinous crimes.

Apparently Greg did not share my fear. It was all he could do to keep from smiling.

"Look, how about I give it a shot first? Here's my phone. If I'm not back in five minutes call—"

"I'm not worried about you," I wailed. "It's my Mama."

"Your Mama will be fine."

Greg thrust the cellular phone into my hands and started up the walk at a brisk clip. I moved to stop him, I really did, but coward that I am, I gave up after a few steps. When it comes to saving my own Mama's life, I was unable to make a possible fool of myself in front of a man I had the hots for. There, I said it. I am pure scum.

I'm not going to trot out any clichés about it being the longest ten minutes of my life. Let's just say that I swear I saw the moss growing on the shady side of Tony D'Angelo's trees. Needless to say I was immensely relieved when the door opened and Mama came out.

"Where's Greg?" I shouted.

Mama came after me like that time I drew a hopscotch pattern on the living-room carpet with her lipstick. Of course I was six then and she could still outrun me.

"Abigail Louise Wiggins Timberlake!"

"Are you all right, Mama?"

"I *was,* young lady, until just now. I've never been so embarrassed in my entire life."

"Yes you have, Mama. Remember when your garter belt broke at my high school graduation? You looked like that woman on *Mama's Family.*"

"Abigail!"

"Well, I was worried, Mama. What happened in there?"

"What happened is that I had a nice long talk with Tony. He wasn't two-timing me, after all."

"They all say that, Mama."

"Not everyone is a timber snake, dear. Tony and Eulonia were never—well, you know."

"Intimate?"

"Yes, that's it. They were only friends and neighbors."

"Oh yeah? Then how was he able to seduce her into deeding over her house and shop? *Friends* don't leave their estate to friends when there are living relatives."

"Because it wasn't hers, that's how."

"What?"

Mama calmly stroked her pearls. "Your Aunt Eulonia was an intelligent woman, but she was terrible at business."

"She was? Her shop was always full of customers."

"That's because she practically gave everything away. She liked people, Abigail, but she had no idea how to run a shop. At any rate, over the years Eulonia got in way over her head financially. She would have gone bankrupt if it weren't for Tony."

"You mean he loaned her money?"

"That's putting it mildly. In the end he just bought her out. Paid her more than she could have gotten on the open market."

"Then what was all that business about a parakeet foundation?"

"That was genuine. It does exist. Although really, it was a misguided attempt on his part to spare her dignity. I don't think Tony, or anyone else he knows, is likely to go tramping around some swamp looking for extinct birds. Tony is an exceptionally generous man."

I shook my head. "I'm still not convinced. If they weren't playing the hootchy-cootchy game, then why did she leave him her bed?"

Mama glared at me. "It wasn't just her bed. Tony gets all her furniture, because it was all his to begin with. Your crazy aunt sold off—or gave away—all the family heirlooms. Of course if either of us had paid more attention to her, we might have noticed that. Maybe we could have put a stop to it."

"Mama, I had a life of my own to tend to."

"And I didn't?"

"Buford left me, remember?"

"And your father left me, dear."

"That's not the same at all. Daddy died!"

Immediately I realized just how stupid and insensitive that must have sounded to her.

"I'm sorry, Mama."

She patted her pearls, as benevolent and forgiving as the Beaver's mom. "So, Abigail, is there something else you'd like to say? About Tony, I mean."

What could I say? I'd jumped to all the logical conclusions, they just weren't the right ones.

"Does this mean you and Tony are back together?"

Mama laughed. "More or less."

"Which is it, more or less?"

"Let's say less. We're still going to see each other, but we're going to take it a little slower. Some things are hard to change, if you know what I mean."

I did. As long as Mama wore her pearls and full-circle skirts, I wasn't going to complain. Which is not the same as saying I was thrilled.

"What is Tony going to do with Aunt Euey's house?"

"Well, that's the really generous thing, if you ask me. Tony is offering to rent it to you. Cheap."

"How cheap is cheap?"

"Become a dues-paying member of the Society for the Reestablishment and Preservation of the Carolina Parakeet, and it's yours. For as long as you like."

"What's the catch? What are the dues?"

"Three hundred dollars a month, including utilities."

I vowed to go swamp-trekking on my next vacation.

21

"So, does this mean you're going to the mountains with me this weekend to track down Penny?"

I didn't like Mama's smile.

"Yes, or no?"

"I said that Tony and I were going to start taking things slower; I didn't say we were going to quit cold turkey."

"Mama, how vulgar!"

"Get a life, dear," she said sweetly, and went back inside.

"Well, I'm going back to Selwyn to talk to Anita!" I shouted at the door. "I'll be there till around five, if you change your mind."

The door opened again, but it was Greg, not Mama. He was, however, wearing Mama's grin.

"I just got off the phone with your friend Peggy."

"How did she track you here?" I wasn't surprised, merely curious. If it involved food or a man, Peggy could find that needle at the bottom of the haystack.

"She didn't call me, I called her. I left one of my good pens there during my interview."

"She still have it?"

"She had a lot more than that. She was full of news."

"She tell you about the Major?"

"Division called me on the lake and told me that."

"I didn't *do* it."

He laughed. "What happened to the Major has nothing to do with your aunt's case. Apparently the accused—who is from Rock Hill, incidentally—went a little heat-crazed and attacked the Major during an argument.''

''M. D. Three flipped?''

''You know him?''

''I went to school with him. He was the class nerd then. How's the Major?''

''The Major's going to be all right, but he's threatening to sue. Everybody! You know any lawyers?''

''Very funny. What did Peggy have to say?''

The blue practically danced out of his head. ''That woman likes to gossip, you know.''

''Do tell.''

''According to Peggy you and I are an item. She says you told her that yourself. She wanted to know if it was true?''

My face stung. If there had been a hole in Tony's lawn deeper than a divot, I would have attempted to crawl into it.

''I have *no* idea what you're talking about. Anyway, that Peggy just blathers on and on about whatever comes to mind. There's not a word of truth—''

''There could be.''

''Excuse me?''

''I can't ask you out now because of the case. But after I wrap this up, we could do something.''

''You mean like a date?''

''Call me old-fashioned, but I like to date a few times first. So, how about it?''

I nodded mutely and dashed for my car. I had to keep my jaws clamped firmly shut to prevent my heart from leaping out of my mouth.

It was nothing short of miraculous that I didn't hit anybody on my way back to Selwyn Avenue. I am also grateful that I wasn't stopped for a moving violation. Had I been, I would have undoubtedly blurted out something about diplomatic immunity on the grounds that I was dating a police officer and was planning to have his baby. Well, the latter isn't quite true—and no longer very likely—but there's just no accounting for my tongue during times of extreme bliss.

''You look fabulous,'' I said to Anita. The truth was that

she looked peaked, which for Anita isn't saying much. Excessive religiosity not only causes constipation, but recent studies have shown that it leads to cancer in lab rats.

"God bless you," Anita said. She patted at her bun in a remarkable display of vanity and then lit up a cigarette. "I bought me a new French gewgaw for my hair. I think it's called a 'bid-*day*.'"

"I don't think so, dear," I said kindly. "Say, do you happen to know a woman named Penny, who dresses up like a mummy?"

"Penny who? Abigail, are you making fun of Penny Jamison who goes to my church?"

I doubted it. Pumpkin Penny didn't appear to be the type.

"I don't know her last name, dear, but this morning she was wearing an orange silk jumpsuit and black leather boots."

Anita shuddered. "The Bible teaches modesty, and orange is not a modest color. Why are you looking for her?"

"Can you keep a secret?"

"You know I can."

"You promise?"

"I don't lie, Abigail."

I told her about the woman's visits to my shop and about the dead fish. She was a good listener, and the bun bobbed up and down or from side to side as was appropriate.

"You really think she might have killed your aunt?"

"If not that, she knows who did. That woman definitely has a secret, and I aim to find out what it is."

"How do you plan to do that?"

"Peggy knows the woman. Only slightly, of course. She says the woman told her she was spending the weekend up in the mountains, at a place called Mossy Lodge." I glanced at my watch. It was four minutes after five. "My Mama was going to go with me, but she had to cancel. You wouldn't want to blow this burg for a trip to the mountains, would you?"

"Well, I might at that," Anita said, nearly knocking me over with surprise.

"You would? What about your shop?"

"Oh, Brandt can mind it, if it's just for one day. There are a few minor repairs I need him to do anyway."

"Perfect. Then you'll go?"

Anita smiled coyly and smoothed a few stray hairs toward her bun. "I wasn't planning on the extra expense of course."

"Of course. I'll pay."

"And I expect my own room."

"You do?"

"It's a sin for two unmarried people to share a room, you know."

"We could stop at one of those charming little wedding chapels in the mountains and tie the knot first. I promise to be gentle."

"What are you talking about, Abigail?"

"I'll be happy to pay for your room, dear. It's no problem."

The hell it wasn't. Despite Tony's generous offer, which I fully planned to accept, I was still going to have to pinch pennies for a while. Three hundred dollars a month might not sound like a lot to you, but it was three hundred more than I was paying then. If, however, our little trip to the mountains was successful, and I was able to pinch Penny, my fortune might improve. I had a strong hunch the woman not only killed my aunt but stole my inheritance.

"In that case I'll go," Anita said. "Just let me stop by the house and pick up a few things."

"Make it quick, dear. You won't need much, since we're no longer eloping."

Anita gave me the fish-eye. One doesn't even dare joke about those things in front of her.

"I'll be back in half an hour. Meet me in front of my shop."

"But I won't allow smoking in my car!" I shouted after her.

While Anita Morgan dashed home to water her violets and pick up her flannel nightgown, I dropped in on the Rob-Bobs. The Finer Things always closes at six on Friday, a full hour after the rest of us dilettantes have bolted our doors. It shouldn't surprise us then that it thrives even in the lean times.

"So how are my babies doing?" I asked cheerfully.

"I watered them this morning," Bob boomed. "Was that the right thing?"

"That was fine. Hey, how about I pick them up on Sunday? I've found a place to live."

"You could pick them up tonight," Rob said. "Bob's making something special for supper. Why don't you join us?"

"It's an iguana salad," Bob said.

"Bob's kidding. Seriously, Abigail, why don't you join us? We owe you."

Bob cast Rob a scathing look. I pretended not to notice.

"Well, if it's all the same to you, anytime Sunday suits me better."

Bob's sigh of relief was flattering. "I'll water them again tomorrow, I promise."

"Please no, you'll drown the dears. Hey, you guys hear the latest on the Major? He's going to be all right."

"Yeah, Peggy called," Rob said. "It's hard to believe a thing like that happening. Someone beating up on him, I mean. I know the Major can be hard to take, but his bark is far worse than his bite."

"That's mighty generous of you, considering the man is practically a Nazi."

"Nah. He's into paraphernalia, not politics. Deep down I think he likes me."

"Rob thinks everyone likes him." Bob sounded slightly jealous.

"Rob, remember when we were talking about old lace?"

"I remember."

"Well, I heard the terms of my aunt's will this afternoon. There wasn't any mention of the lace in it. In fact, she didn't leave me anything. She had nothing left to leave."

"Sorry," Bob mumbled.

I smiled at him. He was trying his best to fit in. And who could blame him if he was a mite insecure about my friendship with Rob. After all, I am an attractive woman, if I have to say so myself. At least Greg Washburn thinks so.

"Well, easy come, easy go, I guess. Anyway, I didn't deserve anything. I wasn't the world's best niece. Not by a long shot."

"You were loyal," Rob said. "That counts for something."

"Yeah, well, I should have done more. Anyway, I just

stopped by to tell you guys that I'm off to the mountains for the weekend. I need to take a few days off and sort some things out. Hopefully it's cooler up there.''

''Speaking of the heat,'' Bob said, ''you didn't warn me that it was going to be so hot down here.''

''You ain't seen nothing yet,'' I said with a straight face. ''In October we get the Bermuda Triangle trade winds. While the North is getting their first frost, we're sizzling in the triple digits. Last year on Halloween we hit an all-time record high of one hundred and twenty-five degrees.''

''She's kidding,'' Rob said.

''Touché.''

''Speaking of Halloween,'' I said casually, ''I found out the Great Pumpkin's name.''

I swear Rob blanched. ''I beg you pardon?''

''It's Penny.''

''Oh? Penny what?''

''I don't know, but I'm working on it.''

''Maybe it's Penny Loafer,'' Bob said.

I am not adverse to glaring at new friends. ''I'll find Penny, wherever she is,'' I said calmly. ''And when I'm done with her she'll fit through a door slot, believe me.''

''I believe you,'' Bob said.

''Have you told the police?'' Rob asked.

''Told them what?''

''That her name is Penny.''

''Of course.''

The phone rang then and Rob scrambled to get it. I am not an eavesdropper by nature, but the way Rob cupped the receiver made me suspicious, and it should have sent Bob into a bolting panic. Fortunately I have excellent hearing and am quite practiced in the art of casually drifting in the direction of whispered speech. Bob's attempts to entertain me with New York humor slowed me down, but they did not stop me.

''No. Now is not a good time,'' Rob was saying, when I got within earshot.

There was a very long pause during which he blinked three times.

''No, I told you, not now!''

He closed his eyes and shook his head slowly from side to side.

"I understand that, and that's why I love you, but I'm not going to be a part of that."

He opened his eyes and caught me staring at him.

"I've got to go now."

Pause.

"No, don't call back. Not tonight."

I turned away. "A word to the wise, Bob," I said kindly.

"What's that supposed to mean?"

I gave him a sad, knowing smile and slipped from the shop before Rob could disengage himself from the phone. I might be a curious person, but I don't like witnessing lovers' quarrels close up.

Just outside their door I bumped into Buford Timberlake. I mean that literally. He was the last person I would have expected to bump into on that stretch of Selwyn Avenue at five-thirty on a Friday afternoon. Had I expected him, I would have bumped harder.

"There you are!" He sounded strangely glad to see me.

"Well, not for long."

"Abby, wait. I've got to talk to you."

"It's hot, Buford, and I've got some place to go. Can you say it in three words or less?"

"Thank you."

Damn the heat, and Penny could wait. This was definitely worth pursuing.

"What did you say?"

"I said 'thank you.' I'm really grateful for what you did for Susan. She had lunch with me today and told me all about it."

"You're welcome. I love Susan."

"I know. You're something else, Abby, you know that? You have a special gift for getting people to see things clearly."

"And I can see right though you, Buford. What is it you want?"

"Tweetie is threatening to leave me."

Two years ago I would have danced with joy. Maybe it was the heat, or maybe I'd changed, but I felt strangely sad. Sad for all of us.

"Tell me about it."

"She found out about Betty Jo and Tammy Sue."

"The two bimbos from Denny's?"

"Yeah. Talk to her, Abb, will you?"

"Excuse me? You want me to talk to the bimbo who bounced me out of leaving you? Doesn't that seem the least bit ironic, Buford?"

"I'll owe you big, Abb."

"You already do."

"I'd give you the house, Abb, but you know Tweetie for sure wouldn't stay if I did that."

"No, she probably wouldn't. Look, I couldn't help you even if I wanted to. I'm headed for the mountains even as we speak. I have a very important appointment up there."

He began to cry. It was a first.

"I'll see what I can do," I said. "*When* I get back. Until then, I suggest you go straight home and stay there. Maybe on your hands and knees."

"Thanks, Abb. You're one in a million."

For the first time I was actually glad Buford hadn't realized that before.

22

Anita was waiting for me impatiently. The toe on one of her sensible shoes was tapping rhythmically up and down.

"It's hot, Abigail. We agreed on five-thirty. Why were you talking to Buford?"

"Tweetie Bird wants to fly the coop. The poor dear needed comforting."

"You shouldn't waste time feeling sorry for him," she snapped. " 'Both the adulterer and the adulteress must be put to death.' It's from the Book of Leviticus, chapter twenty."

"I suppose you would be willing to cast the first stone?"

"Why not? I would be an instrument of God's judgment. That's something to be proud of, if you ask me."

God's instrument was standing next to the largest suitcase I'd ever seen. "What's with the behemoth bag, dear? We're only going away for one night."

"It gets cold up in the mountains, Abigail. Even this time of the year. That's why people go up there. I want to be prepared."

"Good thinking. Maybe we'll meet a party of naked hikers stranded in a blizzard. You can clothe all of them. Maybe feed them, too. Did you bring food?"

Anita's mouth became a thin gray line and stayed that way until we had cleared Gastonia and the crush of rush hour traffic. Then she actually smiled.

"Do you know how to get to Mossy Lodge, Abigail?"

"There's a North Carolina guidebook in the hump. Be a dear and look it up."

"Oh, there's no need for that. I know a shortcut."

"You've stayed at Mossy Lodge before?"

"That's where Brandt and I went on our honeymoon. That's why I decided to go with you. I want to relive a few old memories."

"Without Brandt?"

"Abigail, how you talk! That's a sin, too, you know."

"I didn't mean that, dear. Are things getting a little old in the sack?"

"Abigail!"

"It happens to just about everyone, you know. Marital monotony. It's nothing to be ashamed of."

"Is that why Buford left you for Tweetie?"

The woman could give better than she could receive.

"That's a good question, dear," I said generously. "And one I'm still pondering. Although frankly, I'm more interested in finding the answer to what it was I saw in him in the first place."

"Were you both saved?"

"Anita!"

"Well, the Bible states clearly that a Christian should not be yoked together with a non-Christian in the holy union of matrimony. Of course, if both of you were unsaved, then that could be the problem, too. God doesn't recognize the marriages of heathens, you know."

We were headed almost due west, and the late afternoon sun was hard to avoid. I was beginning to get a headache.

"Not everyone believes the way you do, dear. Anyway, doesn't the Bible say something about not judging, lest we be judged?"

"Oh that! The Bible is always being quoted out of context, you know."

"Really?"

We drove along in relative peace until we got to Shelby.

"Turn right there, Abigail. You want to take two twenty-six north."

I turned right.

The peace prevailed until we were about five miles past Polkville.

"Turn right at the next crossroads," Anita directed.

It didn't seem right to me, but Anita was the navigator, so I made a right turn. I also turned my tape deck on. Mozart is every bit as effective as aspirin for headaches and has the added advantage of being the perfect accompaniment for mountains. Had I not been trying to shake the headache, as well as stay on the road, I might have noticed that the thin gray line had reappeared. At any rate, Mozart worked his magic and the pain started to go.

"They play Mozart in heaven," I said to myself. It wasn't meant for Anita's ears, honest.

"They do not!"

"Excuse me?"

"I wasn't going to say anything, Abigail, but that so-called classical music is really the work of the devil."

"I beg your pardon?"

"It's just as evil as rock 'n' roll."

"That's evil?"

"Of course you Episcopalians wouldn't know anything about that, would you?"

"I dislike heavy metal and I positively hate rap," I said cooperatively.

"That's not what I'm talking about. I'm talking about the role the devil has in all this, making you think that classical music is beautiful. It's a deception on his part, Abigail. Did you know you were deceived?"

"Yes." And I did. But by Buford, not Mozart. "Well?"

"Turn it off then. We can sing some nice hymns instead."

"Please, dear," I said softly, "there's a jackhammer going on inside my head."

"It's the devil! I can pray him out."

"Thanks, but no thanks. There are enough homeless in this world."

"All I need to do is to lay my hands on you. It will only take a minute."

Her hands descended on my unwilling forehead like the talons of a giant bird of prey. Her nails were every bit as sharp as a bird's spurs. I ever so gently pushed them away.

"It's the devil that's making you resist, you know. Fight him, Abigail. Fight!"

The talons came stinging back and fight I did. I didn't mean to slap her hands quite so hard, but a blue pickup was passing me and my attention was diverted. I didn't expect Anita to scream, so when she did, I screamed back. It was a case of being startled pure and simple. Her second scream was pure theatrics, I'm convinced. My second scream was because I had almost sideswiped the truck and had overcorrected. As a result I was ploughing through some tall grass alongside a cow pasture.

I stopped shaking about the time Anita quit praying. That was when the driver of the pickup—a very handsome fellow in his thirties—rapped on my window.

"Hey, y'all all right in there?"

I opened the window. "We're just fine, sir. Sorry about that back there. I didn't mean to get so close."

"You two ladies having a fight in there?" He ran his fingers through a head of thick, bushy hair that I would have loved to have gotten my fingers into. Of course, at another time— in another life.

"Absolutely not."

"Yeah? Well, y'all was waving your arms like a pair of referees at a bad hockey game."

"Everything's cool, honest."

"No it isn't," Anita said, leaning way over me. "She's possessed by the devil."

"I am not!"

The pickup driver grinned. "That's fine by me. I like women with a little devil in them. You sure you ladies are okay?"

"Fine as frog hair split three ways," I said.

He politely extended his hand. "My name's Roy, ma'am."

"Good to meet you, Roy. I'm Abigail. This is—"

"Eve," Anita said coolly. Either that woman had multiple personalities, or she was used to giving out phony names. A televangelist couldn't have been any slicker.

"Pleased to meet you ladies. Say, there's a diner up the road—just a short piece—called The Sitting Duck. Y'all want to have supper with me? My treat?''

Anita recoiled. ''We do not!''

''We'd love to,'' I said.

It sounded like my voice, and I swear my lips moved, but that wasn't me talking. Not the real me. Maybe Anita was right after all, and there was a devil in me.

''Half a mile up on your right. You can almost see it from here.'' He was off.

''Well!''

''It *is* suppertime,'' I said.

''That man doesn't want to eat, Abigail. He's trying to pick us up.''

''He's buying us supper, Anita, not a bed. Besides, look at it as an opportunity to witness. His heart is probably a lot less hard than mine. After all, he had a tattoo on his arm that said MOM.''

She thought it over for a minute. ''It is often easier to reach an outright heathen than it is a backslid Christian. Especially an Episcopalian.''

''Amen!''

As soon as we found a booth I excused myself and called Mama. Much to my relief she answered the phone at *her* place.

''Abby! Where are you? I've been trying to reach you for an hour.''

''I told you I was going to the mountains, Mama.''

''Abby, you turn around and come home right now.''

Mama hadn't spoken to me like that since the first time I went out with Buford—after she had a chance to meet him. If I had listened to Mama then I would have spared myself a whole lot of pain, but a lot of happiness, too. Like Susan and Charlie.

''Mama, I'll be all right. Anita's with me.''

I could hear the pearls clicking against the receiver. ''What is she going to do, pray you out of trouble?''

''Prayer can be a powerful weapon, Mama.''

''The Lord helps those who help themselves, dear. Listen, I've been trying to reach you because I got a call from that detective boyfriend of yours.''

"He's not my boyfriend, Mama. *Yet.*"

"Hush, dear, and listen. He said that he stopped by the lab on his way home and the report showed that the sweat on the bellpull belonged to a female. Probably a postmenopausal female. Is that supposed to mean something, Abigail?"

It is hard to dissemble to Mama. 99 percent of the times I thought I was fooling her in high school, I wasn't. Not that I was a major discipline problem, mind you, but just active enough of a teenager to keep Mama too exhausted to follow up on all her hunches. But the hunches were there, and Mama always had enough energy to peer through the wool I kept pulled over her eyes.

"Mama, it means that Aunt Euey's killer wasn't a man, that's all. It's proof that Rob Goldburg is innocent. Will you call Rob and tell him?"

Mama promised to call Rob, and she promised not to worry. I knew she would do the former and excel at ignoring the latter. As for me, I promised to not worry that she might be worrying. We understood each other perfectly.

Anita was livid when I got back. She held the plastic-coated menu up as a sound barrier and whispered behind it to me.

"How could you leave me alone with this man?"

I smiled pleasantly at Roy and ducked behind the menu. "Because this establishment doesn't have phones that plug in under the tables, that's why."

"Who did you need to call anyway? Your detective boyfriend?"

"He's not my boyfriend."

"Peggy says he is."

"Not yet."

"Well, did you call him?"

"My phone calls are personal, Anita."

"Well, I think it was rude of you to accept this invitation with a strange man and go off and leave me alone."

"I'm sorry, dear."

"He's undoubtedly a fornicator."

Fortunately the waitress, a buxom thing in a too-tight dress, appeared to take our orders. Anita's wrath was temporarily distracted, and by the time the food came she was almost civil.

Of course the credit goes to Roy. He was almost as delightful as the chicken-fried steak and black-eyed peas. He wasn't quite as delightful as the peach cobbler, but close.

"Believe it or not, I ain't never been to Rock Hill. I been to Charlotte, though."

"You ain't missed much," Anita said sourly.

It was obvious she was having a bad time. Roy had not only resisted her attempts at conversion but was addressing almost all his comments to me. I shuddered to think how Anita would act if she knew Roy had tried to play footsy with me under the table.

"Where are you from, Roy?"

"Right around here, ma'am. Born and raised."

"You ever drive down I-seventy-seven to Columbia and then over to Myrtle Beach?"

"Yes, ma'am."

"Then you've been to Rock Hill, dear. By it, at any rate. We're right off seventy-seven."

"Told you it wasn't much," Anita said.

She had a piece of collards hanging from her chin, and I kindly pointed it out.

"If we don't hurry Abigail, it's going to be too dark for me to find the right turnoff. Mossy Lodge isn't that easy to find."

"Y'all headed to Mossy Lodge?"

"To meet our husbands," I said. There was no point in pushing it.

Roy shook his handsome head. "Then y'all need to go back to two twenty-six and head north. Mossy Lodge is up there by Marion."

"I thought it was near Grandfather Mountain."

"Neither of you know what you're talking about," Anita said. "Abigail, I told you that I know the way. Don't you trust me?"

"Of course I do, dear. It's just that Roy is from these parts, that's all."

"On the other hand, I ain't never been to Mossy Lodge," Roy said, sucking on a neck bone. "I just heard about it. Your friend might be right."

"I am right."

It was a risk worth taking rather than offend the woman further. Despite Roy's charm, it had been a touch-and-go meal. For starters, neither Roy nor I had bowed our heads in prayer, and when chided I had the temerity to cross myself, Anglican style. To hear Anita, the Pope and devil were sharing the booth with her.

"Y'all be careful now," Roy said cheerfully. I hoped the eleven dollars our meals cost him hadn't set him back too far.

Anita fished in her purse and pulled out a gospel tract. "Here. Read this."

Not to be outdone I pulled out one of my business cards. "A twenty percent discount anytime you stop by. And I usually take an extra five off at Christmas."

"Yes, ma'am, I'll be there."

"And here," I pulled a comb out of my purse that had my shop's logo on it and handed it to him. With a full, thick head of hair like that, he probably went through a comb a week.

He gave me a friendly good-bye peck on the cheek but wisely refrained from getting within an arm's length of Anita.

"Why, I've never been so insulted in my life," she said as I pulled back onto the highway.

"Anita, dear, I think a little perspective is in order. You would probably have hauled off and plugged him. At the very least you would have called him a rapist."

I got the thin gray line treatment again for the next fifteen or twenty miles. It was just getting dark when Anita ordered me to make a sudden left turn.

I slammed on the brakes. "Where?"

"There, just past that stump."

"But that's nothing but a logging road."

"Turn."

There was a forcefulness to her voice that was strange, even for Anita. I glanced at her and back at the logging road.

"I said to turn, and I mean it."

She did, too. She was holding a gun.

23

"**H**oly shit!"

Anita wagged the gun at me like a fat gray finger. "Don't swear."

"Excuse me? What the hell is that doing in your hand?"

She cocked the pistol. "I said, don't swear. I mean it, Abigail. You swear again and I'll shoot."

"Jeepers! And that isn't swearing," I added quickly. "What on earth has gotten into you, dear?"

Anita extended the gun another couple of inches closer to my head. "I said turn left just past that stump, and I mean it."

I turned left on the logging road and came to an abrupt stop. We both lurched forward in our seats, and I tapped my chest against the steering wheel. My purse went flying off the rear seat, nearly hitting me in the back of the head. Somehow Anita managed to hold on to her gun. In retrospect, I should have hit that damp stump and deployed the air bags. If I'm ever on a country road with a gun-toting looney again, that's exactly what I'm going to do.

"That's wasn't nice," Anita said. With her free hand she patted her Holy-Roller do back into place.

I turned the engine off. "Excuse me! You pull a gun on me, and you say I'm not nice? What on earth is going on?"

"If you give me a chance, I'll explain."

"Well, have at it, girl. Because this doesn't make a lick of sense to me."

Anita actually smiled. "I want you to drive on this road, that's all."

"Well, in that case, just put the gun down, and off we go."

"Oh no, you don't, Abigail. You're not leading me into temptation. That gun stays right here in my hand, trained on your neck. Now turn off your headlights and start the car."

I tried to start the car, I really did, but the engine just sputtered and died. It's my opinion that something happened in the quick stop to flood the thing.

"I said start it!"

I prayed first and spoke later. "It won't start, dear. It must be flooded."

She was a hard woman to convince. After several more futile attempts I found the barrel of the pistol nuzzled against my neck. It felt pleasantly cool now that the air-conditioning was off.

"I am doing my best, dear. Look, why don't we trade places and then you start it yourself. You can even drive if you want to."

She stared at me for an eternity. Maybe she was praying behind those vacant eyes, or maybe she was contemplating what a horrible mess a gaping jugular vein would inflict on her pastel dress.

"We'll sit quietly for a few minutes," she said finally. "If it really is a flooded engine, it'll take care of itself in a few minutes. In the meantime, I suggest you get right with your Maker, Abigail. You're not really saved, you know, or you wouldn't be going to that Catholic church."

"It's Episcopal," I said, and then wisely clamped my lips together as tightly as a clam at low tide.

We sat and sweated in the growing dusk. I kept one eye on Anita and one eye on the rearview mirror. For at least five minutes not a single car passed by on the highway just behind us. Finally the heat inside that metal box got to be too much.

"May I try and start it now?" I asked politely.

"Too early. It's only been a minute."

"May I at least roll my window down."

"You should get used to heat, Abigail. It's a lot hotter

where you're going." She raised her hand and pointed the gun at my brain.

I used to pride myself on being a fast thinker. Good mothers need to be, to stay one step ahead of their children, and my children were bright and very inventive. But nothing in my experience had prepared me for brainstorming with a gun barrel kissing my cranium.

"Well, in that case, may I turn on the overhead light so I can read that tract you gave me? I mean, I'd really rather not go to you-know-where."

To her credit, Anita pondered my request, for a moment. I think she was on the verge of relenting, and giving my poor Anglican soul a fighting chance at salvation, when a pair of headlights whizzed by behind us. Whoever it was, was driving so fast, I didn't even have time to lean on the horn. In a few seconds they were a mile down the road.

"Now try and start the car."

I turned the key, and my dammed car started purring like Dmitri when I scratch his chin.

"Now drive."

"Without lights?"

"It's not that dark. I said 'drive.' "

"What if I hit something? A cow, or deer, or something?"

"The Lord will protect me, Abigail."

You don't really have much choice when there is an armed madwoman sitting beside you calling the shots. If I hadn't been wearing a seat belt, I would have flung open the door and thrown myself on the mercy of the dark. Most people are lousy aims, especially if startled, but thanks to the state law, and common sense, I was trussed like a chicken. A virtual sitting duck. By the time I undid my belt and flung open the door, I would be wearing my brains on my shoulders.

Some car manufacturer needs to invent a seat belt release on the door side. That way I could have been steering with my right hand while my left hand surreptitiously undid the strap. On the other hand, maybe not. Anita Morgan had eyes like a hawk, adding credence to her theory that eye makeup is bad for one's vision, not to mention soul.

I drove slowly. On either side of us there were walls of

second-growth pines. Fortunately the road, which was really two dirt ruts, was easy to follow by feel. But a couple of times there were sudden jogs that thrust me out of the ruts and damn near the trees. Of course at my speed, and due to the fact that pine wood is relatively soft, we wouldn't have been seriously injured—not that it made a damn bit of difference, since I was probably going to die anyway. On the other hand, I would much rather die in an undented and unscratched car, wouldn't you?

I took a deep breath. "There isn't enough room for a snake to turn around on this road, dear. So, you can put the gun away. I'll continue to follow it as long as you say."

"You think I'm crazy, don't you, Abigail?"

"Of course not, dear," I said generously. Stark, raving mad was probably not the answer she was looking for.

"I'm not, you know. You weren't even a part of my plan, until you butted in."

"Excuse me?"

"Eulonia is gone to her eternal reward, Abigail. It really isn't your business who helped her along."

"I can't believe I'm hearing this."

"I had no intention of involving you, I really didn't. After all, you at least go to church, even though it's not the right one."

"So, it wasn't this Penny woman? It was *you*?"

"I had to do it, Abigail. I really did."

"You had to murder my aunt?"

She gave me a swift little tap on the noggin with the gun barrel. "Killing is against the Ten Commandments. Carrying out God's will is not."

"God's will for what? Are you saying God wanted my aunt dead?"

"Your aunt had to die, Abigail. That was the easiest way to do it."

"Do what?" I came close to screaming, and Anita rewarded my emotion with another tap on the head.

"God does not suffer homosexuals, Abigail. They are an abomination unto the Lord."

"Aunt Eulonia was not gay."

"But that Rob Goldburg is."

"So?"

"So, he has to be punished, and he would have been, too, if you hadn't butted your nose into it. I had it all set up to look like he killed your aunt."

"Why didn't you just kill him directly? Why involve my aunt?"

She snorted again. "Killing was too good for Rob Goldburg. Not unless we could do it like in the Bible. You know, stone him?"

"Stone him?"

"They stoned homosexuals in the Bible, Abigail. Adulteresses, too."

"I have never slept with anyone besides Buford," I said quickly. You may think it's sad, but it's true.

Anita sighed. "Too bad the law don't allow stoning anymore. But, the way I figured it, life imprisonment was the best substitute."

"But what did my aunt do? She did not have an affair with Tony D'Angelo, and I can prove it."

"Your aunt had to die because the Lord doesn't suffer fools, and your aunt was a fool. Your aunt had something valuable that the Lord could use to further his work here on earth, but she wasn't doing anything with it. Besides, she had lived her three score and ten years, like the Bible says. Now that your aunt is gone, I'll be able to put that precious treasure to the Lord's use. You understand, don't you?"

"It's as clear as mud, dear."

"Are you mocking me, Abigail?"

My head was too sore to suffer a third blow. "No, dear, I'm not mocking you. However, I have a hard time understanding how the Bible justifies what you did."

"You read the Old Testament, Abigail?"

"You mean the Psalms?"

"I mean Leviticus. It's very clear that God hates homosexuals."

I let that go temporarily. "But little old ladies with messy shops?"

"At various time God's people have been commanded to

kill many little old ladies. Children, too. God has plans, you know, and your aunt was just a part of one."

"Killing my aunt was part of God's plan?"

She gave me a pitying laugh. "If you Episcopalians read your Bible, you would know exactly what I mean. Of course, now it looks like you won't be getting a chance to read it at all."

"I do read my Bible."

"The King James Bible?"

"There are other good translations."

"There is only one real Bible, Abigail, the one God dictated to his people. The one you call King James."

"Did God dictate it to King James, in English?" I asked. I wasn't trying to be a smart-ass; I was trying to stall.

She snorted angrily and I cringed. "Of course not. God dictated the Bible to the disciples and the apostles, and of course it was in English. Sure it's a little difficult to read, but if you spent more time with it, you could sort it out."

I racked my brain, trying to recall one of my college courses. "What would you say if I could prove that English didn't even exist until a thousand years after the apostles?"

"Get behind me, Satan!"

"Okay, let's say you're right and the Bible was dictated in English. I don't recall any passages about—"

"I said, 'Get behind me, Satan.' I will not have you tempting me, Lucifer."

I drove on in silence, a prayerful silence. I don't remember how long it took, but I saw in the rearview mirror that the moon was beginning to rise above the trees behind us, and I took that as an answer to my prayers. I know this is going to sound silly, but I don't want to die in the dark. Not the pitch blackness of a pine forest, at any rate.

After I'd driven about a mile following my moon sighting, Anita tapped me on the head one last time.

"Stop right here."

"And you stop hitting me," I screamed. "Shoot me if you want to, but quit hitting me on the head with that goddamn thing!"

"My, aren't we touchy! I was just about to do the Christian

thing, Abigail, and offer you a chance to pray. But, since you took the Lord's name in vain, I think I'll pass.''

"I'm sorry, Anita. I'll take that chance to pray."

"It's God you have to apologize to, Abigail."

"I'm sorry, God. I really am."

We sat in silence while God and Anita mulled my apology over. A pair of barred owls hooted, one on each side of the car. I remembered old Westerns I'd seen as a kid where the Indians, who were always on the warpath, and who were always sneaking up on settlers, hooted like owls to communicate with each other. The settlers were always fooled. Maybe the hoots I heard were really Indians and not barred owls after all. I would rather take my chances at the hands of a handsome brave than remain in the clutches of a crazed woman with a beehive hairdo who was on a religious warpath.

"The Lord says you have to get out of the car, Abigail. He wants you to kneel when you pray."

"Fine." I was anxious to do God's bidding and immediately reached to undo my belt.

The gun nuzzled, rather than tapped me. Anita was learning.

"Don't you get any ideas, Abigail. I'm an excellent shot."

"Yes, ma'am."

"You think I'm kidding, don't you?"

"No, ma'am."

"I used to practice shooting at trees. Shotguns, rifles, handguns, I learned to shoot them all. Every day I'd practice until I was as good as my brothers. I can hit a squirrel three hundred yards away."

"In Charlotte?"

She cackled. "No, here. Right here. This here was my Daddy's land. All of it—all these woods we've been driving through. We used to live in a cabin up the road a piece, until Mama died. Then Daddy sold the land to a lumber company and moved us all to Charlotte. I was fifteen then."

"This land's been reforested since then, hasn't it?" I asked casually.

"Ha! Don't you be getting any ideas, Abigail. The trees have changed, but the land hasn't. I know this place like the back of my hand. If you try and get away from me, I'll shoot you like a squirrel. Only I won't skin and eat you."

Suddenly I was content to stay where I was. "I've never eaten squirrel," I said brightly.

"Then you've only lived half a life, Abigail. City folks think country folks eat squirrel because they're poor. Truth is, it's right tasty."

"I had rabbit in a French restaurant, once. It was good."

"Rabbit is okay, but nothing can beat squirrel, unless it's possum."

"I had ostrich Wednesday night."

"Ostrich?"

She sounded genuinely interested so I decided to run with it. "Ostrich casserole. Tasted a little like beef. Maybe more like veal. Very low in cholesterol, you know."

"Where?"

"Rob Goldburg—"

"Aha! So you eat with them, too!"

"Jesus ate with everyone."

"Don't you quote the Bible to me, Abigail. You don't even have the right version."

"He ate with them in the King James version, too, dear."

"Jesus did not eat with homosexuals!"

Unfortunately I was riled. "How do we know? The Bible doesn't state their sexual preference. For all we know, Jesus himself might have—"

"That does it! You get out of this car this instant. And remember, I can and will shoot you if you try and get away."

I undid my seat belt and opened my door in slow motion. I slid out an inch at a time. I regret to say that I had to leave both my purse and my car keys behind. Unfortunately Anita is a thin, agile woman, and even though I have bucket seats, she was able to move right along with me. The gun never lost contact with my hair.

"Now kneel. I'm going to give you one minute to pray."

My first prayer was that I wasn't kneeling in fire ants. Those foreign invaders are more vicious than killer bees. Fortunately they weren't mentioned in any version of the Bible that I'm aware of, or Anita might purposefully have had me kneel in those.

I'm not claiming that God spoke to me, but as I was praying for deliverance from Anita, a thought popped into my head. Since it was my nose and my tongue that had gotten me into the predicament, perhaps the same things could get me out.

"So, you plan to shoot me, do you? Well, then what? The next time loggers come up here, or even hunters pass by, they'll find me. Nowadays police can trace bullets, you know."

"Oh, I ain't going to shoot you. As soon as you're done praying, we're taking a little walk. You about done yet?"

"No ma'am, I have a lot of sins to confess."

"I expect you do. Say them fast, 'cause it's fixing to rain."

The woman was turning more corners than a blind man in a carnival fun house. "The moon's out, Anita."

"Not anymore it ain't. I been praying for rain, and the Lord is about to answer."

I wasted a few precious seconds glancing around. She was right. The moon was a thin silver streak and fading fast. The trees, which had been individual shapes, were one black mass again.

I started praying in earnest.

"Ain't you done yet?"

"I've been a wicked woman," I wailed.

She generously gave me a few more seconds. "All right, now get up and do exactly as I say."

"Yes, ma'am."

"Is that sass I'm hearing in your voice, Abigail?"

"No ma'am."

Anita grabbed a hank of my hair and wrapped it painfully around her fist.

"Walk straight ahead, Abigail. Keep walking straight, no matter what, till I tell you different."

I walked dead straight ahead. Just when I thought I was going to hit a tree, it appeared to jump aside. I must have gasped.

"It's a trail," Anita cackled. "Brandt and I came up here hunting over Thanksgiving. Sometimes things don't change as much as you think they do. The loggers might have cut the trees down that was here when I was a child, but they didn't change the trail none when they planted new ones. Dirt's packed down too hard.''

If you can imagine me as a horse, and my hair as the bridle, Anita, with the help of her gun, steered me through the pine forest in pitch blackness. We were a clumsy team, but we covered ground surprisingly fast, even though most of the time it felt as if we were walking uphill. I tried to sense and remember any changes in my environment; the feel of a rock beneath my feet, the smell of a rotting log, but it was all hopeless. The darkness was so intense that even had I been able to overpower Anita, I would never have been able to follow the trail back to my car.

It felt like we had gone about a mile when Anita cruelly jerked me to a stop.

"This is it, Abigail; this is where you die. Are you prepared to meet your maker?"

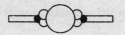

24

"Wait! Can I say good-bye first?"

"Good-bye."

"Not to you. To my family."

She grunted. I took it as permission, although it could have been because of the sudden splatter of raindrops.

"Good-bye Susan, good-bye Charlie, good-bye Mama, good-bye Aunt Marilyn, good-bye Dmitri, good-bye Buford—"

"Enough! Buford isn't your family anymore."

The bottom fell out of the clouds and a million tons of water dumped on us all at once.

"Praise God from whom all blessings flow," Anita sang. "You see, Abigail, I told you I was praying for rain."

It was hard to hear a blessed thing. "What?"

"The rain will wash away your blood. The Lord has truly answered my prayers. Make sure your eyes are closed, Abigail. I don't want to shoot you with your eyes open."

Try thinking of a way to distract a madwoman with a gun, who has you by the hair, in the middle of a pitch-black forest in a downpour. If you can think of any better ways please send them to me in care of the Den of Antiquity, Charlotte, North Carolina.

"You didn't tell me yet how killing my aunt was going to help the Lord!" I shouted.

"Your aunt had earthly riches!" That's what it sounded like. Of course she could have been saying that Aunt Euey had earthy itches, in which case Tony might have been lying after all.

"What kind of riches?"

"Mould-bread face!"

So what's a little name calling when you are about to die? I may as well give tit for tat.

"You slime-sucking, sourpuss Holy Roller bitch!"

Anita did not get to hear all of my epithet, because a bolt of lightning did hit a pine tree less than fifty feet away. For a split second the tree and surrounding area were lit up like a football field on game night. The lightning acted as a giant knife, splitting the tree down the middle for a third of its length. At that point the lightning appeared to gather itself into a ball and roll down the rest of the way until it hit the ground, where it didn't stop. It was headed right for us.

In the brief time it took for this to happen, I could feel Anita let go of my hair. One of the few advantages of being so short is that when I need to take a fall, I don't have far to go. I was able to throw myself on the ground and roll away from Anita before she had time to react. When she did react, it was to the lightning ball, not to me. Fortunately for her, she was apparently able to dodge the ball.

I say apparently, because suddenly we were plunged into total darkness again. I did have an image of Anita flinging herself out of harm's way, but I am ashamed to say that I didn't bother to find out if indeed this happened. Instead of sticking around and acting like the Good Samaritan I pretend to be, I took off into the woods like a deer spooked by hunters. Of course, I was much clumsier than a deer and made more noise than an elephant in a chime shop. I also inflicted a good deal of bodily harm to myself by thrashing through the woods willy-nilly.

I had no idea where I was going, but I have enough common sense to know that I should head downhill. So when I stumbled into a little gully, I followed it. In my part of the Carolinas all valleys eventually lead to the Atlantic Ocean. This one might not lead to my car, but if I followed it long enough I might well end up at Myrtle Beach. Long before then I was bound to hit a jillion towns, probably even Charlotte.

Clambering down a gully in what Daddy used to call a "gully-washer" is no picnic, but it was actually less of a chore then making my way through the woods. Pine needles can be treacherously slippery when wet, and smacking the ground was only slightly less painful that kissing a tree. Besides, there weren't any trees growing in the gully to obstruct my progress. Sure, there were more exposed rocks to contend with, and I did slip a number of times, but all and all it was much faster going.

I am guessing that I had covered about a quarter of a mile when the rain stopped. One minute I couldn't even hear my own gasps, and the next minute the tree frogs were singing. A few minutes later the moon popped into place overhead.

So abrupt was the transformation that I sat down in the gully, muddy water swirling all about me, and cried. At least I think I cried. It's hard to tell if you're really crying when you are all wet. At any rate, I felt my face go through the motions, and despite efforts to the contrary, one very loud sob managed to escape me. Almost immediately I heard someone or something moving in the woods off to my right.

Since the obvious possibilities were Anita or a black bear, neither of which I wanted to encounter, I forced myself up and on my way. It was, of course, much easier to traverse the gully in the light, but more frightening as well. Now that I could see the slippery rocks, and the mud banks about to cave in, my progress was slower. I had taken only a few tentative steps when I heard a loud crack, not far off to my right. Coward that I am, I sat back down in the water with a plop.

There was another loud crack, this one even closer.

"So kill me already," I screamed, and cupped my face in my hands.

"Abigail!"

The voice was not Anita's, and I was reasonably sure it wasn't a bear. I peeked through my fingers.

"Roy?"

A million tons of water can alter one's appearance, you know. Handsome Roy, with the thick head of hair, looked more like a drowned muskrat on a beanpole than the man whose pickup I'd nearly scraped.

Roy grabbed me and gave me hard hug, but I wiggled loose. "You're not *with* her, are you?"

"Me? In cahoots with Anita?"

I stepped back and pried a muddy rock loose from the side of the gully. "Well?"

"Of course not!"

"Then what are you doing here?"

"I followed you."

I discarded the first rock and palmed one with a sharp edge. "What do you mean, you followed me?"

"I've been following you ever since you left the restaurant. I stayed about a quarter of a mile behind till you hit the dirt road. Then I had to lag even further back so as not to raise dust. When you stopped in the middle of the road like that, I had to stop, too. That's when I got out and started walking along the edge of the woods. When I saw her take you into the forest, I tried to head y'all off at an angle, but it was damned dark and I couldn't see where the hell I was going."

"And then it poured."

"Yeah, a real frog-strangler."

I'd known Anita for years, and although I'd always thought of her as a religious fanatic, I'd never thought of her as crazy. Roy, on the other hand, I'd only known a couple of hours. For all I knew, he was one of Anita's sons whom I'd never met or an escaped rapist from the state pen.

"What made you follow me?"

"I had a gut feeling something was wrong, and I guess I was right. I didn't like that woman from the start."

I dropped the rock. "What tipped you off?"

"Well, it wasn't hard to see that the woman was a wacko. When you got up to use the phone she nearly busted an ear-drum trying to hear you. I started to talk to her and she about snapped my head off. Yelled at me for interrupting the Lord's work."

"Apparently killing me was part of that work. She would have gotten the job done, too, if it hadn't been for the lightning. Speaking of which, she could be anywhere. And she's armed, you know."

"Yeah, I figured that. A woman like you wouldn't go off

into the woods with the likes of her unless there was some kind of weapon involved. You know what kind of gun it is?"

"Does it make a difference?"

"It might, if we run into her and she starts shooting. Knowing if and when she has to reload could be a big help."

"All I know is that it was a hard gun. I didn't get a close look."

"How did you get away?"

"You didn't see the lightning?"

"I saw it."

"It nearly killed us. It might have killed her—I don't know. I didn't stick around to see."

"Then we best be going."

Without asking my permission, Roy scooped me up and started carrying me like a baby. I'm not complaining, mind you. At least he didn't hoist me over his shoulder like a sack of potatoes. Still, it wasn't a very practical move on his part.

"Wouldn't it make more sense if I rode piggyback?" I whispered.

"Yeah. But I was planning on using you as a shield if I need to."

"That's not funny. Anyway, the woman would just as soon shoot you in the back."

At the risk of sounding like a wimp, I rode on his back all the way out of the forest. Believe me, with Roy's legs doing all the walking we saved a lot of time. My job was to keep an eye on the rear, which I did. And I don't mean just Roy's rear, either.

Unfortunately Roy was not the great white hunter he would have me believe. After about an hour and a half and two gullies later, we stumbled out onto the road. It wasn't the logging road, however, but a paved highway.

"Hell," Roy said. "I could have sworn I was headed right for the logging road and our cars."

"Turn left, then; it's got to be just down there. I think I see that old stump."

Roy ignored me and made a right turn.

"What you doing?"

"I know what I'm doing, Abigail. Just leave the directions up to me."

"Put me down!"

Unlike the stereotype of the average female, I am a darn good navigator, and I firmly believe most women are. In my case, I became an expert the first time Buford and I ever took a trip into unfamiliar territory. That man would sooner be castrated than consult a map, and he wouldn't stop to ask directions if his life depended on it. If I had a dollar for each wasted mile Buford drove while we were married, I could buy Imelda Marcos's shoe collection. At any rate, while we drove those endless miles in which Buford was lost, but wouldn't admit it, I knew exactly where we were at all times.

I may have had to put up with Buford's stupidity—if only to keep family peace—but I didn't have to put up with Roy's. As soon as my feet hit the pavement I started walking. In the right direction.

"Hey, what do think you're doing?" Roy kept up with me for a few steps but then fell back. "You don't know this area, Abigail. You're going to get lost!"

I kept walking. Unfortunately I had managed to lose one of my sandals during the ordeal in the woods. Although the pavement was a little rough, it was still easier to walk altogether barefoot rather than lopsided. Although I didn't have Imelda's resources, I cavalierly threw my remaining sandal away.

The rain had cooled things down considerably and it was pleasantly warm. My clothes were almost dry. Under better circumstances I could well have enjoyed a nighttime stroll down a deserted country road—preferably with a well-chosen companion, like Greg Washburn. But Roy would do in a pinch, and I had every confidence that he would be joining me in a few minutes. Just as soon as he realized his mistake.

I was very wrong. Not only did Roy not join me, but what I thought was the big stump marking the logging road turned out to be a clump of blackberry bushes draped in honeysuckle. However, much to my joy, further down the road, I could see a light. It appeared to be stationary, perhaps the light from a house.

Adrenaline is a funny thing. One's body can produce great

amounts of it under seemingly opposite circumstances. What had served me well in the pine forest and gully served equally well on the paved road. I flew like Mercury and was there without really having been conscious of the journey.

It was a house, all right. A very ordinary-looking house, but one guarded by a pack of snarling, snapping dogs. Again, thanks to my adrenal glands I sailed right past them. My bravado must have intimidated the dogs because almost immediately they lost interest and slunk off.

I leaped up the steps to the front porch in a single bound. Well, two at the most. Finding no doorbell, I pounded on the door. My internal clock told me that it was no later than ten, and probably much earlier. Besides, the light undoubtedly meant someone was still up. And even if they hadn't been before my arrival, the dogs had surely done their job.

Nevertheless, nobody answered.

The garage door was closed, but there was a car parked in the driveway that looked functional. I would have bet Aunt Marilyn's life savings that the owner was home. I pounded again until the windows rattled.

The door opened just a crack, and I could see a thin slice of pink. "Go away!" a woman said.

"Please, I need help. Do you have a telephone?"

"I said to go away. If you don't, I'll sic them dogs on you."

"Please, this is an emergency. There's been an accident, and I think somebody's dead." That was partly true, because Anita might well be dead, as far as I knew.

The door opened as far as the chain would permit. "There been a car wreck?"

"No ma'am—"

The door started to close.

"Yes, ma'am. Two cars. Bodies lying everywhere."

The door closed just long enough and far enough for the chain to come off. The woman, who was wearing a pink long-sleeved dress, looked surprisingly familiar, although I couldn't place her. A second woman, dressed in blue, darted out of view.

"You in the accident?" Even her voice sounded familiar.

With no shoes, and more scratches than a one-eared tomcat,

it should have been obvious to her. I was forced to lie again.

"Yes, ma'am. May I use your phone?"

She stared out into the night. "I don't see no accident."

"It's down the road about a mile. People moaning and screaming like you wouldn't believe."

"You wait here," she said, and closed the door.

She took forever, and I was too antsy to stand there like a lawn jockey. I started pacing like a caged lioness. It was a small porch bounded by a wrought iron railing, which made my circles tight. I swear I had made a dozen circuits before I realized I could not only see into her garage, but what I was looking at was even more familiar than she was.

"Holy shit!"

A third burst of adrenaline got me off that porch, past the pack of dogs, and smack up against the garage window. It was my car, all right.

"Oh, miss," I heard her calling from the front door.

"That's her, all right!" Anita screamed.

I can't say whether or not the garage door was unlocked, the lock was broken, or I managed to break it. All I know is that I had that sucker open in less time than it took Buford to roll off me and light up a cigarette. Maybe Anita didn't keep a spare key hidden on her car, but I sure as hell did. Two of them, in fact.

Even then, I had just backed onto the road when the first of the bullets came whizzing past my windshield. By the sound of things, more than one person was firing at me, and they weren't firing pistols, either. I ripped the shift stick into drive and stomped on the gas. Charlie would have been proud of me. My car is not exactly prime drag material, but my tires squealed louder than Buford does just before he lights that cigarette.

Thank the good Lord I didn't get hit by one of the bullets, but the rear fender of my car did.

"You'll pay for this, you bitch!" I screamed.

I was still cursing when I almost ran over Roy. He was about a half mile frcm the house and panting with exertion.

"Get in!" I shouted. Frankly, I'm not sure I even stopped all the way.

"Damn if you aren't something," Roy said when he could catch his breath.

I glanced in the rearview mirror for the millionth time. I could just see the pinprick of headlights. It was possible we were being pursued.

"You okay?"

"Damn," he said again.

"Then hold on to your heinie, 'cause you ain't seen nothing yet."

I pressed the petal to the metal. "Eat my dust, ladies!"

25

It was either luck, or divine providence, but somehow we managed to make it back to the main highway and the diner. At that point, neither of us could purposefully have navigated our way out of a paper bag.

I have nothing but praise for the law officials of Cleveland County, North Carolina. They treated me with respect, even an appropriate amount of sympathy. They were also damned efficient. Anita and the pink lady—who, as it turned out, was her cousin—were promptly arrested.

But it wasn't until I got a chance to talk to Greg that I felt really safe. Ironically, that's also when I realized just how vulnerable I had been.

"Stay right there, Abigail; I'll be there as soon as I can."

"Yes, please come," I said.

I couldn't help it. After I hung up, I bawled openly and, for the second time that night, took a thorough drenching. My relief was every bit as intense as my terror had been. Although they all swore I wasn't making a fool out of myself, I could tell that the sheriff and his men were uncomfortable. Eventually even the waitresses at The Sitting Duck cast me get-with-it looks.

Although there was nothing in it for him, dear, sweet Roy stayed with me until Greg arrived. His personal skills were only marginally better than his sense of direction, but he did his best to comfort me until Greg arrived.

"There, there," he said, patting me as if I were a baby.

"They're going to lock her up and throw away the key. You don't need to worry about her anymore."

"It's not just that, Roy. She was my friend—at least I thought she was. She had the nerve to sing at my aunt's funeral—the woman she killed! Can you imagine that?"

"The woman was a real sicko. I overheard the woman deputy say that when they arrested Anita, she was sitting in the middle of the living room in a pile of old curtains."

My heart pounded. "Green velvet drapes? Heavy things?"

"Yeah, how did you know?"

"They were my aunt's. What else did the deputy say?"

"That Anita was ripping them open with a razor knife."

"She didn't!"

"She did. And something pretty spectacular fell out of one of them."

"What?" The only time I regret being a southerner is when I want news in a hurry, while it's still news.

"Something all frilly and gold."

"Mould-bread face!"

He looked hurt. "Sorry, but I don't know about these fashion things."

"Gold thread lace!" I screamed, and gave Roy a long, hard hug.

"I still can't understand why you didn't tell me you had a sister!"

Rob hung his head. "She was only trying to protect me, Abigail. I'm her only brother. You haven't changed your mind about not pressing charges?"

"But a rotten fish on the hottest day of the year?"

"She's really sorry about that and wants a chance to apologize."

"Rotten fish can be forgiven, but I'm not so sure about the threat against my son."

Rob wrung his sculpted hands. "I told you before, Abigail, that it wasn't a threat against your son. She was trying to make a joke."

"A joke?"

"You know, Charlie the Tuna."

"Ha, ha. At the very least, Rob, your sister lacks judgment."

"You're right about that, and I'm very sorry." His contrition was genuine, I'm sure.

"And she has no sense of propriety."

"I couldn't agree more. I told her that the fish was a bad idea. I'll make sure she pays to have your shop fumigated."

"I'm talking about her outfits. Even in Nome, Alaska, they don't wear stuff that heavy this time of the year."

"Told you so," Bob boomed cheerfully.

"And one more thing: tell her to lose that orange getup—unless she plans to inflate it with helium and hang a gondola basket from it."

We walked over and sat down with the others. Mercifully, Peggy Redfern, our new president, did not tap on her water glass to get us started. Neither did she offer up a long prayer.

"Do we have any business this morning?" she asked, eyeing a plate of french toast two tables over.

"I'd like to propose that Bob Steuben be admitted to the association."

"Hear, hear," we all said.

Even the Major was in agreement. Although he was aware that Bob had saved his life, we had yet to tell him just how. I have no doubt that we each were hoping to hold that back as personal ammunition at some later date.

"We also have a petition for membership from a Mr. Tony D'Angelo. He is, as y'all know, the new owner of Feathers 'N Treasures."

There were a few sighs, but mine was not the loudest.

"Now, now," Peggy said, much to her credit, "we have to be fair about this. Mr. D'Angelo has promised to paint the shop, inside and out, and upgrade the merchandise. And of course, no more poster signs in the windows."

We voted Tony in.

"Of course y'all already know that I no longer plan to sell my shop to Major Calloway." I read gratitude in the glance Peggy threw my way. "As unpleasant as all this murder, and attempted murder, stuff has been, business has never been better."

She was right. Our block had become a mecca for ghoulish memsahibs whose lives lacked excitement but who had big bucks to drop. Even the Major was taking a lesson from it and had changed the name of his shop to Guns and Posies. His merchandise still had a military theme with heavy Teutonic undertones, but it now carried some furniture for the first time. One could now buy Eva Braun's daybed, and the Führer's footstool, if one was so inclined.

Peggy's order arrived and she ate a large biscuit, dripping with butter and honey, before continuing. Personally, I think that's too much for one bite. At any rate, I had no doubt that Peggy was going to switch appetites as soon as she met Roy. The lad was going to be in town the coming weekend for a personal tour of the big city by yours truly. However, I had every intention of dumping him on Peggy. Roy had already become a little too sweet on me. That kind of thing can be flattering if you're in the market, so to speak, but I had already found my treasure. Greg and I were having our second date Saturday night.

"And now, I think we should all raise a glass of orange juice—or a cup of coffee—to Abigail. She has generously offered to buy a full page in the *Observer* advertising our shops, to keep the momentum going. It must be nice to be so rich."

"Hear, hear," everyone said.

"I am not rich!"

"How much is gold going for these days?" the Major asked.

"It was gold lace, dear, not Fort Knox."

Actually, Fort Knox wasn't far off, but I didn't want the IRS to start salivating until I'd had a chance to consider all my options. Dear Aunt Euey had not neglected her heirs after all. Sewn into one of her drapes, between the lining and the ugly green velvet, was the front panel of my great-great-great-great-great-great-great-great-grandmother's wedding dress. It was handmade gold lace. I don't mean gold-colored lace but *real* gold lace.

As far as Bob could determine it was late-fifteenth-century Guipure lace, from Ferrara, Italy, of course. Bob says the pattern of flowers, alternating with garlands of leaves, is fairly typical of the times but of exceptional workmanship. Considering that the lace was made specifically for someone very wealthy—a nobleman's daughter—the five hundred tiny pearls that dot it are no surprise. It is no surprise either that the pearls have yellowed somewhat through the centuries, but hey, nothing is perfect—except for the twenty-five small, but very clear, diamonds that dot the centers of some of the flowers. And there's nothing wrong with the rubies on the ten largest flowers, either.

I have been told that I could get upward of three hundred thousand dollars for the panel at the moment, possibly even more if another spectacular royal wedding comes along and the bride wants something truly special incorporated into her dress. Bob and Rob threw up their hands in horror when I suggested removing the gems and selling them and the lace separately.

Teddy, a jeweler friend of Mama's, disagrees. The diamonds would all have to be recut to get them up to current standards, but he thinks they would be worth half that much alone. The rubies, he said, are worth dying for.

I am as sentimental as the next person, and the thought of keeping the panel for Susan's wedding (someday!) has occurred to me. However, while I may be sentimental, I am not brain-dead.

Of course, I would have to give my brother Toy his share, not to mention our Uncle Sam. So, given the fact that I don't own a house and refuse to live indefinitely on Tony's charity, I am not rich. I am, however, indisputably much better off than I have been since the day Buford dumped me in favor of Tweetie.

"Okay. When the waitress brings the checks, pass them down here. But this is a one-time offer."

"For she's a jolly good fellow!" Skinny as he was, Bob could out-bass a bullfrog with a cold.

"Hear, hear!"

The Major wiped milk from his mustache. "I wonder who's going to buy Anita's shop."

We all glared at him.

"I never did like her," Wynnell said, still glaring. It was time to tweeze those hedges again. "If you dig deep enough, you'll find a Yankee in her woodpile for sure. A true southern woman would never have done what she did."

"You haven't read the paper yet today, have you, dear?" I said kindly.

"Well, does this conclude our business then?" Peggy asked.

She paid no attention to our affirmative response because a good-looking man in his twenties had just walked in, *alone*. While she was thus distracted I snitched the last piece of bacon off her plate.

After all, I had paid for it.